A COMPROMISING POSITION

Esme and Lovatt went tumbling head over heels down the slope and right into the stream. It took her a moment to realize what had happened. She was flat on her back in the stream and Lovatt was on top of her, his full length resting on her body. She could feel every inch of him.

Lovatt's eyes registered shock for a moment, then pure devilment. "A lovely sight, Miss Darling," he said, giving her a grin. "I must say you're one of the few women I know who can look delectable flat on her back in a stream."

Esme looked up at him and forgot that she wanted to tell him to get up. "Lovatt, you're incorrigible," she whispered.

"Completely," he agreed. He lowered his head to hers and kissed her, softly at first, and then with warmth. Esme put her arms around his neck and responded in kind. "Umm," Lovatt murmured, raising his head to look at her. "You're incorrigible as well, Miss Darling, and I quite like that."

<u>BOOK YOUR PLACE ON OUR WEBSITE</u> AND MAKE THE <u>READING CONNECTION!</u>

We've created a customized website just for our very special readers, where you can get the inside scoop on everything that's going on with Zebra, Pinnacle and Kensington books.

When you come online, you'll have the exciting opportunity to:

- View covers of upcoming books
- Read sample chapters
- Learn about our future publishing schedule (listed by publication month *and author*)
- Find out when your favorite authors will be visiting a city near you
- Search for and order backlist books from our online catalog
- Check out author bios and background information
- Send e-mail to your favorite authors
- Meet the Kensington staff online
- Join us in weekly chats with authors, readers and other guests
- Get writing guidelines
- AND MUCH MORE!

Visit our website at http://www.zebrabooks.com

A TOUCH OF MAGIC

Juliette Leigh

Zebra Books
Kensington Publishing Corp.
http://www.zebrabooks.com

ZEBRA BOOKS are published by

Kensington Publishing Corp.
850 Third Avenue
New York, NY 10022

Zebra and the Z logo Reg. U.S. Pat. & TM Off.

First Printing: December, 1998
10 9 8 7 6 5 4 3 2 1

Printed in the United States of America

One

"Oh, dear," Mrs. Amilie Pennywhistle said with a note of panic in her voice, "there's a leopard on the lawn."

"Of course there is, Aunt Penny." Miss Esme Darling had her back to the window as she wrote in carefully spaced lines on a clean sheet of paper. "Have you seen Papa this morning? I thought he and Mama would be almost ready to leave by now." There was no answer from Aunt Penny. Miss Darling kept on with her writing, looking up only when the door opened.

Her father, Major James Darling, came in and sat down across from her. "We're almost ready to leave," he said heavily. "Are you sure you won't go to London with us?"

"No, Papa." Miss Darling reached over and put her hand on her father's. "Although I'd like to go and offer you support, I do think I should stay here and watch the house and grounds."

Her father chuckled. "You mean that you need to stay here and manage things and look after that cat of yours. Well, I don't like the idea of leaving you alone here. Your mother and I may be in London for several weeks." He paused and drummed his fingertips on the writing table. "You know how these military hearings are." He grimaced. "But perhaps you're right, Esme, in not going along. The news may be bad for me—for us."

"Nonsense, Papa. I know you'll be exonerated. This charge is all perfectly ridiculous."

"I know that, and you know that. Our only problem is convincing Whitehall."

"You'll convince them. Your reputation is spotless."

Major Darling shook his head. "Or *has* been, up to this point. I just wish I knew who wrote that letter." He slapped the desktop with the palm of his hand. "I knew there was a spy in the garrison. I should have found him."

"You were trying to do that, Papa. And you would have, if that silly letter hadn't been sent to the Horse Guards."

"I know." His tone was tired. "I only hope the powers in London believe that."

Esme smiled at him and thoughtfully rubbed the space between her eyes, leaving a smudge of ink right between her eyebrows. She had, as usual, tried to arrange her thick black hair in a severe knot pinned at the nape of her neck, but, as usual, curls escaped every which way. The curls were completely natural—Miss Darling often said she had no time for fripperies such as curling papers or hot irons.

She pushed the curls from her forehead. "I'm sure you can convince them, Papa. In the meantime, don't worry about me at all. Bram will be in and out, Mimsy is just a few miles away, and I'll have Aunt Penny here with me all the time." She chuckled and shook her head, curls falling again. "Aunt Penny thinks I'm writing to a beau somewhere," she whispered to Major Darling as she folded her letter.

Major Darling looked sideways at her, his favorite of his two daughters, and shook his head. "You could be," he said. "I said providence sent Captain Arno here for a reason."

"Now, Papa, don't bring that up. I'm sure Captain Arno understands that I really don't wish any attachments until these charges against you are resolved." She noted her father looking at her letter, and smiled. "A letter to Spain. Señora Romero wrote that she has a particularly beautiful red dahlia and is coming to London. In fact, she should be there shortly, so I'm sending this in care of her solicitor in London."

Major Darling looked surprised. "General Romero's widow? I had no idea that she would travel out of Spain. That's a dangerous journey for such a lady."

"Things are much safer now, Papa, and I imagine Rodrigo will accompany her. You know how devoted he is to her."

"And she is to him."

"True. Since General Romero's death, I've gotten the impression that she's more concerned than ever about Rodrigo."

Major Darling smiled fondly at Esme. "Well, my dear, he is her only child. Knowing how I feel about my children, I can sympathize with the Señora."

Esme smiled back at him. "And we feel the same about you, Papa. As to the Señora and Rodrigo, the trip will probably be good for both of them. The Señora did say that she had some business in London, and no doubt Rodrigo will want to visit his friends in the city."

"Yes," Major Darling said absently. "Rodrigo certainly enjoys London. I wouldn't be surprised if he moved there some day. He's a fine boy. The last time I saw him he told me that he wanted to be a soldier like his father. I imagine he will be when he's grown."

Esme laughed at him. "Papa, Rodrigo is no longer a boy. He must be almost twenty now."

"Twenty!" He shook his head. "I can't believe it. It seems only yesterday that I was in the Peninsula." He picked up her letter. "Since I'm going to London, I suppose you want me to deliver this to Señora Romero's solicitor."

"But of course. I can't wait to see that red dahlia. I'm going to give her a tuber from my prize violet that you had Señor Morillo send me from Mexico."

"An inspired choice for a birthday gift." He put the letter carefully in his waistcoat pocket.

"One of the two best things you've ever gotten me. The other, of course, is Spot."

Major Darling looked uneasy. "Esme, I really need to talk to you about that."

"We will, Papa, just as soon as you return. Right now I want you to concentrate only on clearing your name." She paused a second. "That and, of course, making sure Señora Romero gets my letter and I get my dahlia."

"You and your dahlias." Major Darling laughed. "I certainly had no inkling that those months in Spain would foster such a hobby with you."

"They are beautiful flowers, Papa, and there are so few of them in England. Perhaps Señora Romero and I can change that."

She picked up a second sheet of paper and sighed. "Unfortunately, this letter won't do any good, but I felt compelled to try again. This complains about the treatment of animals at the circus. I doubt this one will be any more effective than the others, but I intend to keep trying."

Her father's eyes rolled ceilingward as he made a face. "Esme, you are truly incorrigible."

She smiled at him. "Yes, I am. Aren't you delighted that I'm not at all like Bram and Mimsy?"

"At least I'm always sure about Abram and Edwina. And now that they're grown, young lady, I want you to call them by their given names. Bram and Mimsy are for the nursery."

"Whether or not those two are grown yet is a debatable point, Papa."

Major Darling laughed. "Minx. And no doubt *you're* all grown, and ready for caps and a chair by the fireside."

"Hardly that, but you must agree that Bram and Mimsy need assistance now and then."

"And you don't?" He chuckled and patted her hand. "While we're speaking of names, I think it's also time to stop calling Amilie Aunt Penny. That was fine when the two of you were children, but you're grown now."

Esme looked at him, her eyes wide. "Must I, Papa? Aunt Penny sounds so much better then Aunt Amilie. Besides, she's been Aunt Penny my whole life." She made a face. "Aunt Amilie." She shook her head. "I'm sorry, Papa. It just doesn't fit."

He sighed. "It doesn't, does it? Well, my dear, call her what you and she prefer, but just be sure to listen to her advice while I'm gone."

"Oh, I plan to, Papa. I think Aunt Penny and I will rub along famously while you and Mama are gone." She suddenly remembered Mrs. Pennywhistle was in the room. "Don't you agree, Aunt Penny?" Esme turned halfway in her chair and glanced toward the window where Mrs. Pennywhistle had been standing. "Aunt Penny?" There was no one to be seen. Esme looked at her father and raised her dark, arched eyebrows. "I didn't hear her leave."

Major Darling's eyes widened and he leaped to his feet. "Perhaps because she didn't." Esme followed him. "Good Heavens, Aunt Penny!" she exclaimed, rushing to the crumpled figure on the floor beside the window. She shook her aunt vigorously, and Aunt Penny moaned. Major Darling leaned down and helped Aunt Penny to her feet. "Papa, she's much too weak to get up." Esme caught Aunt Penny's elbow as her aunt's knees buckled and she sagged toward the floor again.

"Nonsense, Esme. I've seen a hundred men faint for one reason or the other when I was in the Peninsula, and even more in India when the heat got to them. Best thing in the world is to get them up right away and onto the front lines." He frowned as he unceremoniously dumped Mrs. Pennywhistle onto the nearby green striped sofa. "Any idea what caused this?" He reached down and put his hand under Aunt Penny's head to support her.

Esme shook her head and frowned. "Not at all. The last

thing I recall that she said to me was that there was a leopard on the lawn."

"On the lawn! Esme, how many times have I told you to keep that leopard in the shed, or somewhere out of the way? Spot has terrified half the countryside! We've got to do something about that cat!" Major Darling began chafing Aunt Penny's hands. "Amilie!" he shouted, "wake up!" He tugged on her hands, pulling her upright.

"I'm awake, James," Aunt Penny said faintly. "I assure you I'm quite fine."

"Good." The clock struck the half hour, and Major Darling turned his head to check the time. "Oh, good Lord, I have to hunt up your mother and leave. We're never going to get to London at this rate." He let go of Aunt Penny's hands suddenly and turned to leave. Aunt Penny's head snapped back and hit the wooden frame of the sofa with a crack. Aunt Penny moaned again, this time in real pain. Major Darling did not notice. "I hope Isabel is ready by now." He absently patted Aunt Penny's shoulder, then turned and left the room.

"I'm fine, James," Aunt Penny said, faintly, her eyes closed.

"Papa's gone." Esme sat down on the sofa beside her aunt and picked up one of Aunt Penny's limp hands.

Aunt Penny opened her eyes until they looked like saucers. "Gone! But I haven't said good-bye. Whatever will Isabel think, me letting her go off without a proper farewell?" She glanced over at the window, then paled. "Esme, I do believe I'm coming down with brain fever. I could have sworn that I saw a leopard on the lawn."

"That was just Spot," Esme said absently. "Shall we go say good-bye to Mama and Papa? I think Bram is here as well to bid them good-bye." She pulled Aunt Penny to her feet and helped her out into the hallway.

"Spot?" Aunt Penny asked faintly.

"My leopard." Esme patted Aunt Penny's hand absently. "She's perfectly harmless, I assure you."

Aunt Penny sat back down, and her head fell back against the sofa pillow. "A leopard. No one told me, Esme, or I assure you I wouldn't have come to stay with you."

"Oh, but we need you so, Aunt Penny." Esme sat down beside her and held her hand.

"I know." Aunt Penny's voice was faint, "And there's the quandary. You need me, but I can't possibly go on."

"Nonsense, Aunt Penny." Esme stood up and smiled. "Spot is harmless, and you'll come to like her as much as I do. Now, shall we go bid Papa and Mama a good trip to London?" Esme pulled Aunt Penny to her feet, but had to wait by the door until Aunt Penny held her head and moaned once more.

Esme, her older brother Abram, and Aunt Penny waved a last time as Major and Mrs. Darling rounded the bend in the road and went out of sight. "Do you think Papa can convince them he isn't the spy?" Bram frowned as he turned to go back inside.

Aunt Penny put her hand to her mouth and gasped as she looked wildly around. "Did you see Spot again, Aunt Penny?" Esme peered around. "I'll be glad to introduce you to her."

"No." Aunt Penny's voice was weak. "No, I didn't see your leopard, Esme, and I have no wish to meet him . . . her. I was merely distressed that something might happen to James. That's the only reason I'm here—I came in his time of need."

"And as I said, we do need you, Aunt Penny." Esme patted her arm. "Don't you fret for a moment about Papa. What argument can an anonymous letter have against Papa's illustrious reputation? Do go in and refresh yourself with some lemonade. You've had a most fatiguing morning." Esme smiled at Bram as Aunt Penny turned to go back into the house. She paused and took Bram's arm. "Bram, do let me show you the garden."

"The garden? Esme, I don't care a whit about the garden. I wanted to talk about—"

"Bram." Esme tugged at his arm. "Let's stroll over here. My dahlias are doing particularly well." She almost jerked at his arm.

Bram finally looked from Esme to Aunt Penny. "Oh. Oh, yes. I do love dahlias. Especially yours. Do go on, Aunt Penny. Esme and I will join you in a moment."

"You're singularly obtuse this morning, Bram," Esme said, strolling beside him back to the dahlia patch.

"You're plotting again, Esme. I can tell. As for being obtuse, I seem to be that way every time you begin a new scheme," he said morosely. "It's a matter of self-preservation. What is it this time?"

"Nothing." She smiled innocently up at him. "Bram, Papa will do wonderfully well in London, I'm sure of it. But—" she paused a moment.

"*But* . . . there's always a *but,* isn't there?" Bram groaned. "What are you getting me into this time, Esme?"

"Nothing at all, Bram." She turned and frowned at a dahlia bud that was just opening. "Orange. I do wish these weren't so orange, don't you, Bram? I can't wait until I get the red from Señora Romero. She may also bring me a small yellow dahlia from a friend of hers in Seville, but the red will be the prize. I hope it's the color of your uniform."

Bram grasped her shoulders and turned her to face him. "Enough about your dahlias. I repeat—What are you getting me into this time, Esme?"

She looked directly into his eyes—dark brown, not at all like her deep blue ones. "Bram, we need to investigate and find the real spy. Only then will Papa be exonerated." She held up a hand as Bram started to speak "Hear me out, Bram. Please." He nodded and motioned to a small wooden bench that faced the patch where her prized dahlias grew.

"Go ahead, Esme," he said with resignation. "Just don't count on me if this is another of your crackbrained schemes."

"I do not have crackbrained schemes, Bram." Esme sat down beside him.

"Oh? What about the time you planned to become an actress? Or the time you decided the garrison needed culture, and invited Beethoven here? That must have been a letter that gave him hours of laughter." He shook his head. "Crackbrained."

"That wasn't crackbrained, Bram. Merely overreaching."

"Well, what about the leopard?"

"Spot doesn't signify. Besides, she's quite happy here." Esme pinned him with a look. "Listen to me, Bram. This is quite important." She paused until he shrugged in defeat and looked at her. "As I said, Bram, I do believe Papa will be exonerated in London. Everyone who knows him and knows of his record will be sure that these charges against him are spurious. Major James Darling, a spy! It simply isn't to be believed."

"They have the letters, they say. Whoever sent the anonymous accusation also sent letters to France written in Papa's hand."

"Letters can be forged, Bram, and these have been. All we have to do is discover the forger. Someone is out to ruin Papa by charging anonymously that he's a spy for Napoleon. As I said, I think Papa will be exonerated for lack of evidence, but, Bram, there will always be that stain on his record. It's up to us to eliminate that. Only by finding the forger or the real spy can Papa be restored to his spotless reputation."

"I agree, but—"

Esme threw her arms around Bram's neck, crushing his

uniform. "I knew you'd agree with me, Bram! I knew you'd help me! After all, both of us have Papa's best interests at heart." She released him and leaned back slightly to look at his face. "Thank you so much, Bram. Now all we have to do is figure out how to go about catching this person."

"Don't tell me you haven't given that some thought."

"Yes, I do have a plan," Esme began, but she stopped when Spot came ambling up to her. Bram cringed slightly, but Esme just began scratching Spot absently behind her ears. Spot stretched and put her head on Esme's knee.

"Spot has certainly grown during the past few months." Bram moved to the end of the bench.

"Yes," Esme agreed, patting the leopard on the head. "I had no idea leopards reached this size. But you don't need to fear, Bram. She won't scratch you. Look how affectionate she is."

"Thank God for small favors," Bram said fervently.

Spot had indeed grown in the past few months since Esme had rescued her from the circus that was a permanent part of town. She, Bram, and Mimsy had gone to see the circus, and Esme had spotted the tiny cub covered with sores. It had been so weak that it was unable to walk. One of the men who owned it picked it up and took it around to the back of a shanty. Esme ran after him, and Bram ran after her. The man threw the cub onto a pile of refuse and picked up a club to kill it. Esme shrieked and climbed right up the garbage, snatching up the cub and threatening the owner and the circus with everything from the local magistrate to a Higher Power. The cub's owner had turned on her, and Bram had been thankful that he was there. Esme refused to relinquish the scrap of cat, so Bram, Esme, and the cub soon found themselves back at Rouvray, facing Major Darling. He first told Esme to return the cub, but she refused. Esme, unlike her sister, seldom shed tears, but she had on this occasion. What could Major Darling do but relent and allow her to keep the tiny leopard?

There had been a terrible row between the family and the cub's owner. Major Darling had finally offered to purchase the cub for her to nurse back to health. He had, however, stipulated that she must give the cub to a zoo as soon as it had healed. Somehow Esme had never gotten around to doing that. She had named the tiny cub Spot, and cared for it almost incessantly for weeks. When she wasn't actually with the cub, she was worrying about its health. Esme had been afraid Spot was going to die, but, miraculously, the cub survived and had become quite attached to her. For her part, Esme had come to love Spot, and insofar as Spot was capable of love, that feeling was reciprocated.

"That cat is still a wild animal, you know," Bram said, moving to the very edge of the bench as Spot rubbed her head against Esme's knee. "She could get violent and tear you limb from limb."

"Do you think she would? I rather doubt it." Esme scratched Spot's neck and then patted her absently as Spot draped herself across Esme's feet. "Back to my plan, Bram." She paused. "I rather thought you might start asking questions at the garrison. After all, you're in the army, and who better to ask?"

"I'm on leave. I can't just walk in there and begin asking this and that. Why not get Captain Arno to do it?"

"Because," she explained patiently, sliding her feet from under Spot and propping them against Spot's back, "it's something we need to do ourselves. Everyone must be suspect. We know the letter came when Papa was investigating the garrison. The investigator from the Horse Guards said that the intercepted letters to Napoleon's network came from this garrison, so that much is known. The anonymous letters and the letters purportedly written by Papa were only sent to London after Papa began asking questions."

"Your point?" Bram had always been mystified by Esme's thought processes or, as he usually put it, lack of them.

"My *point*," Esme said patiently, "is that Papa must have been close to discovering the spy. The anonymous letter implicating Papa is a smoke screen designed to draw attention away from the real spy. Papa must have heard something or asked something that would have unmasked the real French sympathizer."

"We don't have to do anything of the kind." Bram shifted uncomfortably, almost falling off the end of the bench. "This is something that is best left to the authorities."

"Horsefeathers!" Esme snorted. "You see what a muddle the so-called authorities have made of this so far. To actually think that Papa would spy for Napoleon! It isn't to be borne!" She nudged Spot aside and stood, facing Bram. "It's our duty to clear his name, Bram," she said, her fists on her hips. "We have no choice. Are you going to let the Darling name be smirched?"

"Of course not, but—"

Esme threw her arms around his neck again. "I just *knew* you'd agree with me, Bram! Our family must stick together and save Papa! You're quite wonderful, Bram!"

Bram put his hands on her arms and looked up at her. He knew from long experience that it was no use to argue. "All right, Esme. What happens after I ask all these questions?"

Esme smiled happily at him. "That's the beauty of this, Bram. After that, we improvise, depending on what you discover."

"Improvise?" Bram's voice was weak. He'd learned long ago what Esme's improvisations usually meant: total disaster.

"Oh, Lord," he croaked.

Two

Esme walked slowly along the edge of the meadow, Spot's leash firmly in her hand. The leash was merely for form, to reassure the neighbors that a vicious leopard wasn't running unrestrained. Actually, Esme had discovered through experience that Spot, although not heavy, was all muscle and could go about anywhere she wished, dragging Esme along on the leash.

Spot sniffed here and there as she ambled along. The grass was growing nicely, and at a particularly bare place in the meadow, Spot stopped to investigate a new smell in the grass. Esme, as usual, waited patiently for her to resume their walk. She tried to take Spot out every day, and intended, just as soon as she returned home, to honor her promise to Papa to keep Spot out of the yard. Papa had called in a carpenter who had built Spot a very nice little house inside a tall fence. It was pleasant and shady, located right under a large tree in the backyard. At first, Spot had been so sick that Esme hadn't forced her to stay inside the pen. Later, Spot had enjoyed prowling the yard and garden so much that Esme spoiled her by letting her roam close to the house by day and sleep in the pen at night. Those days were over—Spot was just going to have to go inside the pen and stay. Esme pondered the problem as Spot rubbed against her leg and nuzzled contentedly. There was no other way, she decided. Spot had to stay penned up, or she and Bram would spend the next weeks with Aunt Penny in a permanent state of the vapors.

She let the leash dangle from her fingers as she watched Spot stretch in the warm sunshine. Esme closed her eyes for a moment, savoring the quiet day and the midsummer smells of the meadow. She was quite satisfied with her day so far. Bram had agreed to go to the garrison and ask, as he put it, "a few delicate questions," Aunt Penny had settled in nicely after accepting that Spot's presence was permanent, and the post had brought a letter from her father's friend, Señor Morilla, the dahlia enthusiast in Mexico. He had come by a particularly fine white with a yellow center and promised to send her a tuber if the plant thrived. Between this and Señora Romero's promised gift, Esme's collection was steadily growing.

In addition, the weather was perfect—sunny, but not too warm—and there were wonderful summer smells in the air that just made a person glad to be outdoors. Esme sat down on a small rock and watched Spot as she wandered around poking her nose in the grass. The leash had slipped from Esme's hand, and it dangled uselessly from Spot's collar as the leopard slithered through the grass.

Esme turned her face upward to the sun, hoping Aunt Penny wouldn't notice any change in her complexion. She always enjoyed the feel of the warm sun on her skin and, in her more daring moments, had even bared her shoulders. Now, she smiled at the sun, then closed her eyes and breathed in the heady smell of flowers, grass, and earth. Bees were buzzing in the background, and somewhere a bird was trilling plaintively, most likely calling to its mate. Esme took a deep breath, reveling in the sensations.

Suddenly there was an earth-shattering roar, a strange sound Esme had never heard before. Esme jumped to her feet and looked wildly around, then realized that the sound was coming from Spot. It was a terrible, jungle sound. Spot was in the middle of the meadow almost hid-

den by the grass, and she made another sound, a low, men-
acing rumble in her chest and throat. Then she crouched
low and began slithering through the grass, almost crawling along the ground. Esme ran toward her, calling her
name. Suddenly a shot rang out. Spot moved as Esme
called to her and the bullet went wide, missing the leopard.
Esme threw herself down and grabbed the leash. Another
shot rang out from the woods at the far edge of the
meadow, this one going over Esme's head. "Stop!" she
screamed. "Whoever you are, stop!"

Esme lay in the grass for a moment, her heart pounding.
Spot lay just as quietly, and Esme feared the leopard had
been shot. She looked at Spot and realized the leopard
was tensed in every muscle, just waiting to spring at whatever was threatening them. Esme reached out and touched
Spot gently. Spot was instantly on her feet, teeth bared,
facing Esme. "It's me, Spot," Esme said evenly, holding
out her hand, trying not to let Spot see the frisson of fear
that had gone down her spine at the leopard's savagery.
This wasn't her Spot.

Spot relaxed a second, then turned. Once again, the
leopard moved to a crouching position, looking at the
woods, clearly waiting to attack the danger there.

Two men came out of the woods, carrying rifles. Esme
slowly stood up, still holding onto Spot's leash. She looked
at the men walking toward her, rifles at the ready. One was
dressed all in white and wore a turban of white. His skin
was dark, very dark, and he was slightly built. The other
one was dressed in clothing one would see on any well-
dressed man of the *ton*, but there the similarity ended. He
was dark as well, but he hadn't been born that way. The
sun had bronzed his skin to a rich color, the same color
Esme had seen in men who spent long hours on a ship's
deck or on a battlefield. The man was tall and well-built,
and walked with the same air of command that Esme had
long recognized in ranking army officers. He was one who

was accustomed to being obeyed. He wore no hat, and his hair was longer than most men wore, curling almost to his shoulders. It was brown, threaded with golden streaks. He seemed foreign, somehow, almost as incongruous in the calm English countryside as Spot. As the man drew closer, his rifle trained on Spot and her, Esme was caught by his eyes. They were green, a glittering green, and they made him look like a dangerous jungle animal.

As the men drew closer, Esme stepped between them and Spot.

"Move," the taller man ordered, holding his rifle steady, aimed right at her. "Just do it slowly so you won't frighten the leopard."

"No." Esme tried to keep from trembling. Her hat had fallen off in her tumble to the ground, and now a breeze caught her hair and blew her curls across her face. "This animal is mine."

"Yours?" His face mirrored his disbelief as he lowered his firearm. "This is the animal that's been terrorizing my horses for the past fortnight. It hasn't harmed one yet, but I intend to kill it before it can do any mischief. Now move." He raised his rifle again.

"No." Esme tried to be firm, but she heard the tremor in her voice. "Spot is perfectly harmless." She tried to look coolly at him. "Which is more than I can say of you, sir. Do you usually run about the countryside shooting at innocent bystanders?"

"I have done so. Especially when they get in my way." He lowered his rifle again and looked at her steadily. "Do you move, or do I move you?"

Esme attempted dignity. "You will touch neither my person nor my animal." When she saw him move toward her, she stepped back and relied on threats. "If you try it, sir, I'll report you to the magistrate. My father, Major Darling, is well known here, and I advise you to make no moves you may regret."

The man stopped in his tracks, looked at her from her toes to her head, and then did it again. Esme was growing increasingly uncomfortable under his scrutiny when he began to laugh. "Well, I'll be damned. You must be Esme Darling. I wouldn't have known you at all." He lowered his rifle. "I suppose I should hold off disposing of the animal until you've had your say. It should be good." He settled the rifle familiarly in the crook of his arm. "Would you like to tell me about the cat?" He grinned at her. "Will this be as big a hummer as the story you told me about being related to William the Conqueror?"

"My family does happen to be related to the Conqueror, although I own it's distant," Esme said icily. "And you have the advantage, sir. While you appear to know me, I have no idea who you might be."

"Well, I daresay I've changed." He turned to the man with him. "Samad, I believe things are well in hand here. If you wish to go back, do so. I'll be there shortly."

The man called Samad bowed slightly and, without a word began walking back toward the woods. In just a moment he had disappeared, all without a sound. "Now, Miss Darling, do tell me about the cat." He glanced around her to make sure Spot was still standing there quietly. "Unusual pet. While you're telling family secrets, how's Mimsy?"

"Her name is Edwina, not Mimsy." Esme stopped short. "How do you know Mimsy?"

He grinned at her again, his teeth very white against the dark bronze of his skin. "Oh, I was thoroughly in love with her when I was twelve. Let me see, she should be nine and twenty now. Is that correct?"

"Mimsy would not appreciate you discussing her age, I'm sure." Esme frowned as she looked at him, wondering how he knew her family so well. She had no idea who he might be.

"And her twin, Bram? How is he?" He walked casually

over to the rock where Esme had been sitting, looked at it, and turned to face Esme.

"Bram is quite well," Esme said stiffly. "You didn't answer my question, sir. I don't believe you've introduced yourself."

"Ah, Esme," he said, sitting down and eyeing Spot warily, "how soon you've forgotten. I should think you would remember me from the time I tossed you in the millpond. As I recall, you had a most extensive vocabulary for a child. You were—what?—six years younger than Mimsy, and Mimsy is my age. You must have been six, then." He paused. "That would make you three and twenty now. Am I correct?"

"Lovatt," she breathed, "Chalmers Lovatt." The words still conjured up all the hate a six-year-old had ever felt. "You blackguard! You rogue! How dare you! You . . . you . . ." She ran out of words.

"Ah, quite so. You've discovered me. And, from the perspective of my advanced years, permit me to apologize for tossing you in the pond. I probably shouldn't have thrown a female into the water, but, as I recall, you deserved it at the time."

"I most certainly did not. As I recall the incident, you and Bram had been tormenting me all morning. I was quite right to pour a bucket of mud on your head."

"We'll call it even, then." He grinned at her again. "I knew Major Darling was posted here, but I had no idea you were still living with the family, as well." He patted the rock beside him. "Do sit down and catch me up on the years between. Let's see, your father was in India the last time I saw him. What has he done since that time?"

"He came home when Grandmother died, and then he was sent to the Peninsula, where he saw action. He had hoped to be posted here so we could live at Rouvray again, so this was a dream come true." Esme circled and sat down warily across from him, where she could watch Spot. "Papa has been in charge of the garrison here for the past two years, ever since he was wounded in the Peninsula."

"Not wounded severely, I trust?" His tone was light, and there was a smile on his face, but Esme sensed something else. There was something about him. *Wary,* she thought. That was the word. He was wary, just like Spot.

"It was severe, but he recovered completely." She put her hand on Spot to reassure him, in case he was uneasy around the leopard. "I assure you Spot is perfectly harmless," she said.

Lovatt glanced at the cat, who stared right back at him, her round pupils large. "I was in India myself, Miss Darling, and saw many leopards there. She doesn't look quite grown yet. How did you come by a leopard here at Rouvray?"

"I rescued the poor thing from the circus. Her owners there had mistreated her and were going to kill her. She was so tiny and malnourished that I thought she was going to die." She made a face. "Papa thought so, as well. That's the only reason he purchased her from the circus and allowed me to keep her."

Lovatt laughed and picked a blade of grass, which he put negligently into the side of his mouth as he leaned back and stretched his feet out in front of him. "Fascinating. And what are you going to do with her now? You can't have a full grown leopard wandering around the countryside. She might attack someone—no matter that she seems domesticated. I don't think leopards ever lose that sense of the jungle."

"I know." Esme sighed. "I'm supposed to keep her in a shed and a little pen that Papa built for her, but she hates it. She likes to get out and wander."

Lovatt nodded. "And terrorize half the countryside, no doubt."

"She most certainly doesn't!"

"Ah, but she does. Those of us who aren't familiar with her good qualities are terrified. Leopards have terrible reputations, you know. My horses don't like her at all. I suppose she hasn't learned the jungle tricks about staying downwind. The horses get restless and scared at night when she prowls."

"Is that why you were trying to find her?"

Lovatt nodded. "Actually, I was trying to follow the tracks. Samad swore that the tracks looked like those of a leopard or wildcat of some kind, but I couldn't imagine what one of those would be doing here in England. I'm sure he'll give me grief when I get back home." He grinned at her again, the smile lighting up his eyes. "But enough of that. Do tell me about your family. I haven't heard anything about them in forever."

"And where have you been?"

"India most of the time. I, too, fought in the Peninsula for a short while." He flipped the blade of grass aside. "My father wanted me to come home because of his illness."

"I'm sorry he's not well. Mama and I went for a visit when we were in London, but Redferne was not at home. I thought he must have recovered."

"He's improving. That's why I decided to come down to Shad Abbas for a fortnight or so. The house is mine, now."

"So we're neighbors." Esme wasn't sure if this was good news or bad news. "Do you plan to spend a great deal of time here?"

"As much as necessary." He moved as Spot came over to him and began to sniff at his clothing. Esme could see him stiffen and get ready to slide away, just as Spot had done in the grass. Spot moved away and Lovatt slowly let out his breath. "Would you like me to see you back to Rouvray?"

Esme stood and picked up Spot's leash. "It' isn't necessary for you to walk us home." She grinned at him. "Spot and I are seldom bothered on our walks."

"I daresay not." Lovatt's tone was dry. "Still, I believe I'll walk with you. I'd like to say hello to your father."

"He isn't there." Esme moved along as Spot decided to head for home. She hesitated to say anything else, as she had no idea if Lovatt had heard about her father's difficulties. "He and Mama have gone up to London" She had to call out the last over her shoulder. Spot was in a hurry.

Lovatt caught up with her, his long strides covering the distance in just a second. He grinned, watching Spot break into a lope and Esme break into a trot. "Perhaps you should just let her go and follow her home," he said, his voice full of laughter. "Otherwise, I do believe you're going to have to begin running, and it's much more pleasant to walk back to Rouvray."

Esme started to answer him, but Spot jerked on the leash and began to quicken her pace. Esme was already out of breath. She hated to do it, but she followed Lovatt's suggestion. The moment Spot felt the leash go slack, she was off toward Rouvray. Esme stopped to catch her breath as Lovatt stepped up beside her. He put his hand on her elbow and chuckled. "That was quite a sight, Miss Darling! You're going to have to learn to ride that cat." He looked down at her, concerned, as Esme took a deep breath. "Are you all right?" He put his hands on her shoulders and looked right into her eyes, his green eyes meeting her deep blue ones. Esme felt herself go quite breathless again, but this had little to do with Spot. She blushed and turned her head.

"I'm quite fine, thank you."

"Of course you are." He stepped beside her and put her arm through his, absently patting her hand as it rested on his wrist. "Tell me, how is Mimsy? I would have thought she'd be married and have a houseful of children by now." He began walking toward Rouvray, following Spot's lead. Esme had no choice but to walk along beside him.

"Mimsy is married," she said, and to her ears her voice sounded far away. *Whatever was wrong with her?* she wondered, stumbling. Lovatt paused and looked down at her with concern. She gathered her wits and began chattering, walking on. "She's been married for almost twelve years." She paused a moment, still not looking at Lovatt, intensely aware of the pressure of his arm linked with hers. "She married a baron—Lord Evers's heir. Perhaps you remember him."

"Vincent?" he asked in surprise, guiding Esme around a protruding rock with pressure against her arm. "She married Vincent Jeffereys?"

"Yes. Do you know him?" Esme was uncomfortable. It must be, she decided, that she still disliked Lovatt so much. She had hated him so that the feeling must have stayed with her.

"I know him well. We were in school together, and I stayed with him for several weeks during one summer. He was a year or two above me, but still we were friends." He paused. "Any children?"

Esme shook her head. "No. It's a great tragedy for both of them. Oh, Vincent never says anything, but his mother . . ." Esme made a face.

"I know Lady Evers," Lovatt said with a chuckle.

"She's not Lady Evers now, just the dowager, and she's anxious for the family line to continue." Esme shook her head.

"I remember that well. Even when Vincent was in school, she was impressing on him that it was his duty to marry and continue the line. She was, I suppose, very proud of marrying old Evers. She hasn't changed, then?"

"No. According to Mimsy, the woman mentions the lack of an heir every five minutes. Especially since old Lord Evers died and Vincent came into the title." They topped a small rise, and Rouvray came into view. Esme could see Spot ambling her way into the back of the garden. She paused and looked at Lovatt. "Thank you for escorting me, but it isn't necessary to go farther. I do appreciate it." She smiled at him, thinking she would be polite even though she still hated him. He smiled back, and it took her breath again.

"Oh, I wouldn't think of leaving you alone here in the wilds," he said. "I'll take you to the door."

"That really isn't nec—" Esme began, but stopped as Lovatt began walking, pulling her along.

"Is that Mimsy?" he asked, looking toward Rouvray. "I'd know that blonde head anywhere."

"No. Mimsy hasn't been at Rouvray for several months. She and Vincent were traveling on the continent, and now Mimsy is with Vincent and his mother at Eversleigh House. I don't expect—" She was cut short by a scream of terror.

Lovatt paused only a second, then shoved her out of the path. "Stay here," he ordered, breaking into a run.

Esme wasn't about to stay anywhere, especially after being ordered to do so. She inelegantly lifted her skirts to her knees and began running behind him. She reached the garden gate in time to see Lovatt swoop Mimsy up into his arms just before she swooned. Spot was sitting right in front of them, grooming her paws, looking on with disinterest.

Three

Mimsy put her arms around Lovatt's neck and clung to him. Her blond curls fell artlessly around her perfect face, and her eyelids had a blue shadow to them, while her lips trembled slightly. She looked, Esme thought, rather like a painting that would be found in one of Mrs. Radcliffe's books.

"It's only Spot," Esme said, putting her hand under Mimsy's head and shaking her slightly. "I wrote you that Spot had grown."

Mimsy's eyes fluttered open, revealing all their china blue beauty. Poems had been written about Mimsy's eyes before she was married to Vincent. Mimsy blinked, tightened her hold on Lovatt's neck, and parted her full, pink lips slightly. "Who . . . ?" She sighed weakly. "Who?" Her eyes widened further. "Chalmers Lovatt!" she whispered, a smile flickering across her face. Mimsy made no move to release him, and Esme noted that Lovatt didn't seem to be concerned about loosening his hold on her body. *Papa would not like this at all,* Esme thought. Mimsy was a married woman, and Vincent's jealousy was legendary.

"Very good, Mimsy," Esme said briskly. "You recognized him." She moved to put her arm about Mimsy's shoulders. Mimsy still didn't release Lovatt.

"Perhaps I should carry her inside so she can lie down," Lovatt suggested. His eyes never left Mimsy's lovely face.

"That would be wonderful." Mimsy sighed and closed her eyes languidly. She sagged imperceptibly, just enough to lean even closer to Lovatt.

Esme snorted in disgust as Lovatt carried Mimsy through the open French doors into the house. She had seen Mimsy faint in just the same way with Vincent, and to Esme's annoyance it had worked in the same way then. If Esme recalled correctly, that was the occasion when Vincent was so overwrought about Mimsy's sensibilities that he had proposed on the spot. Mimsy, of course, had recovered immediately and accepted him.

Lovatt placed Mimsy down carefully on the striped couch in the room that was used as both library and drawing room. He patted Mimsy's hands for a moment, then went to the sideboard to get her a small glass of brandy. Esme leaned over until she was within an inch or so of Mimsy's face. Mimsy had her eyes closed again, and reached up to touch Esme's face with her fingers. "Chalmers Lovatt, is it really you?" she whispered weakly.

"No, it isn't Lovatt, you goose," Esme hissed. "Stop this charade immediately! How could you do this to Vincent? What if someone should tell him?"

Mimsy's eyes flew open and she glanced across the room to Lovatt's back as he was pouring the brandy. "I've left Vincent, so I don't care what you tell him," she whispered back. Lovatt turned, and Mimsy fluttered her eyes, then closed them again, sighing deeply.

"Would you like to give this to the patient?" Lovatt asked, handing Esme the glass of brandy. "Slow sips, and not too much at a time."

"I'd be delighted," Esme said. Lovatt put his arms around Mimsy and sat her upright. Esme held the glass to her lips, and Mimsy took a small swallow. Mimsy gasped as though she had never had brandy before, and then her eyes fluttered open. "Oh," she said, putting her hands on Lovatt's strong biceps. Esme held the glass to her lips again, and tipped it just as Mimsy moved. The entire contents of the glass went right down Mimsy's chin and onto the front of her dress. Mimsy leaped to her feet, banging into Lovatt's head, screamed, and flung her arms outward.

Lovatt sat back in a chair in surprise, while Esme was pushed back onto the couch.

"You did that on purpose, you little twit!" Mimsy screeched, fully recovered. "I know you! Well, it isn't going to work this time!" She ran across the room and grabbed the brandy decanter, tossing the stopper aside as she turned back toward Esme. "See if this matches *your* dress."

Lovatt stood up and reached for her. "Really, Mimsy," he began, stepping in her path. Before Mimsy could stop herself, she had soused Lovatt liberally with the brandy. His cravat was sopping, his waistcoat was drenched, and his face was dripping Major Darling's best brandy.

Mimsy stopped and put her hand over her mouth. "Oh, Chalmers, I'm so sorry. I truly didn't mean to . . . to—"

Lovatt ran his tongue across his upper lip, tasting the brandy, then looked down at his dripping clothing. He tugged at the end of his cravat and wiped his chin. "You certainly haven't changed in all these years, Mimsy," he said.

"I have changed." Mimsy put the brandy decanter down on the table next to Esme. "You just don't realize. You just don't understand." She burst into tears, put her hands over her eyes, and ran from the room.

Lovatt and Esme looked at each other in silence. Lovatt picked up the brandy decanter and looked at the level in the bottle. "Just about enough for the two of us, I'd say, Miss Darling. Shall I pour?"

"Please." Esme handed him the glass she had used for Mimsy and Lovatt poured half the brandy in it, then got himself another glass from the cabinet and poured the rest. "To old times," he said, raising his glass. He drained it in one gulp.

Esme had taken only a sip of her brandy when Abram came in. "Glad to see you here, Esme. I wanted . . ." He stopped and looked around, staring first at Esme and then at Lovatt, taking in with one shocked look the dripping cravat, ruined waistcoat, and empty glass. "Good Lord! What happened here?" He paused and looked again. "Lovatt?" he asked.

"Yes, indeed."

"Good afternoon, Bram. You're looking particularly fine this afternoon. I'm glad you remember our neighbor." Esme smiled, as if nothing were amiss. Bram followed her lead, making himself look at Lovatt's face rather than his ruined clothing and the empty glass. Esme stifled a giggle—Lovatt's face was drying, but still had drops of brandy here and there. Bram studiously ignored them.

"It's been several years," Bram said. "Warm weather this afternoon." He sat down and smiled. "It may rain later, though. I walked from the post and thought I saw clouds gathering."

Lovatt removed a handkerchief from his pocket and mopped his face. He looked at Esme and began to chuckle. Esme couldn't help herself—she began laughing, as well. Bram looked from one of them to the other as they laughed. Finally, he frowned in Esme's direction. "I do wish you'd tell me what's so funny here. I was just talking about the weather."

"It isn't you, Bram," Esme said as she rubbed her eyes. She had laughed so hard they were watering. "It's Mimsy."

"Mimsy? What does she have to do with anything?"

"She's the one who liberally coated my clothing with your father's brandy," Lovatt drawled. "By the way, this is excellent brandy. If you'll tell me where Major Darling acquired it, I'll replace it."

Bram turned bright red, right up to the roots of his blond hair. "Oh, Papa just . . . it just—"

"Papa bought it from a smuggler like everyone else, I'd

say." Esme's tone was matter-of-fact. "Don't even think of replacing it, Lovatt. If anything, we should be reimbursing you for your clothing. I'm sure Mimsy is mortified."

"Knowing Mimsy, I doubt that." Lovatt's tone was dry.

Bram nodded. "You remember her well, then. She's just as spoiled as ever." He stopped suddenly. "Mimsy did that?" He stared from Lovatt to Esme. "How? Is she here?"

Esme nodded. "She was here when I came back from taking a walk with Spot. Lovatt had tried to kill Spot, and was walking me back home."

"Kill Spot?" Bram was more and more confused.

Lovatt laughed and recounted the afternoon's events. "At least I understand why you'd try to rid the world of that cat," Bram said, shaking his head. "But I don't understand about Mimsy. What's she doing here without Vincent? Sounds havey-cavey to me. What's going on there?"

Esme shot him a warning look. "With Vincent and Mimsy, who knows?" She decided it was time to change the subject. "Have you had an interesting afternoon, Bram?"

"Yes and no." He sighed. "I went off to the garrison to ask questions as you wanted me to, but I found out nothing. Everyone there knows all about Papa being accused and they think it's a hum, but no one knows what to do about it."

"They know!" Esme was horrified. "Bram, really . . ." She tried to move her eyes in Lovatt's direction to warn Bram to be quiet.

Bram did not take the hint and looked at her blankly. "Of course they know. Everyone knows. I'd say that Lovatt here knows." He looked at Lovatt. "Don't you?"

"Know what?"

"Bram," Esme said, frowning, "mind your manners. This is a family matter."

"Horsefeathers. I'm telling you, Esme, the whole town knows about this. The whole post knows every detail. And they're fighting mad about it, too. Everyone there believes—*knows*—that Papa is innocent. As for the real spy, I don't think he's here. I think the men would have ferreted him out and hung him up by his thumbs." Bram began pacing. "No, Esme, that spy has to be someone in town."

"Spy?" Lovatt looked interested. "There's a spy here?" He frowned. "And what does your father have to do with whatever is going on?"

Esme sighed. "Why don't you just put something in the *Gazette,* Bram? How did you ask discreetly at the post, if I may ask? Did you go to the door and shout inside, 'Did anyone here write a letter implicating Major Darling as one of Napoleon's spies?' "

To Esme's horror, Bram turned red. "Well, not exactly, but I did go in and ask." He looked annoyed. "Dash it all, Esme, how was I to find out anything if I didn't ask?" He stopped pacing and sat down across from Lovatt and Esme.

Esme peered down into her empty glass and tried to think of something to say that wouldn't embarrass the family in front of Lovatt. She couldn't think of a thing.

Lovatt regarded Bram for a moment. "Are you saying, Bram, that someone has accused Major Darling of being a spy?"

"That's about it." Bram looked at the floor unhappily. "Whitehall has suspected there's been a spy here at the garrison, and someone in the Horse Guards even talked to Papa about the possibility of him spreading around some erroneous information to try to trap the culprit. Then . . ." He paused, and his voice shook. "Then someone in Calais intercepted a letter which implicated Papa in the plot. He's been called to London to look at the evidence and discuss the problem."

"It's the most ridiculous thing that has ever been proposed!" Esme said with heat. "To think that Papa would do such a thing! The army is his whole life. He's been to

India, to the Peninsula, and at Gibraltar. He would never, never betray England."

"I agree with you." Lovatt's voice was low and warm. "I served under him in India if you recall, and have never met a finer officer." He paused for a moment. "The problem, as I see it, is how to discover who implicated him. If we find that person, we should find the real spy."

"Exactly what I told Bram!" Esme said.

"No you didn't. You told me to go to the garrison and ask questions. That's what I did."

Esme opened her mouth to answer him, but Lovatt interrupted. "No matter. Our immediate problem is to find the real spy here, before the army takes any action about your father. Many people in London admire him, so we may have a while."

"We?" Esme asked. "Lovatt, our family certainly can't expect you to assist in any way. I assure you that Bram and I will track down the culprit. Although I do thank you for your generous offer."

Lovatt raised an eyebrow and looked at her. "Of course I intend to help, Miss Darling. After all, as a child I was here as much as I was at Shad Abbas. Major Darling was always very kind to me. Then, when I was in India, he taught me everything I know about the army. I owe him much, and my helping now would be an excellent way to repay him."

"Thank you," Bram said, "we can certainly use your help." At the same moment, Esme looked at Lovatt coolly and said, "Thank you, but I think we can manage on our own. I certainly don't want you to risk your career by getting involved."

"I think I mentioned that I am home on leave because Redferne is ill, so my career is on hold at the present. I don't mind being involved at all. I'm happy to help." Lovatt stood and waved her objection aside. Turning to Bram, he put out his hand. "Perhaps the best way for us to go about this is to think about what we might do, then get together and discuss it. Will you and your sisters join me for supper tonight at Shad Abbas? We'll put our suggestions together and come up with a plan of action."

Bram agreed while Esme sat and fumed. She was completely unaccustomed to being ignored, especially in favor of Bram. True, he was the male and Major Darling's heir, but Major Darling had always discussed things with Esme rather than Bram. Ignoring her was, Esme thought as she watched Lovatt walk out through the garden and take the path to Shad Abbas, one more thing to add to her list of black marks against Lovatt. Nothing could be as bad as the time he tossed her in the millpond, but this was close. She would, she decided, ignore Lovatt, while she found the spy. She certainly knew much more about the men at the garrison than Lovatt did. She had not only met them socially, but her father had discussed each of them as he talked about the day-to-day activities of the post. Lovatt was not needed. If she refused to have anything to do with him, surely he would see that his help wasn't necessary.

"I'm certainly glad Lovatt is helping us," Bram said, rubbing his hands together briskly. "We want to keep on his good side, as well. He has a great deal of influence in London, I understand."

"Worse luck," Esme muttered, mentally adding another black mark. She picked up the brandy decanter and glasses and started toward the kitchen.

"Worse luck? Esme, whatever do you mean? Papa may need an influential voice."

"Well, if he does, let's try to find someone other than Lovatt. I can't abide the man."

Aunt Penny came into the room, her cap on backward. "Did I hear someone, dears?" she asked, looking around. Her eyes widened as she saw the glasses and empty decanter. "Oh, my dear," she said in a strangled tone. "I had no idea. And in the middle of the afternoon, at that. Do your parents know?"

Esme took a step back so Aunt Penny couldn't smell the brandy on her breath. "We had a visitor, Aunt Penny. He spilled brandy on him."

"What kind of visitor would do that?" Aunt Penny walked to the sofa and picked up the sodden handkerchief Lovatt had forgotten. "There's just no delicate way to put this." She paused. "Does he have a . . . a problem?"

Esme took the handkerchief from her. "He *is* a problem, Aunt Penny," she said, skirting the furniture on her way to the door. "Now, if you'll excuse me . . ."

Mimsy came to the door, almost running into Esme. She glanced at the empty decanter, then at Esme. "Esme, really!"

Luckily, Bram interrupted. "What are you doing here, Mimsy? Where's Vincent?"

Mimsy draped herself on the sofa again and put her hand up to her forehead. Her feet dangled over the edge, showing new kid slippers that matched her gown. "I've left Vincent," she announced. "I know it will cause a scandal, but it can't be helped. I can't go on!"

Aunt Penny screamed, clasped her hands to her chest, and collapsed onto the nearest chair. "Fetch my vinaigrette," she moaned. "Hurry!" She closed her eyes and leaned back. "Whatever will James and Isabel say? To think that this has happened while I'm responsible!" She sat up suddenly and looked at Mimsy. "My dear, you must go back. If you return tomorrow morning, no one will think anything. Just tell them you came to visit your family. You can swear that Esme was sick and needed you. It will be no problem at all. Tell them that Esme has . . . a problem."

"I told Vincent's mother," Mimsy said, opening her eyes.

"You told her that Esme has a problem? Excellent." Aunt Penny nodded.

"No." Mimsy frowned. "I told his mother that I was leaving Vincent. And I told his sister. And I left a letter for Vincent.''

Esme walked over and sat in the chair Lovatt had used. "A letter? You didn't tell him yourself?"

Mimsy shook her head. She looked miserable. "I just couldn't tell him."

Esme frowned. "Why, Mimsy? What would cause you to take such a shocking step? It isn't as if Vincent is Lord Byron or someone of that ilk. He's madly in love with you, and has always been excessively good to you."

Mimsy began sobbing. "That's part of the problem. The other part is his mother. We had a terrible fight—his mother and I—and she told me that if I really loved Vincent I would divorce him and let him remarry and beget an heir."

"And you listened to her?"

"Not at first." Mimsy shook her head. "But that night I asked Vincent if he would like a baby, and he said that he would." She burst into tears, "I just couldn't bear being blamed for that anymore. I'd love a child more than anything. Do you know how this breaks my heart?"

"Of course, dear." Aunt Penny patted Mimsy's ankle. "Now you just rest, and tomorrow you can go back home."

"I'm not going back. Not ever." Mimsy's mouth narrowed and straightened. Bram and Esme looked at each other. They had seen that look before, and it did not bode well. When Mimsy looked that stubborn, she never changed her mind.

Mrs. Hinson, the housekeeper, came to the door. "Pardon, but there's a visitor."

"Tell whoever it is that we're not at home," Bram said testily. "Get a name and I'll write him a note."

"Very good." Mrs. Hinson looked over her shoulder as someone began shouting and cursing at the door. She shut the drawing room door, but returned in a moment. Her face was flushed, and she appeared all at sixes and sevens.

"He doesn't believe that no one is at home. He demands to be let inside. Now."

"Who would be that rude?" Esme asked, annoyance tinging her voice. Without thinking, she wiped her face with the handkerchief she had in her hand. The smell of brandy filled her nostrils.

Mrs. Hinson rolled her eyes. "He's going to come in. He said that if I didn't let him in, he'd break down the door."

"Who said that, Mrs. Hinson? Who?" Esme's eyes were watering from the brandy fumes.

"Lord Evers." Mrs. Hinson sounded quite put upon.

"Oh, Lord, Vincent's here," Esme said, looking down at Papa's decanter. This was no time for it to be empty.

Four

Mrs. Hinson turned just as the front door crashed open, a sound accompanied by fluent cursing. Esme, Bram, and Mrs. Hinson ran to the front door to discover Vincent inside, in a towering rage, with Mrs. Hinson's husband on the floor, blood flowing from a cut in his forehead.

"You've killed him!" Mrs. Hinson screeched, throwing herself on her beloved. Hinson made a gurgling sound when she landed on him. Mrs. Hinson was not a small woman.

Esme knelt beside Hinson and began swabbing at his wound with Lovatt's handkerchief. The brandy stung the wound and Hinson yelled, prompting Mrs. Hinson to even louder screeching. Hinson struggled to get up, waving both Esme and his wife away. His thin face and crooked nose were covered in blood streaked with brandy. He rolled Mrs. Hinson away and stood with as much dignity as he could muster.

"What happened, Hinson?" Esme asked.

"The door," he said groggily. "It was the door."

Esme looked at the cut in his forehead. It was long and straight. The door had caught him right down the side of his face. She turned to Vincent. "You should be ashamed of yourself, Vincent. We would have let you inside."

Vincent pulled Hinson to his feet. "My apologies," he mumbled, then sniffed. He locked at Esme, the brandy decanter, the empty glass, and the handkerchief, then paused. "Esme, I had no idea. No idea at all. And this early in the afternoon, too."

"Don't be ridiculous, Vincent." Esme stood, gathering the glassware, and glared at him. "Mimsy is in the library. She's quite overset, so don't say anything to her." She started toward the kitchen, thought the better of it, then put the glassware and handkerchief on the second step of the stairs. "I'll go with you."

"I don't want to distress her," Vincent said. "I just want to take her back to Eversleigh House with me." He paused. "She . . . she left me a letter."

"I know." Esme sighed. "Come along, Vincent."

Mimsy's mouth was still in a straight, stubborn line when they went into the drawing room. Vincent demanded, he raged, he shouted, and it was no use. Mimsy refused to speak to him for a good half an hour. Finally she spoke. "Vincent, you might as well return to Eversleigh House. I am not going back there. In the meantime, it's too late for you to return this evening, and I know how much you hate inns, so you might as well stay here." She stood. "Mrs. Hinson will see you to your room, Vincent. Bram, Esme, I wish to speak privately." Mimsy swept out of the room as Bram and Esme looked at each other. This wasn't the Mimsy they had known.

Esme got Vincent settled in the upstairs bedchamber at the opposite end of the hall from Mimsy's room, then hunted up Bram. They went together to Mimsy's room. She was there, sitting in a chair, her mouth still in a straight, stubborn line.

"All right, Mimsy," Bram said, sitting down in the only other chair in the room. Esme stepped up on the footstool and perched on the edge of the bed. Bram pulled his watch from his pocket and flipped the lid on it. "I don't have long. I promised Papa that I would see to his business, and I want to check on some things before we get ready to go over to Lovatt's this evening."

"Lovatt's? What's this?" Mimsy sounded peevish. "Were we invited to supper and no one told me?"

"We were invited, and no one told you because we hadn't seen you," Esme said.

"What about Vincent?" Mimsy glared at her. "We just can't leave him here alone."

"I'm sure Lovatt won't mind another for supper. See if Vincent wants to go, then send Lovatt a quick note." Bram frowned. "What did you want, Mimsy? I need to be going."

"I'm not going back to Vincent." Mimsy's voice was flat. "And furthermore, I don't want you to tell him why I left." Her shoulders began to shake, and tears rolled down her cheeks. For Esme, this was worse than the loud crying she had done before. For the first time, she realized just how deeply it hurt Mimsy that she was unable to have a child. "Mimsy," Esme said quietly, "perhaps he should know. I think Vincent loves you, child or no child. He doesn't care. After all, his cousin Anne already has two small boys who could inherit."

"Yes," Mimsy said bitterly, "but as Vincent's mother said, they won't have the right name. They won't be carrying on the *real* Jeffereys line, as she put it."

"From what I've heard about the Jeffereys line, it really isn't worth worrying too much about," Bram said. Mimsy frowned at him and he added hastily, "Vincent excepted, of course. He's really not like the rest of them."

"Unfortunately, you're right, Bram," Esme said with a sigh. "And I do recall Papa had some reservations about Vincent because of the dowager's past. Papa wouldn't tell me, but he did say such things weren't for my ears. Once I overheard him telling Mama that Vincent's mother had a scandalous reputation in her youth."

Mimsy waved that all aside. "Oh, I've heard all the stories, and I really wonder about them. She's such a stickler now. She spends half of her time at church, and the other half telling me what I should do. The divorce thing was a

terrible decision for her, she said. She's against it in prin-
ciple, but that overrode her concern about Vincent fathering the next heir."

"So those stories are true?" Esme's eyes widened. "I
wondered why Papa later told Mama that Vincent certainly
didn't resemble the Jeffereys because he was so good and
responsible."

"Responsible or not, I'm not going back to him. I've
made up my mind. To *think* that he would tell me that he
wanted a child!" She started crying again. "He'll just have
to have one by someone else." She stood and mopped at
her eyes. "That's all I wanted to tell you. I want you to
promise me that you won't tell him why I left."

"Dash it all, Mimsy, he needs to know. How can he fix
something if he doesn't know what to fix?" Bram looked
annoyed.

"This is something he can't fix, Bram. Now promise
me." Mimsy stared right at him.

Bram reddened, then promised. "Although I don't
agree with you, Mimsy. I'm just promising to keep you from
crying again." He looked at his watch again, and stood.
"I'll meet you later, and we'll all go together to Shad Abbas
for supper." He turned and left them.

Mimsy turned and looked at Esme. "Now *you* promise."

"All right, Mimsy, I promise." Esme slid down from the
bed and went to the door. "But I agree with Bram. You're
wrong. Vincent deserves to know."

"No matter." Mimsy's mouth straightened again and she
wiped her eyes. She walked to the mirror and looked at
herself. "I may even remarry. Perhaps I can find someone
with a house full of children, and he won't want any
more."

"You're in love with Vincent, and you know it. You would
never admit it, Mimsy, but I know you. You've been in love
with him since the first time you ever saw him."

Mimsy smiled into the mirror. "Yes. That was at Lady

Brockhaven's ball. He was the handsomest man there. He looked at me over the head of that insipid Sarah Lewis, who was chasing him at the time. Our eyes met, and I knew right then that I was going to marry him. He told me that he knew the same thing." She paused. "He was so wonderful on our trip to the continent, Esme. He was so kind and loving. Just perfect."

"Well, if you love him, go back to him. He's quite beside himself."

Mimsy shook her head. "No. I've made up my mind." She turned away from the mirror and faced Esme. "Now, if you don't mind, I think I'll take a short nap before I get ready to go to Shad Abbas." She glanced out the window. "Esme, Vincent is in the garden, and I do believe that your leopard is thinking of attacking him. Poor Vincent is standing on a bench. I believe the leopard is thinking of a late lunch."

"Oh, good heavens!" Esme hit her forehead with the palm of her hand. "Ned isn't coming today, and I haven't fed Spot yet. Don't worry about Vincent, though—Spot isn't carnivorous. Well, she is, but she hasn't eaten humans."

"Yet," added Mimsy.

Esme gave her a horrified look and ran down the stairs.

Vincent was standing on the garden bench, while Spot stretched luxuriantly on the ground in front of it. "She won't hurt you, Vincent!" Esme called. "She just wants to be scratched."

"Scratched! I say, scratched! Look what this vicious animal did to my coat!" Spot moved as Esme came near, and Vincent tried to take a step back. He missed his footing and fell backward off the bench, right into Esme's carefully nurtured violet dahlia. She screamed as she heard the stems snap. Spot was surprised at the confusion and leaped onto the bench to see what was happening. Vincent opened his eyes to see Spot perched right above him, yellow eyes gleaming. He swatted at her and Spot swatted back, as she always did when Esme played with her. Vincent went rigid. "She's. Going. To. Kill. Me." His voice was a hoarse whisper.

"Nonsense." Esme waded to the broken dahlia, picking up stems and leaves wherever she could. "Vincent, stand up and get out of my flowers. These flowers were the ones Señora Romero sent me last winter, and I've pampered them through the whole spring. I was going to send a tuber to the Horticultural Society. How could you have done this?"

Vincent didn't answer her. Instead, his eyes large, he scooted back as far as he could until he ran into some dahlia stakes. Then he slithered to his feet slowly, never taking his eyes from Spot, who was waiting patiently for him to move his hands again and play with her.

"Captain William Arno to see you," Mrs. Hinson announced from the French doors that led into the garden. She looked at Spot with loathing, Mrs. Hinson was a dog person, and had informed Esme that she didn't hold with cats of any kind—not even big ones. Esme did her best to keep Spot out of Mrs. Hinson's way, but Spot seemed to know the woman hated her and did her best to be around Mrs. Hinson often. Esme had once remarked to Bram that it did not make for a happy situation.

"Ask him to wait if you will, Mrs. Hinson, and I'll be there in a moment," Esme called out. "And bring me some garden shears, please. I'll save as many of these flowers as possible."

"Allow me to help." Captain Arno came across the lawn to the dahlia patch. "I followed Mrs. Hinson, thinking you might be out here." He took in the situation in a glance. "An accident?"

"Yes." Esme held out a hand for Vincent and guided him out of the dahlia patch. He was dirty from top to toe. Spot had evidently tried to jump up on him and give him a hug, judging from the pawprints on his coat. "Are you all right, Vincent?" she asked. Actually, he looked wretched.

"I'm fine," he said, glancing at Spot and edging sideways. "I believe I'll just go wash up a little. It was a dusty trip." He took off across the lawn at a lope.

"My brother-in-law, Lord Evers," Esme said to Captain Arno. "I'm sorry I didn't manage the introductions before he left. He was in something of a hurry, but please don't think he's at all rude. Lord Evers, as you saw, had fallen into the dahlias."

Arno chuckled. "I noted." He looked sideways to see that Spot had gone off to a shady spot and stretched out. Then he looked at the crushed flowers. "Could I help you with these, Miss Darling? I'm no gardener, but if you would tell me what you wish, I'll be glad to assist."

Esme sighed and looked at the bouquet of dahlias she had salvaged. Mrs. Hinson appeared with the shears, and Esme snipped a few more and handed them to Arno. "I do believe that's all I'm going to save," she said sadly. "I'll have to cut the rest and try to save the tubers when fall comes." She turned with a determined smile and took the flowers from Arno. "Thank you for your assistance. Would you like to come inside for some tea? I'm afraid Bram isn't here right now."

Arno glanced again at Spot to make sure she hadn't stirred, then offered his arm to Esme. "Actually, Miss Darling, I didn't come to Rouvray to see Lieutenant Darling. I had pleasanter prospects in mind." He smiled down at her and Esme was struck, as always, by just how handsome he was. Arno wasn't tall, not as tall as Lovatt, but still had a presence. His hair was dark, and was cut so that the ends curled slightly. His skin was becomingly tanned from his being outdoors, and his features had, if gossip were to be believed, sent many a young miss head over heels during the short time he had been in London. There had been no scandal attached to Arno, and he always seemed a model of decorum. He was simply unbelievably handsome, and always created a stir at every rout and ball he attended.

In his spotless uniform, he was always the center of attention, especially with the ladies. Esme had remarked once that Arno should make a very good marriage, but her father had noted that Arno's origins were somewhat suspect. He had no family that anyone knew of, other than an uncle in trade who had bought his colors. "For all that," Major Darling had remarked, "he's a good man, I think, and will go far. Many men have overcome a lack of background. Arno may even have a good ancestry. He certainly has manners enough."

Arno's manners were impeccable as he sat Esme down in the small drawing room and took the flowers from her. Esme rang for Mrs. Hinson, and she came and took the flowers and a request for tea.

As they sipped tea, Arno smiled at her over his cup. "In truth, Miss Darling, I'm glad to find you alone, as I wish to discuss a matter of some delicacy with you." He paused. "As you know, Lieutenant Darling asked at the garrison about . . . about the problem your father is facing."

Esme closed her eyes for a moment. She would kill Bram the next time she saw him. That was a certainty.

Arno read her expression. "Don't be embarrassed, Miss Darling. As your father's aide, I, of course, was aware of this. I was even with him when he received word about the letter that implicated him." He took a sip of tea and put his cup down on the table in front of him. "I wish to offer my help to you, Miss Darling. I know how much this must hurt you, since Major Darling is one of the most loyal soldiers in the realm, and I would like to do something to help."

"That really isn't necessary, Captain Arno, although I appreciate your offer." Esme smiled at him warmly. He really was a nice person.

He leaned over and took her hand. "Please allow me to assist, Miss Darling. You know how much I admire your father, and I want to do something to erase this stain from his record. After all, who knows the garrison better than I? I could be a great help to you in your search."

Esme looked into his dark eyes and was impressed by his sincerity. "Thank you, Captain Arno. I accept your offer. You don't know how much it means to me to know that Papa's friends are rallying around him."

"He's both an excellent commander and a good man." Arno turned her hand over and rubbed his thumb across her palm. "Miss Darling, why don't I see what I can discover and then meet you to discuss it?" He looked right into Esme's eyes, his dark eyes warm. "Tomorrow?"

Esme felt strange. She knew her father would approve if Arno came to see her. In spite of the question about Arno's origins, Major Darling liked the man, and had often hinted to Esme that she might foster an acquaintance. And, yes, Arno was the most handsome man she had ever known. More handsome than Lovatt, she thought. Still, there was something about Lovatt. . . .

"Tomorrow?" Arno repeated.

"That would be good," Esme said, glancing at her hand. Arno's fingers were warm. "Do you think you might discover something by then?"

"I don't know, but I intend to try." His voice was low and husky. "Miss Darling—" he began, but stopped as Mimsy ran into the room.

"Esme, I wanted to know if you had—oh, do excuse me!" She stopped and her eyes widened as she looked at Arno, then at Esme, then at Arno's fingers clasping Esme's hand.

Arno stood and Esme made the introductions. "Lady Evers," Arno said, bowing. He looked at Mimsy in much the same way that he had looked at Esme. "It's such a pleasure to meet you. I've heard so much about Major Darling's other daughter. I must say that you surpass all the compliments."

Mimsy, to Esme's disgust, smiled and batted her eyes at him. Esme looked anxiously at the door. Vincent's jealousy was legendary, not only in the family, but in London. The last thing the Darling family needed was for Vincent to call out Captain Arno at daybreak. Esme decided to act.

"Captain Arno, I do hate to cut your visit short, but we have a supper engagement." Esme stood aside so he could get to the door.

Arno took the hint at once. "Of course. A pleasure to meet you, Lady Evers." He turned to Esme as she shepherded him out the door. Hinson was never around when she needed him.

"Good-bye, Miss Darling. I'll see you tomorrow." He bowed slightly to the two of them and then left.

"Where did you find that one?" Mimsy asked as soon as the door was closed. Now that he wasn't needed, Hinson wandered in to see what was happening and then wandered out again, headed for the kitchen.

"He's father's aide. And don't hint at any kind of *tendre* there. There is nothing."

Mimsy looked shrewdly at Esme. "There could be, I believe. Marrying James Darling's daughter could be a step up for a career army man."

"I have no intention of marrying Captain Arno, or anyone else," Esme said.

"Nonsense. You merely need some lessons in how to get on. It's a good thing for you that I'm here. I'll be glad to teach you."

"Never. Now if you'll excuse me, I need to get ready to go to Lovatt's for supper."

Mimsy sighed. "Ah, Chalmers Lovatt. I could have married him. Do you know he was desperately in love with me when we were twelve or so?" She followed Esme up the stairs.

"So he said," Esme answered woodenly. "Why didn't you wait for him and marry him?"

"Lovatt? Good heavens, Esme, use your head. Lovatt and I would be at each other's throats within an hour. He's much too independent and strong-willed. No, he needs a woman just as strong as he is." She paused on a step and mused a moment. "Still, Esme, if the gossip about his family and their fortune is true, Lovatt would be quite a catch." She stopped at the top of the stairs and looked at Esme. "Good Lord, Esme, are you considering Lovatt?"

Esme sighed. "Must you always give everything the wrong interpretation, Mimsy? No, I have no interest in Lovatt. I have no interest in Arno. My only interest right now is in proving that Papa is innocent."

"Perhaps. But it wouldn't hurt to indulge in a little flirtation while two such handsome gentlemen are around. Just watch me tonight, and I'll show you how to do it."

Esme turned, her hand on the doorknob. "Mimsy, you know how Vincent is. Don't even think of it!"

"Vincent might as well get accustomed to it. After all, we won't be married for long. So just watch me, and learn how it's done." Mimsy laughed and went into her room.

Esme closed her eyes and put her head on the cool, painted white door. "Oh, good heavens," she moaned, "how could things get any worse?"

Five

Supper at Lovatt's was everything Esme had thought it would be—a disaster. She had known the evening would be bordering on calamity when, in spite of Esme's hints, Vincent insisted on going along with them. Trying to dissuade him, Esme had mentioned that Lovatt had just invited them on the spur of the moment, and Vincent seized on that.

"Then he certainly won't mind one more," he said, echoing Bram. "After all," he explained, "I've known Lovatt's family for years, and it would look strange to everyone if I were here and didn't go visit. We were in school together."

"Yes, he told me," Esme said, sighing. "He even spent a summer with you, I believe."

Vincent registered surprise. "Why yes, he did. I had forgotten that. All the more reason for me to go to Shad Abbas with you." It made sense, so Aunt Penny dispatched Hinson to inform Lovatt that Lord Evers had arrived and to ask if he could be included in the invitation. Lovatt wrote back that nothing would please him more.

Esme had not been to Shad Abbas for several years—the last time before her family went off to Spain. Esme had been only fourteen at the time. Now, the house looked much different than it had then. Shad Abbas wasn't the principal seat for Lovatt's father, Lord Redferne, but it had always been Lovatt's favorite place as a child. His mother had loved it as well, preferring it to the larger country

house, and she had stayed at Shad Abbas at every opportunity, usually bringing Lovatt with her. That was why the
Darling children were so well acquainted with him.

Lady Redferne had seen to the gardens at Shad Abbas,
and they were lovely and meticulously kept. She had spoken
with Esme about some dahlias when she was visiting the
previous summer. Esme had sent her three of the tubers
from Spain, but hadn't heard how they had done. She
didn't see them in the garden as they approached the
house. They were probably, she decided, in the informal
back garden.

As Esme and her family rode up the front drive, she noted
that Lovatt had refurbished the outside of the house, not
really adding anything to it, but cleaning the stone and
applying paint to the trim. The side gardens had been ex-
panded so that they complemented both ends of the house,
setting it off nicely in the lawn. When they went inside, she
saw that he had redone the interior, as well.

"When did you see to all this, Lovatt?" she asked as they
were taken to the drawing room to chat for a few minutes
before supper. "This must have called for several visits, or
an extended stay. I hadn't heard about you being in the
neighborhood."

"I wasn't, except for a few very short visits." He looked
around. "I must have written a hundred detailed letters,
though, and Mother saw that the work was done. She had
everything done exactly as I asked."

Esme nodded approvingly. "I commend your taste,
Lovatt. I had no idea you had such an eye." She looked
at him and smiled, only to discover him looking at her in
an odd way. Disconcerted, Esme looked back quickly and
followed Mimsy into the drawing room. Lovatt caught her
arm as she went in the door. "I've redone the gardens, as
well, although they're just beginning. After seeing your
garden at Rouvray, I thought perhaps you would come over
and give me the benefit of your advice."

Before Esme could answer, Mimsy turned and gave Lovatt her most brilliant smile. "You've done wonders with this place," she said, attaching herself to his other arm. "Do show me about." Lovatt smiled down at Mimsy and agreed. Together, Lovatt and Mimsy walked around the house, while Esme walked behind them with Vincent, who was glowering at Lovatt. Esme held Vincent's arm throughout the house tour—she was afraid he'd plant Lovatt a facer if she didn't.

"I can't believe Lovatt would do this to me," Vincent muttered as they looked at the library. "We were friends."

"I'm sure you still are," Esme whispered back, trying to stand between Vincent's line of sight and the scene of Mimsy chattering away with Lovatt. "Remember that Mimsy and Lovatt have known each other for years. Of course they're familiar with each other."

"It just isn't proper," Vincent muttered back, scowling.

Esme sighed. There was nothing she could say—Vincent was entirely correct. Worse, during the entire evening at Shad Abbas, Mimsy seemed to make a point of flirting with Lovatt at every opportunity. After the short house tour, Vincent sat on the sofa until supper was announced, smoldering, watching every move that Mimsy made.

"Remember," Esme noted, sitting down beside him and nodding toward the pair, "they haven't seen each other for years, so they have a great deal to discuss. And Vincent, even though I have never cared much for Lovatt," she surprised herself by the words, "I must own that he is the consummate gentleman."

"Since when?" Vincent's voice was bitter.

Esme stared at him. "Since forever, I suppose. What makes you think differently?"

"I knew him in school," Vincent said morosely. "Furthermore, any lightskirt in London can tell you what kind of gentleman Lovatt is," Vincent said, his eyes never leaving Mimsy. "He's been back from India for six or eight months, now, and I hear he's cut quite a swath."

"But you and Mimsy were gone for four of those months, when you were on the continent, Vincent, so how could you know for sure? How can you credit gossip?" Esme was surprised to find herself again defending Lovatt.

"All right, it was gossip. But there was enough of it so that some of it had to be true." He paused. "Well, Brockhaven told me, so perhaps one or two things may be true."

"And perhaps none."

Vincent ignored her, glaring as Lovatt touched Mimsy's arm. "Another thing, Esme—does it not seem strange to you that Lovatt would choose to come to Shad Abbas just now? Just at the time Mimsy has gotten such a feather in her brain about dissolving our marriage. As if I'd agree to any such thing!"

"Lovatt couldn't possibly have known that. I didn't know myself until today."

"I didn't know until today." Vincent stood and scowled as Mimsy attached herself to Lovatt to go in to supper. Esme noted that Lovatt had been prepared to escort Aunt Penny into the dining room, but Mimsy had intervened. Bram took Aunt Penny's arm, and Vincent walked in with Esme. "Look at that," Vincent whispered hoarsely. "Look at the two of them. They must have been planning this for weeks."

"Planning what?" Esme looked at him in confusion.

"This." Vincent gestured vaguely. "To make fools of themselves in front of everyone. To make a fool of me."

Esme paused before they went into the dining room. "Don't be silly, Vincent. First, no one knew you were going to be here. Second, no one knew Mimsy was going to be here, or that she was going to leave you. I was with Lovatt when he first saw her, and he was as surprised to see her as I was."

Vincent sighed and patted her hand. "I apologize, Esme." He looked at her. "It's just that . . . I simply

couldn't bear it if Mimsy left me. We had the most wonderful time in Europe—it was almost as if we were newly-
weds again. I just don't know what happened to cause her
to do this." His voice broke slightly. "Do you know?"

Esme bit her lip. She had promised Mimsy, and a promise was a promise. "I can't tell you, Vincent. If Mimsy ever
gives me permission, I will. But I *can* tell you that it had
nothing to do with Lovatt."

Vincent sighed and walked with her into the dining
room, where Lovatt had evidently arranged the seating
according to Mimsy's whispered instructions. Lovatt and
Aunt Penny were at the ends of the table. Mimsy and Bram
were to one side, while Esme and Vincent faced them.
Every time Vincent attacked his food with his knife, Esme
knew exactly what he was thinking.

The food was wonderful, although some dishes were
strange. "From India," Lovatt explained when she asked.
"I brought back a cook from India. He cooks for me. I've
also retained Cooper, our cook for years. This way, we have
a mix of both English and Indian food. While I was in India,
I came to enjoy the subtle flavors and spices of their food."

"Do tell us about your stay there," Mimsy said, batting
her lashes at Lovatt. Vincent's knife slipped and went flying
across the table. "Sorry," he muttered, retrieving it. Esme
kicked him under the table.

Esme hardly realized that she had eaten when supper
was over. Between kicking Vincent and fretting about what
Mimsy was doing, she hadn't been aware of eating. She
resolved to enjoy her dessert, a dish made with rice, sugar,
and some spices, but as she took the first spoonful, Mimsy
changed the subject.

"Lovatt, you know people in London. Would you help
Papa?"

This time Esme's spoon went flying. "Really, Mimsy, that
is hardly Lovatt's province. He has already offered to assist,
and although I appreciate his interest, I don't wish to im-

pose." She reached out and retrieved her spoon from Lovatt's plate. "So sorry," she muttered.

"On the contrary," Lovatt said, discreetly wiping rice from his waistcoat with his napkin, "As I told you earlier, I would be delighted to assist. I do have friends in the army." He turned to Esme and smiled, a warm, open smile that made her feel strange. "As I said this afternoon, I do feel that your idea is a good one. If we discover who sent the letter implicating your father, we should be able to get him exonerated of any charge."

"Just what I said," Bram said, nodding.

Esme turned to him, her mouth open. "Really, Bram, that was hardly—" She stopped, not wanting to discuss intimate family matters in front of Lovatt. Then she glanced from Mimsy to Bram, and saw that they were both frowning at her. She gave up. "Thank you, Lovatt. We appreciate your help. I'm sure I speak for Papa, as well."

"What's going on here?" Vincent asked, looking from one to the other. "What's happened?"

Mimsy looked at him. "Oh, Vincent, you didn't know! Papa has been accused of being a spy for Napoleon!" She glanced back at Lovatt and batted her eyelashes again. "Lovatt, I *know* you can help him. Your family is so influential."

"So is mine," Vincent said belligerently. "How was he accused? Who accused him? Just haul the chap up and ask him what's going on."

"That's the problem," Esme explained. "We don't know. Someone working for the Horse Guards intercepted a letter in Calais that implicated Papa. The letter implied, I understand, that Papa was a loyal and trusted spy for Napoleon." She bit her lip, her dessert untouched.

"There was another letter," Bram continued. "One from someone at the garrison. This one, like the other, was anonymous."

Mimsy put her hand on Lovatt's arm. "So you see, Lovatt, you could really assist us."

"And I certainly plan to do that. Thank you for asking me." He pushed his chair back. "Everyone seems to be finished, and I, for one, could use a cigar. Gentlemen?" He looked at Bram and Vincent.

"Certainly," Bram said.

Esme glanced at Vincent and knew that she certainly didn't want him in the same room with Lovatt. Bram, however many his good qualities, was useless in stopping a situation like this. "We really need to leave early," she said, "so perhaps we should just discuss our plans now."

"Oh, not for another hour or two," Mimsy said, putting her hand on Lovatt's arm again. Vincent growled in his throat. Esme tried to kick him again, but he had caught on and moved his leg. Instead, she leaped to her feet and took Vincent by the arm. "We really need to return to Rouvray. I need to check on Spot, and besides, I do have a crashing headache."

"Chicken pox and the ague as well, I suppose," Lovatt said with a grin. "Very well, I'll call for your carriage, but you must promise me that you'll return later in the week. I have a new pianoforte that needs a talented female to play it."

"Not something you'll get out of this family," Bram said. "Talented females, that is."

"I wouldn't say that," Lovatt answered, letting his eyes meet Esme's for a moment. His grin fairly sparkled with devilment.

Mimsy's temper flared when they got in the coach. "Just why, Esme, did you concoct that Banbury tale about having a headache? I wanted to stay a while longer. I enjoy Lovatt's company, even if some of you don't."

"I noted you enjoyed his company," Vincent said, his voice shaking.

"Hush! Hush, you two!" Esme yelled. Then she lowered

her voice. "I don't want to hear another word from either of you. If you must argue, do it alone." She stared hard at Mimsy and Vincent, who were sitting on opposite sides, glaring at each other in the moonlight.

"I must agree," Bram said. "This sort of marriage thing just ain't my dish, at all."

"What did he say, dear?" Aunt Penny asked, touching Esme's arm. "What's that about a dish?"

"Lovatt's dishes were attractive, weren't they?" Esme asked, trying to distract her.

"Oh my, yes. What a lovely rose pattern! A little old-fashioned, but I liked it very much. Did you notice that man in white lurking behind the screen in the dining room? Very strange, I thought. He must be a foreigner, as he is so very dark. Very dark, indeed."

"Lurking?" Esme hadn't seen a thing, but she remembered the man in white who had been with Lovatt when he shot at Spot. "Did he wear a turban?"

"Oh my, yes. Did you see him, too? That certainly makes me feel better! He slipped away so quickly that I thought my eyes had deceived me."

Esme was saved from replying by their arrival at Rouvray. Mimsy and Vincent stalked off to their respective chambers, and Esme began wearily climbing the stairs to her room. "We've got to get Vincent back to Eversleigh before they kill each other," Bram said, falling into step beside her.

"Or worse," she said gloomily, "before *we* kill the two of them."

She went to sleep and dreamed of dark men in white turbans, strange jungle creatures, and, superimposed on everything, Lovatt smiling that devilish grin. It was not a restful night.

The next morning, Esme got up early to check on Spot. The leopard ran to see her and gave her a hug, putting both front paws round Esme's neck. "Good girl," Esme said. "I'll take you for a walk this afternoon if you behave." Spot stood still so Esme could scratch her behind the ears. "I thought you'd like that." She glanced around. "Ah, here comes Ned with your breakfast." Major Darling had had to hire a boy from the village to go by the butcher's daily for meat for Spot. Then they discovered that they also had to have the boy, Ned, feed the leopard. Esme didn't wish to put her hands into the bucket of raw meat and Hinson absolutely refused to get near, as he put it, "them big fangs." Ned didn't seem to mind, and had been a model of punctuality. He seemed quite taken with Spot, and she liked him, as well. Spot liked the bucket of meat even better. It seemed to be her favorite part of the day.

Spot taken care of, Esme went back inside. She planned to garden during the morning, then take Spot for a walk. After that she planned to send Bram back to the garrison to ask more questions.

After breakfast, Esme went upstairs to put on her gardening brogans and an old dress. Hearing a noise, she went into Mimsy's room. Mimsy was in bed, quite pale. "Have you been ill this morning?" Mimsy asked. "I feel terrible. It must have been all those Indian spices at Lovatt's. I can never eat spicy foods and Vincent can't, either. I wonder if he's ill."

"I don't know. Do you want me to ask Bram to check?"

"Yes. No." Mimsy frowned. "I don't want him to think that I'm worried about him. If I'm going to leave him, then I can't be asking about his health."

"Of course you can." Esme turned. "I'll let you know what Bram discovers."

Vincent was fine. "Those spices," he declared, shaking his head. "We spent every meal in Europe dodging spices. Give me good English cooking any day." He paused. "Do you really think it's the spices? Could she have contracted some deadly disease while we were in one of those foreign cities?" He wanted to send to London for a doctor, but Esme persuaded him that Mimsy had only a touch of indigestion. Then she sent him off with Bram while she went into the garden to tend to her dahlias.

That afternoon, Esme kept her promise and took Spot out for a walk. She retraced her steps to the field where Lovatt had shot at them. A small voice in her head asked if she were hoping to see Lovatt, but she dismissed the thought. She really didn't like the man at all.

Spot played and ran, tracking butterflies through the grass. She crouched and sprang, jumped and stretched. The day was warm and sunny, and Esme sat quietly and watched her, savoring the soft, warm breeze and the sight of the leopard enjoying herself. Finally, after an hour, no one had happened by, so Esme regretfully gathered up Spot's leash. "Come on, it's time to go home. Supper!"

As usual, Spot declared her independence by stretching and waiting until Esme got near with the leash. She played her game of waiting until Esme had attached the leash to the collar. Then Spot jumped up and ran back, dragging the leash. Esme followed, grabbing for the leash, but Spot kept jumping back, keeping just out of reach. Finally Esme grabbed the leash and pulled. Spot ran toward her, and the sudden slack on the leash sent Esme backward. She tumbled down into a small gully and wound up flat on the bottom, with Spot standing over her, looking quite pleased. Esme sat up, dirty all over. "Spot, I'm going to discontinue our walks if you don't stop this."

Lovatt's face appeared at the top of the gully. He had hunkered down on his heels and was laughing as he looked down at Esme and Spot. "I, for one, hope she doesn't stop," he said, giving her his wicked grin. "An entertaining sight if I've ever seen one." He looked approvingly at Esme sitting in the bottom of the gully. "And a fetching turn of ankle, as well."

Esme felt herself blush and stood. "Hardly a thing to say to a lady, Lovatt. I thought gentlemen ignored those things."

He held a hand out to help her. "Gentlemen probably do, Miss Darling. Unfortunately, or fortunately as the case may be, I've never been accused of being one of those."

"So Vincent said, although I must own up to defending you." She dusted off her dress and felt her hair. It had pulled loose from her pins and was standing out in all directions, while her hat had fallen off and was almost crushed. Lovatt dusted it off and put it back on her head. "Hold still while I tie these ribbons," he said, tipping her chin up.

"I won't ask where you learned that particular skill," Esme said when he had finished, straightening the bow until it suited him.

He grinned at her again. "I'm a man of many talents, Miss Darling." He took Spot's leash from her. "Here, let me hold that before this cat takes you galloping off across the field."

"Spot won't allow anyone to hold her leash except me."

"Really?" Lovatt held the leash with one hand and offered his arm to Esme. They began walking across the field, Spot behaving better than usual.

Esme looked up at Lovatt. "Don't gloat, Lovatt. It isn't becoming."

He laughed, throwing his head back in delight. "Perhaps not," he said, "but it's very enjoyable. Especially in this instance."

"It's a half a mile to Rouvray, Lovatt. Spot may have her revenge yet."

"I doubt that." He gave her a smug look. "Haven't you heard about the noted Lovatt way with ladies? Spot, after all, is female."

"Lovatt, you are, as always, incorrigible."

He grinned at her again as Spot trotted docilely beside him. "As are *you*, Miss Darling. One incorrigible meets another. Who knows what may happen next?"

Esme had no reply.

Six

When they got in sight of Rouvray, Lovatt paused, leashing in Spot. To Esme's amazement, Spot sat down on her haunches and waited. "Before we go in, I want to say something," Lovatt said. Esme looked at him and he continued. "From your remarks last night, I realize that you feel your father's problem is something for your family alone, but I do want to help. As I told you, in many ways Major Darling was more of a father to me than Redferne, and I want to repay him in any way I can. However, I don't want to cause you any distress." He turned and looked at her. "Does my participation in this meet with your approval?"

Esme tried to look at him, but couldn't. His gaze was doing strange things to her. She looked at the gardens at Rouvray instead. "I didn't mean to imply that your help isn't appreciated, Lovatt. Mimsy and Bram know you much better from years past than I do, and both of them think you would be able to add a great deal to our search."

"Yes, those few years made a difference. Not so much now, I hope." He grinned wickedly at her again.

Esme blushed and went on. "At any rate, I've been thinking about what Bram said. You are familiar with the army and how things work. You do have many connections there." She paused. "So yes, thank you for offering to help Papa. I know he would appreciate it."

Lovatt put his hands on her shoulders and turned her

to face him. "There," he said softly, "that wasn't so difficult, was it? Now we can work together and do what's best for Major Darling." He ran his fingertip along the line of her jaw and chin, stopping to straighten the bonnet ribbons. "I would have to say that I missed much by not knowing you better as a child. Perhaps I can rectify that situation now that both of us are grown." He stopped and chuckled. "But you were so furious when I threw you in the millpond. I've cherished that memory for years."

"You, Lovatt, are indeed incorrigible. Shall we go? I believe I see Mimsy in the garden walking with Captain Arno. He's Papa's aide, and has offered to help, as well. Shall we go see if he's discovered anything?" She reached for Spot's leash and began walking. Spot bounded ahead, and Esme was forced to lope into the garden behind the leopard.

"Get that thing away from me!" Mimsy screamed as Spot headed directly for her.

Arno stood between Spot and Mimsy, and was rewarded with one of Spot's hugs. He blanched and flinched while Esme pulled Spot away. "She won't hurt you. Truly, she won't," she told Arno. He did not look convinced.

Lovatt took the leash away from Esme and helped get Spot into her fenced lot. Spot rubbed against Lovatt's boots, then looked up at him. Esme could have sworn Spot grinned. Lovatt patted the leopard on the side as she rubbed against him once more. Then she went to a shady spot to flop down and rest. "Well-behaved animal," Lovatt observed.

Esme couldn't resist. "It's my influence."

When they returned to Mimsy and Arno, Mimsy was sipping lemonade, fanning herself, and declaring that she had never been so frightened. Vincent came charging through the door at that moment, coming to a halt beside Mimsy's chair. He pulled another chair up beside her and glared at Arno and Lovatt. Aunt Penny ran out to them. "Did I hear someone scream?"

"Spot frightened Mimsy," Esme explained, "but she's all right now."

Aunt Penny patted Mimsy on the shoulder. "You poor dear." She then patted Lovatt's shoulder. "You, too," she said, nodding her head as she wandered back into the house.

"Aunt Penny doesn't care for the outdoors," Esme explained. "She thinks gardening should be left to gardeners, and walking is only for those interested in punishing their bodies."

"Don't forget her dictum that reading should be left only to men of God," Mimsy added.

Lovatt laughed. "In other words, a thoroughly modern woman."

"We need more of those," Arno said. He paused, looking at Lovatt. "I don't believe we've been introduced."

"Oh, good heavens, my manners!" Esme quickly made the introductions, noticing that there was a definite coolness between Lovatt and Captain Arno. They seemed to have taken each other into instant dislike. Esme couldn't pinpoint anything overt, but there were currents in the air.

Shortly after Mrs. Hinson had brought more lemonade and macaroons for everyone, Bram came in and pulled a chair up so that he sat between Esme and Captain Arno. "Well, William, I hear you've been asking questions around the barracks. Have you discovered anything?"

Arno shook his head. "Nothing of note. I did discover that a thin, dark man was at the butcher's, where he mentioned Major Darling's name. He shouldn't be difficult to locate. My source said he wore a white turban."

Bram grunted, and Esme expected Lovatt to identify the man who had been with him when he shot at Spot, but he said nothing. Esme decided to wait and see what was going on between the men. Lovatt was certainly an enigma.

"Also," Arno went on, "one of the men who had been posted to London last year reported that there were some in the government who were determined to blame someone for the failure to crush Napoleon decisively. They were ready to pick any scapegoat, no matter who."

"But why would anyone pick Papa?" Esme asked. "His reputation is impeccable."

Lovatt raised an eyebrow. "As I see it, there may be one of two reasons, or both, for that. First, he might have been selected because his reputation is impeccable and the investigation would prove nothing, so he would be exonerated. This would be an effective red herring. The second reason may deal with time. If the army spends a great deal of time examining these charges, it gives the real spy some working room to do whatever he needs to do."

Esme frowned. "True, Lovatt. But what if this person is effective with these false charges, and Papa is ruined?"

"That would be good for the spy, as well. The army would look no further." Lovatt sipped his lemonade and grimaced. Esme thought he must have been wishing for brandy.

"None of the options are good here," Bram said thoughtfully. "We have to find the real culprit."

"I think you're all being ridiculous," Mimsy said. "Everyone knows Papa is innocent, and this will all pass. Why don't we discuss something more pleasant?" She turned to Arno. "Tell me, Captain Arno, have you been to the town assemblies? Are they as dull as they used to be?"

Captain Arno smiled at her as Vincent made a strangled noise in his throat. The conversation turned to social events. Esme didn't pay much attention to the gossip bandied about—she was much too busy trying to make sure that Vincent didn't say anything offensive to either Captain Arno or Lovatt. At last Arno rose to leave, and Mimsy declared that she was going inside to rest. Vincent stayed only long enough to announce to Bram and Esme that he was going to stay at Rouvray until Mimsy came to her senses and returned to Eversleigh with him. Then he stomped away into the recesses of the house.

"Another quiet family gathering," Bram observed.

"Many more, and I'm going to take to my bed with a permanent headache," Esme said, touching her temples with her fingers. "Vincent and Mimsy we don't need while all this is going on with Papa."

"No, it's a distraction," Lovatt said, pulling his chair up to the table and leaning on his elbows, "but they're here, and one can't ignore them."

"True," Bram said, "but Mimsy has the brains of a gorse-bush. She's not worried about Papa at all." He paused. "Of course, I suppose she has enough on her plate without that."

Esme, as Lovatt and Bram had done, pulled her chair closer to the table and then leaned toward them. "Granted, but she and Vincent will have to work that out. We really can't do much. Our main concern right now must be Papa. Does anyone have a suggestion?"

Lovatt hesitated, and Esme caught it. "Out with it, Lovatt. No matter how something sounds, we need to explore it."

He sighed. "All right, but it sounds farfetched and I can't make a connection." He leaned forward slightly, as did Esme and Bram. "As you know, there's a circus based in town," he began.

Esme nodded. "That's where I rescued Spot. A terrible place."

"Well, it's much like all circuses." Lovatt bit his lower lip for a moment. "I was thinking about a cover for a spy, and how a spy would need to move from place to place without being suspected, and I thought about the circus. There would be no better way to move in and out of town without anyone noticing."

"Or," Bram added, "no better way to hide. There's an assortment of unusual people there. A stranger wouldn't be remarked at all."

"Exactly. There are even two families from India there." He stopped and ran his fingers through his hair, tumbling it around his face. "I sent Samad to the circus with instructions to make their acquaintance and see if anyone in either family had noted anything at all unusual." He paused. "The families had noted nothing, probably because their English is poor and they stay to themselves, but while Samad was there, he noticed two soldiers going into the animal trainer's tent. Now, this wouldn't be strange, but Samad reported that the two looked around before they went inside, almost as though they were worried about being followed. He didn't know the word to use, but I gathered that the two looked furtive."

"They could be carrying information!" Esme whispered hoarsely.

"I hate to be cynical or embarrass you in any way, but they could also have been visiting the keeper's wife, if you get my meaning," Lovatt said. "However, I do think the circus deserves further investigation."

Bram frowned. "True. Well, why don't we visit the place and see what we can turn up? I'll speak to Arno about it, as well. I saw him there one day, and when I asked why he was there, he said he had an acquaintance in the vicinity. Arno might be able to find out something."

Lovatt hesitated before replying. "I know you trust Arno implicitly, but I would like to keep our suspicions to ourselves for a while. The more people who know about our investigation, the more likely it is that the spy will be alerted."

Esme laughed at him. "Really, Lovatt, Captain Arno is Papa's aide. He's as distressed as we are, and he's offered to help."

"Probably so, but please humor me in this. Let's keep this private until we see if there is anything to question at the circus. Then, if we need to, we can bring in Arno."

"All right, Lovatt," Bram said. "Shall we go tomorrow?"

Esme heard a noise behind her and turned. It was Hinson, showing Ned out the back, toward Spot's pen. "I have to help Ned," she said with a sigh. "I dearly love Spot, but her eating habits are terrible. Raw meat."

"The responsibilities of pet ownership," Lovatt said with a laugh as he stood up. "Allow me to help Ned. It's the least I can do since Spot behaved so nicely today." He strode toward the pen to join Ned.

Lovatt walked home, deep in thought. For an instant he had considered telling Esme why he had come back to Shad Abbas. He had been in London after his tour in India, and had toyed with various things to do with his life. Just before he left India, he had helped his commanding officer ferret out two soldiers who had been selling army property and pocketing the proceeds. It had been noted on his record, so when word reached London about the spy in Major Darling's command, he had been tapped to investigate. He felt totally inadequate for the job, and only agreed because he felt he owed a debt to Major Darling. Now here he was, and he seemed to have run into a wall. It didn't help at all that Arno and the Darlings were asking questions—that only served to push the real spy, whoever he was, further underground.

Right now, his problem was to distract Esme and Bram so they didn't further alarm the real spy. He had wondered what might send the Darlings off in another direction, and had rejected several plans involving the garrison. If that was where the real spy was based, he certainly didn't want Bram or Esme asking questions or putting the spy on guard. The idea of the circus had sprung full-blown into his head when Esme was telling him about rescuing Spot. There were enough odd things at the circus to keep Esme busy for months. Samad could stay there for a while and feed information to Esme. That should distract her.

Esme. He smiled briefly as he topped the small hill above Shad Abbas and looked at the property. He always thought of Shad Abbas when he thought of home. It was where he always wanted to be. He looked at the house for a moment, then walked toward it, thinking again of Esme.

The last time he had seen her, years ago, she must have been all of ten years old. He remembered that she had been all arms and legs, and had thoroughly despised him.

Now she has grown into a beautiful woman, he thought. *A beautiful and intelligent woman,* he amended. Even better, she had no time for all the things he hated about society: the gossip, the flirting, the manipulation. He wasn't much at being a man about town. Lord knew he had tried, since his father expected it of him. He had been to every rout and function in London for months, meeting every insipid miss in town, creating gossip at every turn. No, that life was not for him—Lovatt much preferred Shad Abbas.

As he went into the airy, marble hall of Shad Abbas, he wondered how Esme would look seated in the little yellow parlor, waiting for him. The idea startled him so that he went to his study and poured himself a glass of brandy. *Impossible,* he thought. Esme had always disliked him, and there was no reason for her to have changed her mind. If anything, she had seemed attracted to Captain Arno. He shook his head to rid it of the image of a smiling face and tangled black curls. Resolutely, Lovatt poured himself another brandy and sat at his desk to write a note to London informing them of his lack of progress.

The next day, Lovatt presented himself at Rouvray early. Esme was waiting for him. "Bram said he had something to do, but he would meet us at the Three Dogs Inn. He wondered if we could wait for him there."

"Fine." Lovatt looked at Esme. She looked quite fetching in a cherry and white striped dress trimmed with white. Her bonnet was trimmed with a bunch of artificial cherries, and her hair was tamed and pinned. Lovatt wondered how long that would last. He helped her up into his curricle and they went off to town.

The day was again warm, and there was a wonderful, soft breeze blowing in from the sea. "I just love the smell of the coast in the summer." Esme took a deep breath, closing her eyes. "Don't you?"

"That depends," Lovatt answered. "Of course, some parts of the coast smell of seaweed and dead fish. Some smell of sea salt."

Esme made a face at him. "Don't be so practical, Lovatt. You know very well what I mean."

He smiled at her. "Yes, I do. I love the sea smell, too." He settled back and looked at her. "Tell me about the years I've been gone, Esme. What have you been doing all that time? I know you went to school for a while. Where was that? What did you do then, and afterward?"

Esme raised an eyebrow. It had never occurred to her that Lovatt could be interested in anything she had done. She began just sketching out her life for the past few years, but his questions made her reveal more than she knew. "So, you prefer here to London," he said, as they approached town.

"Yes, I dislike London very much. Mimsy loves it. She and Vincent have a town house there, but don't stay very much because Vincent's mother doesn't like the city. It bothers her lungs."

"Vincent's mother, unfortunately, is something of a tyrant."

Esme sighed. "Yes, I think that's the whole problem between Mimsy and Vincent. Mimsy is terribly in love with Vincent, and he's completely besotted with her. But the dowager is an opinionated, overbearing woman."

"Why don't you tell Vincent that? If he's as he used to be, he's so accustomed to his mother that he can't see it."

She looked at Lovatt. "I can't say anything. I promised

Mimsy that I wouldn't tell Vincent why she left. I can't break that promise."

"Well, why did she leave? I wondered, because Mimsy's too old to be acting the flirt, and I had heard she was very happily married."

Esme hesitated. "Mimsy and Vincent have no children. That's really all I can say."

They drove on in silence until they were at the edge of town. "So Mimsy has no children, and Vincent is an only child. Do I deduce that the dowager has suggested that Mimsy do the right thing and allow Vincent to find another wife?"

Esme's eyes opened wide. "How did you know that? Did Mimsy tell you?"

Lovatt chuckled. "No, I merely added two and two. Knowing the dowager, I have an idea how she would think. Someone should tell Vincent."

"I can't. I promised, and so did Bram." Esme shook her head. "Over there is the Three Dogs Inn. I don't know how long we will have to wait for Bram. If he doesn't come in an hour, perhaps we should go on without him."

"A good suggestion." Lovatt gave her that devilish grin that caused her breath to catch in her throat. "In the meantime, let's engage a private parlor and have something to eat. I've eaten here before, and the food is excellent."

They were just getting their food when Bram ambled in. He ordered a plate, as well, and looked in puzzlement at Lovatt. "I've been thinking, Lovatt. What made you come back to Shad Abbas?" he asked bluntly.

"Bram! How very rude!" Esme exclaimed.

Lovatt raised an eyebrow and shrugged. "I'd had enough of travel, and wanted to see the house after the remodeling had been finished. I've always preferred Shad Abbas to anywhere else." He paused and pinned Bram with a look. "Why do you ask?"

"Arno," Bram said, shoving roast beef around on his

plate with his fork. "He got me down and wanted to talk about you. He said it was strange that you should appear out of the blue just at the time a spy is wandering about."

Esme gasped. "I can't believe that! We've known Lovatt for years." She stopped, surprised to discover herself defending him.

Lovatt gave him a level look. "I understand your concern, and all I can do is tell you that I'm certainly no French spy. It's just coincidence that I'm here right now."

"What I told Arno," Bram said. "Said that theory about you was ridiculous, but he said he wanted to pursue it." Bram absently ate a forkful of beef.

Lovatt chuckled. "Thank you for the warning. If I see any strange characters hiding behind various potted palms, I'll know that Captain Arno's minions are watching." He paused as a serving girl came in with wine and an apple tart. "Tell me," he continued after she had gone, "have you heard anything from your father?"

"He sent word that they'd arrived all right. That's about all. I expect a long letter any time." Bram dug into his apple tart. "Esme, we really need to have Mrs. Hinson make some of these." He ate all of his, and looked over at Esme's untouched tart. "Go on and take it, Bram," she said, laughing. He did.

Over Bram and Esme's objections, Lovatt insisted on paying the bill. They all walked down to the circus and paid to get in. Esme looked around. "I haven't been here since I rescued Spot. I've written letter after letter trying to get the magistrates to investigate the treatment of the animals here. To no avail, I might add."

"So am I to understand that you are *persona non grata* here?" Lovatt offered her his arm.

Bram laughed. "I'd say! One of the men threatened to run her off if she came here again. If it hadn't been for father, those two men might have actually tried something."

"Well, Miss Darling," Lovatt said, smiling down at her,

"try to keep a low profile, and perhaps we'll learn something interesting."

Esme looked around at the garish paint and signs that hid the squalor in back. "If those men are any indication, Lovatt, anything could be happening here."

It was only later that Esme realized how very correct she had been.

Seven

The circus was much quieter than the last time Esme had visited it. Before, it had been a noisy place full of many people, especially soldiers. Now, there were only a few people milling around, mostly mothers who had brought their children for the pony rides. The magician was halfheartedly trying to bamboozle some off duty soldiers, and the man with the walnut shell game had two gullible farmers standing in front of his facile fingers. There were a few other attractions, but most of the circus seemed shut down. The appeal of the animals in cages had lured several smaller children, who stood near the bars with their parents, pointing to the strange animals.

"What on earth is that?" Bram asked, looking at a strange hoofed animal.

Lovatt peered at an elegant animal that looked out of place in its painted cage. "I've never seen one in the flesh, but I've seen pictures. I believe that's called a llama. It's from high in the Andes of South America."

"Poor thing," Esme said, looking at the animal. It looked as if it should be running in the open wind rather than standing in a cramped cage. The animal looked at her with large, liquid eyes. "Bram, we've got to do something about this," she said. "This isn't the kind of animal that can live in a cage."

"What kind of animal can?" Bram said. "Esme, we can't get into this again."

"Bram's right." Lovatt looked at her quietly. "We don't want to call attention to ourselves right now by making any demands. Perhaps we might try to buy the animal later, and find it a home. Usually these animals can't be sent back. They've forgotten how to live in the wilds."

"Like Spot," Esme said sadly. "I'm not sure she could ever survive in the wild."

"I don't know—she might. Leopards are usually quite self-sufficient." Lovatt took her arm and guided her away from the llama's beseeching gaze. "But I promise you that we will do something later about the llama. I won't forget."

"I know you won't," Esme said, looking up at him. She knew in her heart that she could depend on his word—no matter that he didn't think himself a gentleman. Lovatt couldn't escape it—he had been *born* a gentleman—even if he *had* tossed her in the millpond.

They walked around the circus for an hour or so, seeing nothing out of the ordinary. Lovatt talked her into buying a trinket, a golden cross that she admired. "I fully expect to see a green circle around your neck from this," he said, laughing, as he put it into her hand.

"And you probably will," she said, laughing back at him. He looked so at ease, so comfortable here. Lovatt was the kind of man who was at home anywhere.

They wandered toward the back of the circus, away from the attractions and near the living quarters of the circus folk.

"Look!" Esme said, gesturing to a shanty that was placed close to the back fence. The shanty was made of boards of various widths and ages, and had planks covered with canvas for a roof. A window had been put into each side, but the window sizes didn't match. The door was a stout, timbered affair, and looked as if it had been removed from an old barn or mill. Two men were standing outside the shanty, talking. "Those are the scoundrels who mistreated Spot," she told Lovatt.

"They look like thoroughly disagreeable types," he said.

"Damned rascals," Bram agreed. "As I told you, one of them even threatened Esme. The one on the left, if I recall."

Esme nodded. "Wilson Sipes is his name. The other one is named Bradshaw. I don't know what his first name is." She turned so that her back was to the men. Bram did the same.

Lovatt paused and seemed to be examining a circus wagon standing beside them, but Esme noted that he was really taking a good look at Sipes and Bradshaw. "And Sipes threatened you?"

Esme frowned. "Yes, although he denied his statement when Papa and the magistrate went to see him. The magistrate refused to investigate further, saying there was nothing he could do."

"Legally, he was correct," Lovatt said.

"I don't think either of them would be the man we're looking for," Bram said. "They're merely petty criminals."

"Perhaps." They drifted back to the main path and Lovatt paused, buying bonbons for each of them from a passing vendor. "Never discount anyone," he said. "They could be in someone else's employ." He glanced back at the men and then stiffened slightly.

"What is it?" Esme turned to see Captain Arno walking up the path toward the shanty. He stopped and looked around, then took a tentative step. When he did, he caught sight of Esme, Bram, and Lovatt. He abruptly changed direction and walked over to them. "Good afternoon, Miss Darling, Darling, Lovatt." He gave Esme his best bow. "What a surprise seeing you here. I came looking for two of my men. I thought they might be here, since I couldn't find them anywhere else." He looked at Bram. "You haven't seen them, have you? Hoskins and Padgett."

"No, I saw a few off duty men, but not them," Bram answered.

Arno sighed. "I was afraid of that. I'll be forced to look elsewhere, I suppose." He smiled at Esme. "And what are you doing here this fine afternoon, Miss Darling? The best time to come is early evening. The place is usually crowded by then."

"Do you come here often?" Lovatt asked casually. Esme found that she was getting to know the nuances of Lovatt's speech and gestures, and, although he seemed casual, she sensed something else there.

"Not really. As I said, I'm merely looking for two of my men. They come here often." Arno's voice was easy. He turned away from Lovatt, ignoring him.

Bram frowned. "I thought you said you have an acquaintance here. Wasn't that what you once told me?"

"Well, yes." Arno said. "Just someone I met once or twice." He waved his hand as though dismissing the subject. "By the way, I stopped by Rouvray and talked to Lady Evers before I came here. She's a charming woman. She tells me that she may be living at Rouvray permanently." Arno couldn't keep the curiosity out of his voice. "Lord Evers came in as we were talking. He told me that they had just returned from the continent."

"Did he mention anything else?" Esme asked warily. She was afraid Vincent might have called Arno out, or some such ridiculous thing.

Arno shook his head. "No. However, Lady Evers did invite me to supper tomorrow night. I'm looking forward to it." He pulled his watch from its pocket and flipped the lid. "I hate to hurry, but I must be on my way." He smiled at Esme. "Until tomorrow night." He nodded at them and disappeared into the small crowd that was milling toward the gate.

"A strange man at times," Bram said, looking at Arno's uniformed back vanishing into the crowd. "He's right about one thing, though, Esme—there's not much of a crowd now. It's time to leave. Everyone seems to be going home for the evening. By the time we get back to Rouvray, it'll be time for supper."

Esme sighed. "I hate to leave that poor llama alone. Don't you ever think about anything except supper, Bram?" She frowned in annoyance as he laughed. "I know there's something to be discovered here. I feel it in my bones."

"You'll have to feel it in your bones another day," Bram said. "I'm going home."

Lovatt took Esme's arm, and they followed Bram toward the exit. "We'll come back another day, I promise."

"Tomorrow?"

Lovatt hesitated. "We don't want to be too obvious. Why don't we wait two or three days, and then come back?" He grinned down at her as they went out the gate. Lovatt had that wicked grin she was beginning to know so well. "We probably need to get back to Rouvray, anyway, just to keep Lord Evers from being jealous. Hinson is still at home, you know. And then there's Ned."

Esme laughed. "You think you're teasing, Lovatt, but you're closer to the truth than you know. Vincent is insanely jealous. He'll be following Captain Arno next."

"I'm counting on it," Lovatt said.

Back at Rouvray Mimsy was feeling ill again, and was on the sofa. Vincent was beside her, plying her with Mrs. Hinson's macaroons and lemonade. Mimsy managed to sit up when Bram, Esme, and Lovatt came in. Vincent held her hand and looked at Esme with anxious eyes. "Do you think we need to call the doctor?"

"I'm fine, Vincent," Mimsy said. "Just fine."

"You *were* fine until Captain Arno arrived," Vincent said.

Mimsy gave him an annoyed look. "I'm going to my room," she said, standing and stalking from the room.

"That's it," Vincent said, sitting down and putting his hands over his eyes. "It must be Arno. They have to have met on the continent when I wasn't with her. I left her for two days when we were in Portugal."

"Vincent, really!" Esme said impatiently. "Mimsy has no interest in anyone, especially Captain Arno."

Vincent stood up. "I think you're wrong, Esme. Today, she became ill right after he left. If that isn't suspicious, I don't know what is."

"Wait a moment, Lord Evers," Lovatt said, looking interested. "Did you say that Mimsy met Captain Arno on the continent? When was this?"

"Yes. Well, no. That is, I don't know for sure that they met, but they could have. I do know Captain Arno was there, because he said so. We were talking about our trip, and Arno mentioned that he was there at the same time. I got the impression that he was in Italy, but he and Mimsy began talking about Lisbon, and even discovered that both of them knew Señora Romero. Granted, Arno said he knew her only slightly, but it was still a connection."

Lovatt lifted an eyebrow. "Interesting. I wonder how Arno got to Lisbon during the past few months. I thought he had been stationed here for a while."

Esme shook her head. "Lovatt, you're reading something into nothing. I know that answer to that—Captain Arno had to leave for a few weeks to attend to some family business. I don't remember exactly what it was— something about one of his relatives being critically ill. He went through the proper channels and got the proper authorization. I remember Papa talking about it."

"All the same," Vincent said, "he was in Lisbon when we were. I don't recall his mentioning any ill relatives. He probably followed us there so he could speak to Mimsy. I'm going to get to the bottom of this." It was his turn to stalk out the door.

"Two well-matched," Bram said with a sigh. "Papa said that, and I didn't know at the time what he meant. I do now."

Lovatt shrugged. "At least he'll keep watch on Arno, and we won't have to."

"There's nothing to know about Captain Arno," Esme said. "I trust him implicitly."

"Trust no one," Lovatt said. "That's the first rule of espionage."

"Espionage? I'd hardly call Vincent jealously following Captain Arno espionage."

"Not that, Miss Darling. Spying is definitely espionage. The game here is being played for much higher stakes than either you or Lord Evers realize."

"And how do you know that?"

Aunt Penny came in at that moment as Lovatt stood to leave. "Surely you're not leaving," Aunt Penny said, sitting down and searching for her embroidery. "There's roast beef for supper, and I'm sure there's plenty."

Lovatt made his apologies, got his hat, and was ready to leave when Hinson came in to speak to Esme. "It's that boy from the village who feeds the cat," he explained. "He says it can't wait."

Ned appeared right behind Hinson and came on into the room. He looked ill at ease. "It's Spot, Miss Darling," he said, looking at his feet. "She's not here."

"What do you mean?" Esme looked blank.

"She's not here." Ned looked from one to the other. "The gate to her pen was open, and she was gone. I went to feed her, but she wasn't there."

"That wild animal is loose!" Aunt Penny turned pale. "My vinaigrette! What shall we do?"

"It's all right, Aunt Penny." Esme rummaged through Aunt Penny's things piled on top of one of the little tables, searching for her vinaigrette. "Spot has never come in the house. If you stay in here, she won't bother you."

Aunt Penny stared at the French doors, then at the stairs. "Please ask Mrs. Hinson to send a tray up to my room. I do believe I have a headache." She took one last look around and fled.

Lovatt turned back to Ned. "What do you mean, the gate was open, Ned?" he asked. "Had she broken out?"

Ned shook his head, miserable. "No, it looked like someone had opened it deliberate like, and just let her out. I don't know who would do such a thing."

Esme was incredulous. "You must be wrong, Ned. No one here would do such a thing. After all, Mr. and Mrs. Hinson were here, as well as Aunt Penny, Vincent, and Mimsy. None of them would let her out. They're all terrified of her."

"Don't forget that Captain Arno was here, too." Lovatt spoke softly.

Esme gave him a sharp look and shook her head. "That isn't a possibility," she said, picking up her bonnet. "Show me the gate, Ned. I'm sure that she managed to open it from the inside. Spot is quite intelligent."

"I'll say she is. She knows how to get you to do exactly what she wants," Bram said with a grin. Esme ignored him and went out the door.

"Come on, Ned. Perhaps we can discover which way she went. Someone will shoot her if she gets out into sheep or cattle."

The gate bore no marks at all, just as Ned had said. Lovatt and Bram examined it carefully. "Major Darling saw to this, didn't he?" Lovatt asked.

"Yes, how did you know that?" Esme frowned.

"Because there is absolutely no way this gate can be opened from the inside. Once Spot is in there, she's in to stay." He looked back at the latch. "I agree with Ned. Someone opened the gate and let her out."

"Nonsense. Everyone's afraid of her." Esme gave Lovatt a warning look. "Don't say it, Lovatt! Right now, we don't need to argue that point. We need to find Spot before someone else harms her."

Bram wandered up and examined the lock again. "Or before she attacks someone or something," he said.

Lovatt dropped to his knees and looked at the grass. He looked all around, as did Bram. "I don't know. There are no real tracks here that would give us a clue. As a guess, I would say that she's gone to the field where you usually take her for a walk. I'll check there. Darling, you go the other way. Miss Darling, you stay here in case she returns. She'll go into the pen for you more easily than she will for anyone else." Lovatt looked at Ned. "Do you have time to go with me? We'll both search this way. She might come to you since you've been feeding her." Ned nodded, and they walked off beyond the break in the hedge.

Esme put her hands on her hips and glared after them. "Well, can you believe that? He just thinks he can walk in here and take charge, just like that!"

"Good thing, too," Bram said. "Someone needs to. I'm off to search this way. Tell Mrs. Hinson to hold supper for me." He walked off, clearly annoyed.

The search for Spot produced nothing. Lovatt, Ned, and Bram returned to Rouvray at dark. They were ravenous, and met in the kitchen, where Mrs. Hinson had seen to it that the cook saved the roast beef for them. "I saw absolutely nothing," Bram said, forking out some roast beef and ladling gravy over it.

Lovatt served Ned a plate and handed it to him, then got some for himself. He motioned for Ned to sit down opposite him and began to eat. "We saw some tracks that looked fresh. Ned has got to get back home, so I thought I might go to Shad Abbas and get a man or two to help me search." He looked at Esme. "You're right about one thing, Esme. If Spot causes any damage, she'll be shot. I don't want that to happen."

Esme was flooded with a strange feeling. She averted her eyes and blinked back tears. "Thank you, Lovatt," was all she could manage. She glanced up at him and he smiled at her, a different kind of smile this time. This smile was warm and caring, and seemed to hold a secret. She felt herself grow warm all over, and turned away again.

Lovatt stood and looked out the small kitchen windows. "I'm off to Shad Abbas to get those men to help search. Luckily the moon is good tonight, so we'll be able to see." He turned and grinned ruefully. "That is, if Spot gets out where we can see her. That spotted coat is the world's best camouflage."

Bram stretched. "I'll go back toward the barracks and search for another hour or so. If I don't find anything, I'll come back here and begin again in the morning." He and Ned walked out the front together, leaving Esme and Lovatt in the kitchen. "You don't have to do this," Esme said. "Spot isn't your responsibility."

"No, but we're friends, aren't we?" He stood closer to her and put his fingertips lightly on her arm. Esme felt a chill and a strange, giddy sensation. "Friends help each other."

She stepped back, trying to gather her thoughts. "All right, Lovatt. And thank you. I'll search near the field."

"You'll do no such thing." His voice was firm. "Someone needs to be here in case Bram finds her. I think she may come back with me if I find her, but he'll need help. You stay here so that we'll know where you are if we need you. Besides," he added with a grin, "Spot may just decide to come home on her own. In that case, you'll need to send someone out to tell us to stop searching."

"I'll wait right here for you," she said.

Lovatt opened the kitchen door, then turned and gave her a last look. "That's nice to know," he said softly, closing the door behind him. Esme went to the window and watched him go through the break in the hedge, the moon giving him a silvery look as the light washed over him. Every feeling she had experienced in many summers of following him around as a child came back to haunt her. Much as they had taunted each other as children, there was affection. *Is that what this is?* she wondered. *Childhood affection?* Somehow, it didn't feel that way.

She turned back to the table and saw Lovatt's hat still there. She picked it up, inhaling his scent, which still clung to it. He didn't wear heavy perfume as many men did—instead, the scent was of soap with a touch of spice. Esme ran her fingers over the brim, then put the hat down. The last thing she needed or wanted, she told herself angrily, was to have feelings for Lovatt. If Vincent were to be believed, Lovatt had cut a swath through the females of London during the previous months. He would never have any feelings for a country miss, especially one with only a modest prospect.

She felt tears in her eyes again, coming suddenly and without any warning. Quickly she wiped her eyes with the back of her hand. It wasn't Lovatt making her feel this way, she insisted to herself. It was merely worry about Spot. That was all.

She picked up her candle and started for the drawing room, where she could look out the French doors into the night while she waited. At the kitchen door, she turned and went back to the table to pick up Lovatt's hat. She carried it with her to the small drawing room and sat down, the candle beside her and the hat on the table where she could see it.

Eight

Aunt Penny wandered back down into the room and offered to make the sacrifice of sitting up with Esme until someone returned with news about Spot, but Esme declined. Aunt Penny was visibly relieved and went on to bed. Mimsy, usually a person who stayed up until the small hours of morning, had gone on to bed, too, and was sound asleep. Vincent was nowhere to be found, but Esme didn't worry about him. She had other things on her mind.

With every noise, she started, wondering if it were the distant sound of a gun. Spot, for all her ferocious look, was really at a disadvantage away from home. She had grown accustomed to people who wouldn't harm her, and if she found someone who would, she wouldn't know how to defend herself. She could run, or she could stop and fight, but a pack of dogs or a bullet could end that.

Esme paced for a while, then sat for a while. She tried reading, but couldn't concentrate. She tried embroidery, but snarled her thread beyond redemption. Finally she just sat, worrying.

It was almost midnight when she heard a noise at the front door. She jumped to her feet and ran toward the door, colliding with Bram in the hall. Bram was covered with mud. Vincent was right behind him, and looked worse.

"What did you discover?" Esme blurted. "Did you find Spot?"

"Spot?" Vincent was blank as he went across the floor to the brandy decanter, trailing little clumps of mud as he walked. "Is Spot lost?"

"Isn't that where you've been?" She watched as Vincent picked up the empty brandy bottle and then sadly put it back down. "Nothing here," he said.

Esme wheeled and turned to Bram. "Did you find Spot?"

Bram shook his head and wearily sat down on the floor. He was too muddy to sit on the furniture. "No, the only thing I found was Vincent. I thought I had Spot—I heard some twigs snapping, and then some rustles in the grass along the stream outside the garrison. When I went down there, I discovered Vincent." He looked down at his uniform. "But not until Vincent thought I was someone else, and tried to drown me."

"I wasn't trying to drown you," Vincent said to his brother-in-law. "I thought *you* were someone else, so I was trying to teach you a lesson."

"He thought I was Arno," Bram explained to Esme. "Vincent was outside the barracks, trying to watch Arno. He had the maggoty notion that Mimsy was going to meet Arno after dark."

Esme looked at Vincent as he stood in the middle of the floor. It was too much. "Vincent, I don't see how Mimsy has been able to bear eleven years of your jealousy. I couldn't abide a week of it."

"I can't help it. I've always been terrified that she'll leave me. And now look what's happened."

"Mimsy's leaving has nothing to do with you," Esme said before she thought.

"Then what? If you tell me, I'll fix it. I swear I will."

Esme paused, remembering her promise. "I can't, Vincent. I promised Mimsy I wouldn't tell, so I can't. But I assure you that it wasn't because of anything you did. I also promise you that Mimsy has no interest in any other man."

Bram stretched and looked at the mud on his uniform.

"So you needn't go chasing around behind Captain Arno anymore."

"But he did leave the barracks after dark," Vincent said. "He appeared to be sneaking out."

"What?" Bram looked up at him sharply.

"He was sneaking out of the barracks. I saw him. I was just going over to the front of the building to follow him when I ran into you. I thought you were Arno, and that's why I threw you down and tossed you in the stream. I was going to give you the thrashing of your life. Now I realize that Arno didn't have time to get to my side of the building. He must have gone the other way—toward town."

Bram frowned. "He's on duty tonight. Why would Arno risk sneaking out? Furthermore, why would he be going to town?"

"With his position, he's able to come and go with few questions, isn't he?" Esme asked.

"Well, yes," Bram answered, still frowning, "but he's not supposed to leave when he has duty."

"From what I can gather, Arno is a dab hand with the town girls," Vincent grumbled. "Ought to stay with his own class instead of trying to insinuate himself with Mimsy."

"Don't be ridiculous, Vincent," said Esme. "I told you that Mimsy has no interest in Captain Arno. As for his class, I think the man is of good birth. He hinted to Papa that he was, at any rate." She frowned. "You're probably right about one thing, though, Vincent. I dare say that there's a possibility that Captain Arno had an evening . . . um . . . an evening assignation."

"Probably so." Bram nodded wearily and stood. "I'll try to find out." He looked at his clothing again. "Esme, I'm going to clean up and go on to bed. I'll get out and start searching for Spot in the morning." He went across the room to the door, dropping little bits of mud and leaves as he walked. "Coming, Vincent?" Bram asked. Vincent looked thoroughly miserable as he nodded in agreement and followed Bram up the stairs.

Esme picked up some lumps of mud and threw them out the window. She left the window open so she could see out toward the field, but there was nothing there except the moonlit grass. She stood at the window, wondering if Lovatt had given up the search and gone to bed. She hadn't heard or seen anything at all. The clock struck the half hour and she sat back down, worried and wide awake.

She sat for a while, watching the candle dwindle, then went to look out the window again. The moonlight made the landscape a lavender silver, but nothing seemed to be moving. No Lovatt, no Spot. The night was warm, and there was a faint breeze wafting the spicy scent of sweet peas into the room. Esme could stand it no longer. She blew out the candle and picked up her thin shawl. Before she could change her mind, she went outside and toward the field where Spot loved to play.

It was a strange, nighttime world. She could see quite well, although there was little color in things. Everything was silver, lavender, gray, and black. She had often walked after dark, but this seemed different. This time she noticed the silence, and that familiar things looked unfamiliar in the moonlight.

At the field she walked all around the edges, watching where she stepped. The ground was difficult to see in the half-dark, and there was little moonlight there. There was no sign of Spot. She thought about calling out Spot's name, but hesitated because the world seemed asleep, and she didn't want to disturb anyone. Instead she went back out to the path and sat on the rock she frequently used when Spot played. She saw nothing. She thought she heard a noise that might have been a muffled gunshot in the distance, very far away. Then she heard dogs barking. The sound was very faint, and must have come from the other side of Lovatt's house. Afraid for Spot, she stood and began walking toward Shad Abbas.

She had barely reached the end of the field when she saw something. At first she couldn't make out what it was, so she stepped to the edge of the woods and hid, worried that it might be a footpad out late at night. A figure drew closer, and she saw Spot in the lead, held by a piece of rope. "Not so fast, you damned feline," the man growled as Spot loped along the path. Spot stopped suddenly, right in front of Esme, and began sniffing the air. Esme ran out to the path. "Spot! Lovatt! You found her!" She knelt and gave Spot a hug.

"Rather, she found me," Lovatt said wearily.

Esme looked up at him. He was sweaty and dirty, covered with leaves. His coat was torn here and there, as though he had been in the brambles. He walked into the field, pulling Spot along behind him, and sat down on the rock where Esme had been. Esme moved to sit beside him. She noticed that instead of letting Spot loose, as she usually did in the field, he held fast to the length of rope that was tied to the leopard.

"Where did you find her?" she asked, resisting the urge to reach out and smooth a dark tangle of his hair that had fallen over his forehead. A leaf was stuck in it. After a moment's hesitation, she reached up and pulled out the leaf. Lovatt looked at her, then at the leaf, and grinned, his smile a contrast to his skin in the moonlight.

"You wouldn't believe where this cat has been," he said with a chuckle. "I think I've been through every bramble patch on Shad Abbas. I'm just glad she went in that direction—at least I know where all the patches are."

Esme held the leaf in her fingers. It was still warm. "I'm sorry."

He smiled at her again. "Don't be. It wasn't your fault at all. And not Spot's, either. Any animal will prefer freedom to being caged." He paused. "No, the fault belongs to whoever let her out. And there's no doubt that someone did."

"The questions seem to be *who,* and *why,*" Esme said, not daring to look at him further. Just the closeness of him in the quiet darkness was unsettling. She was intensely aware of him sitting close beside her, his arm pressing against hers.

His scent, that faintly spicy smell she had noticed before, mixed with a faint tinge of sweat, which in turn melded with the fragrant odors of the night air. The warm roughness of his coat rubbed familiarly along the length of her arm. Esme's senses reeled, and she felt faintly disoriented in space and time, almost as if she were dreaming this scene instead of living it.

Lovatt broke the sensation by turning to look at her again. "You shouldn't be out here, Miss Darling. What would Mrs. Pennywhistle think?" He smiled again, more warmly this time, more intimately. "I'd hate to think that Bram or Major Darling would feel the need to call me out for enticing you into the fields at night."

"I was worried about Spot." Esme didn't look at him. He was right, of course. Her reputation would be ruined if anyone found out that she had been out alone with Lovatt at night. Instinctively she knew that Lovatt would never tell anyone. She pulled her thin shawl up around her shoulder and arm so that there was that fragile barrier between her arm and Lovatt's. "Bram came back home emptyhanded and went on to bed, promising me he'd search in the morning. I was just afraid that something would happen to Spot tonight."

Lovatt raised an eyebrow. "I think that was someone's plan. The question is, whose plan was it?"

Esme shook her head. "I have no idea. Several people in the community have complained, even though Spot has never bothered them. Just knowing there's a leopard in the area seems to have made people nervous." She looked up at him in the moonlight. "Even you, Lovatt." Looking at him had been a mistake—she shuddered visibly, although not from cold.

Lovatt noticed her shudder and misinterpreted it. He reached around her and pulled her shawl up on her other shoulder, touching her arm and shoulder as he did so. Esme shuddered again, and could see goosebumps on her arm. "The night air," she said, trying to explain herself. "It's a little cool."

"I hadn't noticed." Lovatt pulled out his handkerchief and mopped his sweating forehead. The hair around his face was sweaty and clinging in points to his face. Esme found herself staring at it. "Actually," Lovatt said, putting back his handkerchief and getting a firmer grip on Spot's rope, "I think it is extraordinarily warm tonight." He grinned at her. "Of course, my nocturnal adventures might have contributed to that."

Esme looked away from his smile quickly and reached out to touch Spot. "On Spot's behalf, I apologize. Where did you find her?"

"In the bramble patch on the hill above my stables. I had gone inside to get a horse because I was exhausted from tramping all around the countryside on foot, and I noticed that the horses were extraordinarily nervous." He chuckled. "I believe I registered that complaint with you once before."

"Yes." Esme still didn't trust herself to look at him. "She's gone that way before when we've gone out on walks. I believe I had forgotten to put her up on the night you mentioned." She moved to scratch Spot's ear. "I won't do that again. I intend to check that latch every night." She moved to touch the other ear and brushed against Lovatt's arm. The goosebumps popped back up.

Lovatt ran his finger along her arm, making the goosebumps even worse. "Miss Darling, you must be freezing. Perhaps you're not well." He turned to look at her before Esme could avert her eyes. His gaze held hers for what seemed like forever, although Esme knew rationally that it was only for a moment. Lovatt turned his body to face hers, placed Spot's leash in his lap, and ran the fingertips of his right hand along the edge of her jaw. Esme could feel his other hand on her arm as he touched her lightly. "Esme," he whispered softly. "Esme." He leaned toward her, and Esme knew that he was going to kiss her. She put her hands on his chest and slid her fingers up toward his neck. She wanted him as she had never wanted anything else. "Lovatt," she whispered, turning closer to him.

As she turned, Spot's rope fell around her feet. She felt Spot tug at the rope, and then it came loose. With a bound, Spot sprang loose and began running across the field, the rope flying behind her.

"Hell and damnation!" Lovatt yelled as he sprang to his feet. Esme had been leaning heavily into him, and she tumbled backward off the rock and rolled a few feet. When she managed to sit up, she could see the moonlight outlining Spot's shape as the leopard bounded off into the trees encircling the field. Lovatt was right behind Spot, yelling.

Esme jumped to her feet. "Lovatt!" she yelled. "Don't scream at her. You'll scare her. Just talk!" She lifted her skirts and ran across the field after them. Lovatt slowed down as he approached the woods, and Esme was able to catch up with him. She was sweaty now, her shawl had dropped during her run, and she was gasping for breath.

"Don't scare her," she said to Lovatt between gasps.

"Scare, hell! I'm going to wring her neck." He stomped off into the bushes, parting them with his hands.

Esme followed right behind him. "You'll do no such thing. Lovatt, be quiet. She's right over there." She pointed to Spot, who was standing quietly beside a tree on the other side of a small hollow formed by a tiny stream. "All we have to do is go get her." She stopped and called out in her sweetest voice. "Nice Spot. Stay there, Spot."

Spot looked at them curiously and stood still. "See," Esme said. "Now all we have to do is just go over there very quietly and pick up the rope."

"All right," Lovatt muttered, "but I can promise that the second we reach for the rope, she'll run off again."

"Not if we're careful and quiet." Esme shoved her hair back. It had caught on the branches and was sticking out every which way.

Lovatt carefully started down the slope of the hollow. "Stay there. There's a small stream down there, and you'll get wet."

"I need to go with you." Esme put her foot where his had

been and began following him down the slope. Her blue kidskin shoes were slick, and she slid through the leaves and mud, right into Lovatt's back. He reached out to steady himself and grabbed her arm. Both of them went tumbling head over heels down the slope and right into the stream. It took Esme a moment to realize what had happened. She was flat on her back in the stream, and she could feel the cold water rippling around her body, turning her back colder and colder. Her hair was floating around her head. Lovatt was on top of her, his full length resting on her body. While Esme's back was cold from the running water, her front was on fire as soon as she registered Lovatt's presence. She could feel every inch of him down her body.

Lovatt's eyes expressed shock for a moment, then pure devilment. "A lovely sight, Miss Darling," Lovatt said, giving her a grin. "I must say that you're one of the few women I know who can look delectable flat on her back in a stream."

"Lovatt, you're completely incorrigible." Esme looked at him, and forgot that she wanted to tell him to get up. "Just completely incorrigible," she whispered, feeling him on her and seeing a strange look in his eyes. She forgot about the cold water, forgot where she was.

"Completely," Lovatt agreed. He lowered his head to hers and kissed her, softly at first and then with more warmth. Esme put her arms around his neck and responded in kind. "Umm," Lovatt murmured, raising his head to look at her. "You're incorrigible as well, Miss Darling, and I quite like that." He bent and kissed her again. This time he lingered on her lips only a long moment, and then began kissing her face. He left a line of kisses from the corner of her lips to her ear. He paused there to nuzzle her ear, then kissed below her ear on her jaw. Esme forgot completely about the water, forgot about Spot, forgot about everything except the feel of Lovatt on top of her and the touch of his lips on her skin. "Lovatt," she whispered, licking a drop of water from his lip with her tongue. She was going to say more, but a rough tongue slurped up the side of her face, sloshing water into her ear. She turned her face and found herself nose to nose with Spot.

Lovatt closed his eyes. "God is against me," he muttered, getting to his feet. He stood and reached down for Esme, helping her to stand. Esme was wobbly, not from the fall, but from Lovatt. "Spot," she said shakily. Lovatt reached down for Spot's rope just as the leopard danced away, nimbly bouncing from rock to rock to keep out of the stream. In just a moment she was up on the bank and headed back to the field.

Esme and Lovatt looked at each other. "We might as well go," he said with a disgusted sigh. Then he paused and grinned at Esme again. "I should apologize to you, Miss Darling, but I don't intend to. In fact, at the first opportunity I plan to resume where we were interrupted."

He held out his hand to her as he stepped to the rocks on the edge of the stream. "But for now, I assume our plan is to recapture Spot and then get you into your house without Mrs. Pennywhistle, Bram, or Mimsy seeing us. As I said before, I'd hate to be meeting Bram at daylight with drawn pistols."

"Knowing you and knowing Bram, I don't think that's a possibility," Esme said as she took his hand, then followed along behind him. He carefully held the branches for her and once untangled her hair from a flying twig. When they reached the field, Esme felt her hair. It seemed to be about the size of a bushel basket, and was full of twigs and leaves. Lovatt retrieved her shawl where it had fallen and wrapped it around her, following that with his coat. "That should keep you from freezing until we get you home," he said, smoothing his coat over her shoulders.

"Look over there. Spot is waiting for us.," Esme pointed to the end of the field where Spot sat patiently. As Esme and Lovatt walked toward her, she moved ahead. "I believe she's going home," Lovatt said wearily. "If we had known that, we could have just sat down with a pot of tea and waited."

He was right. Spot trotted ahead of them through the

break in the hedge and went right into her pen. To Esme and Lovatt's annoyance, she wandered over to the corner under the tree where she slept, stretched out, and yawned hugely. In moments, she was asleep. Lovatt rigged the latch closed, and leaned against the gate in exhaustion. "Now, our next problem is to get you inside without anyone hearing us," he said.

"I left the door open here. I'll just go in, and no one will know I've even been out." She walked toward the door. Lovatt followed her, pausing by the French door. "I have to say, Miss Darling," he said with a grin, "that my life certainly has changed since I met you. Goodnight, and I'll see you tomorrow." He smiled at her again and, before Esme could move, gave her the briefest of kisses on her lips. "Sleep well," he said, touching her nose with his fingertip. He turned and walked away toward the break in the hedge. Esme watched him, marveling at how broad his shoulders looked in his shirt. She stepped inside, pulling his coat tighter around her. She was halfway up the stairs before she realized she was still wrapped in his coat. Quickly she ran into her room, shutting the door behind her. She hurried to the window, looking out over the moonlit countryside. She could make out Lovatt walking toward Shad Abbas, the white of his shirt gleaming in the moonlight.

Esme sat down on the edge of her bed and shivered, not from cold, but from emotion. She pulled Lovatt's coat closer to her, reveling in the scent of him that lingered on it, and imagining the feel of him on her. Quickly she stood and stripped off her wet clothes, ran her fingers through her hair, and put on her night rail.

As she crawled into bed she saw Lovatt's coat, and wondered briefly what she should do with it. There was only one logical thing to do: she crawled under the covers and pulled the coat into bed with her, hugging it to her until she got warm.

Nine

Lovatt strode across the field under the moon, passing by the place where he had sat with Esme. He paused and sat down again, looking out toward the woods where they had fallen down into the hollow, and he had almost forgotten himself. *Damn me for five kinds of a fool,* he thought. The Horse Guards had sent him here to find out who was trying to send messages to Napoleon at Elba, and what had he done? Nothing at all except get tangled up with the daughter of the finest man he had ever known. He hit his knee with his fist, realizing for the first time that he was without his coat. He had left it wrapped around Esme. He wondered what kind of tale she would come up with to explain that. He felt sure she would come up with something. Miss Darling was nothing if not inventive.

That thought brought him back to his problem. He had volunteered for this detail as soon as he had heard that Major Darling had been implicated. Lovatt knew the major would never betray England, never. Lovatt himself had heard Major Darling rail against Napoleon. Lovatt had assured the powers at Whitehall that Major Darling could never work for Napoleon, a man he despised. The reply had been, quite logically, that the spy, whoever he was, had to be located before he could do any damage. Lovatt had then convinced them that he could unearth the real spy.

Now, other than his admiration for Major Darling, he had

another reason to find the culprit. He intended to find the man. After all, he had given his promise to Esme, and he knew how much a promise meant to her.

"Esme." He said the name to the night breeze, letting the syllables roll softly off his tongue. He hadn't seen her in years, not since she was a gangling girl, and hadn't thought about her at all. There had been other women across the years, but something had happened to him the moment he saw Esme protecting that leopard. A flood of memories had engulfed him, but there was something else. He was afraid to say the word. He was a man who had promised himself he would never be entangled unless he could be the kind of husband and father that Redferne had never been. His career in the army and his life didn't allow for the time involved in being a husband and a father.

Lovatt stood and began walking slowly toward Shad Abbas. His life, the spinning out of time that he had done, had been satisfactory until he had come back here. His only truly happy times had been at Shad Abbas, the happiest when he was with the Darling children. It had been a mistake to think that he could come home again, and that things would be the same. He shook his head, trying to get those thoughts out of it. He had a task: he would find the man responsible for accusing Major Darling, and then he would go back to London and ask to be posted somewhere. The Indies, perhaps, or even Canada. There were all sorts of places he could go—the farther away, the better.

Even as he thought this, the top of Shad Abbas came into view, and he realized that this was the only place he wanted to be.

He ran his fingers through his hair. This wasn't in his plan. He had mapped out his life, and it didn't include entanglements. It didn't include Shad Abbas, except as an occasional place to visit and see his mother. He would just have to withstand temptation. If he didn't, the first thing he knew he'd be making a complete cake of himself, just like Vincent.

He went inside Shad Abbas and sat down to write a report to Whitehall, detailing his actions to date. He edited it heavily.

The next morning Esme woke up and stretched. The wool of Lovatt's coat was against her cheek, and she was instantly flooded with memories. She could feel Lovatt on top of her, and the warmth of his kiss. She stretched again, smiling smugly. The door opened and her maid, Abby, came in. Quickly Esme pushed Lovatt's coat underneath the covers. The second Abby left the room, Esme scrambled out of bed, Lovatt's coat in her hand. *Whatever can I do with it?* she wondered. Hearing Abby returning, she quickly shoved it under the bed, hoping no one would clean under there until she could retrieve it and return it to Lovatt. He would probably be duly appalled that his superbly tailored coat looked as if someone had slept in it, but then it was all torn and dirty, anyway.

Esme giggled, thinking of how Lovatt had looked being dragged along by Spot. She tried to be serious as Abby knocked on the door and opened it, bringing in Esme's morning chocolate. As she sipped, she looked in the mirror at her hair. "Abby," she said, surreptitiously pulling a twig from her curls, "why don't we try something new today? Perhaps we could use the curling iron to tame the front."

Abby stood up and dropped the hairbrush she was holding. "Curling iron?"

"Curling iron." Esme nodded. Out of the corner of her eye she saw her ruined clothes and shoes. She needed to take care of those before Abby discovered them. Quickly she sent Abby down to the kitchen for another pot of chocolate—no matter that half of hers was still left.

Esme jerked up her still wet clothing, as well as her sodden shoes. This was all wadded up and stashed under the bed to join Lovatt's coat. She quickly checked her hair for leaves and twigs, finding more than she could have imag-

ined and pulling them out. Hair, of course, came out with
them, and tears sprang to her eyes. She didn't have time to
be gentle—she could hear Abby coming back up the stairs.
Catching a glimpse of a leaf on her pillow, she brushed
frantically at the bedclothes and then dashed back to her
seat, just settling into her chair as Abby came in the door
with a fresh cup and a new pot of chocolate. To Esme's
surprise, Mimsy was right behind Abby. Mimsy, to put it
kindly, looked wretched.

"Are you no better?" Esme asked, offering her a piece of
toast.

Mimsy shook her head and nibbled on the toast. "I'll feel
better after a while. Vincent has already asked me if he
could call a doctor, but I said no. A doctor can do nothing
for food poisoning. It's one of those things that you have to
wait and get out of your system. Lobster has an evil reputation on that score, anyway."

"So I have heard," Esme said dryly, "but in my circles it
isn't usually a problem." She paused and poured Mimsy a
cup of chocolate. "Why don't you tell Vincent why you're
leaving him? Give him a chance to defend himself."

Mimsy shook her head. "No, his mother is right. Vincent
needs to sire an heir. The Evers line goes back almost to the
Conqueror." She polished off her chocolate and held out
her cup for a refill. "This is good. My food poisoning must
be better." She sipped at the second cup. "As for Vincent,
he'll get disgusted and go back to Eversleigh in a day or so."

"I doubt that." Esme looked at Abby getting things ready
to try to tame her hair. It didn't appear to be a pleasant
process. She almost called a halt until she glanced in the
mirror and saw the frizzy mass of curls around her head.
Mimsy noticed what Abby was doing and immediately took
charge. "Esme!" she crowed. "You're finally dabbling in
fashion! Captain Arno?"

"Don't be ridiculous," Esme said, tears springing to her
eyes as Mimsy grabbed a hank of hair and wound it around

the curling iron. Esme heard her hair hiss as it hit the too hot iron.

When Esme went downstairs later, she wanted to hide her head in a basket somewhere. No matter that Mimsy said that she was ravishing—Esme had seen ravishing before, and knew that tale wasn't true. After Mimsy's ministrations she looked all right, but she certainly didn't look herself at all. Actually, she thought, getting a muffin from the sideboard in the dining room, she looked rather like a dark version of Mimsy, except not nearly as pretty. Mimsy had given Esme the same haircut that she had—"Monsieur Marc said this was just right for my face."—and had cut the hair around Esme's face before Esme could stop her. Now all around the front, it was too short to pin out of the way and, as usual, had a life of its own. Right now, the curling iron had tamed it, but as soon as it got damp—Esme didn't even want to think about it. She wondered what Lovatt would think of it.

The moment she thought of Lovatt she was flooded with warmth. Again, she had a sharp memory of the way he had felt on top of her, the way his lips had touched hers. She looked down at her breakfast and grinned foolishly.

"I fail to see what's worth smiling about this morning," Bram said grumpily as he came in and filled his plate. "What a wretched night. I'll get Vincent up and we'll go hunting that cat again, but I warn you, Esme, someone may already have shot it. As a matter of fact, I'd almost pay someone to shoot it."

"Bram! How could you say such a thing!" Esme glared at him. "You don't have to go anywhere this morning. Lovatt found Spot and brought her back last night."

Bram looked at her in amazement, then smiled. "Well, that is good news. No wonder you're smiling. I'll do the same." He grinned up at Hinson, who poured coffee. Hinson did not smile back.

Spot was no worse the wear for her adventure, although Esme herself felt greatly changed. She spent most of the morning thinking about Lovatt, not even answering

Mimsy's gentle probes about Captain Arno. "Good heavens, Esme," Mimsy finally said in exasperation. "Answer me. Is that the reason for the change in your hairstyle?"

"What?" Esme asked, trying to bring herself back from thinking of the feeling of the faint stubble of Lovatt's beard on her skin.

"Captain Arno coming to supper, of course. What have I been talking about for the past hour?"

"Oh." Esme tried to think.

"I've been discussing Captain Arno, and pointing out the fact that you're not getting any younger." Mimsy stood and frowned. "If Captain Arno doesn't appeal, why don't you let me take you to London? It's too late for you to have a season, but I could introduce you to numbers of men. Vincent knows . . ." She sat down suddenly, looking surprised. "I can't do that now, can I?"

Esme shook her head. "Not unless you make it up with Vincent."

"That I cannot do." Mimsy closed her eyes.

"I understand your motive, Mimsy, but you're being ridiculous. Vincent is besotted with you, and you with him. Ignore the dowager and live happily ever after with Vincent."

"Impossible." Mimsy turned slightly at a noise in the front. "That must be Hinson." She sighed. "He's getting worse and worse. Papa is going to have to replace him."

"That will never happen. Hinson has been with Papa since their early days in the army." Esme looked off into the garden and fought the impulse to lapse into a daydream about Lovatt. "Papa has a sense of loyalty about Hinson. He'll be with us until he dies."

"I suppose so." Mimsy turned to her and smiled. "Now back to my topic. Shall we discuss Captain Arno?"

"Arno?" Vincent asked hoarsely from the doorway. "Why do you mention Captain Arno?"

"No reason, Vincent." Mimsy looked at him coolly. "I thought you were on your way back to Eversleigh House."

"Bram asked me to stay on a few days."

Esme stared at him, amazed, but Mimsy got right to the point. "Did he ask you, or did you finagle an invitation out of him?"

"It really doesn't matter," Esme said quickly. She liked Vincent, even if he weren't going to be her brother-in-law any longer, and certainly didn't want to offend his sensibilities. Vincent was very sensitive. "You know we're always glad to have you, Vincent." Mimsy glared at her, then at Vincent. Vincent glared right back. Mimsy got up without a word and flounced up the stairs. Vincent looked at the empty stairs for a moment, put one foot on the bottom step, changed his mind, then went out the front door, slamming it behind him.

Aunt Penny wandered into the room, looking around. "Did I hear someone come in?" she asked.

Esme shook her head. "No, Aunt Penny. Just Vincent and Mimsy again."

"Oh, dear." Aunt Penny sat down on the sofa and looked distressed. "Whose hat is this, dear?" She picked up Lovatt's hat, which Esme had left on the small table.

"That belongs to Lovatt. He must have left it when he was last here."

"Oh." She put the hat down and glanced around. "Did you say that Mimsy and Lord Evers were at sixes and sevens again? James and Isabel leave, and the whole household falls down around my ears." She looked at Esme. "Thank goodness you're such an example of propriety, my dear."

Esme glanced down at a small scratch on her arm. She must have gotten that when she was rolling in the stream with Lovatt. "Thank you, Aunt Penny," she said, rising. "I have got to check on Spot. She's back, you know."

"Yes, dear, I heard," Aunt Penny said as Esme went out the door. She sounded vastly disappointed.

Outside, the sun was shining over her head, but there were dark clouds in the west. Esme knew this meant it would rain soon. She looked in at Spot, who was sleeping quietly just as though the uproar of the night before had never happened. Esme left her curled up in the shade under the big tree and went to tend to the dahlias. She could hardly wait until Señora Romero arrived in London with the new plant for her. A red dahlia would be perfect right between the white and the red and white stripe Esme had in her collection. Esme could visualize it already. She smiled as she looked at the dahlia patch. Her collection was coming along nicely.

She put on her bonnet and gloves, then went to work, digging around the dahlias and making sure the stakes were supporting them properly. Vincent's fall had done a great deal of damage, but the dahlias would recover, she thought.

The sky darkened and she hurried to finish her work. She cleared a place for the new plant, and was standing back admiring her work when Lovatt walked into the yard.

He paused and looked at the flowers admiringly. "You and my mother have the two greenest thumbs I've seen," he said by way of a compliment. "I have no talent for gardening."

Esme turned and smiled at him, unsure how to proceed. Should she run to him as Mimsy often did with Vincent, or should she wait for him to let her know if he still felt as he had last night? She opted for the latter. "It's necessary to love gardening to be good at it," she said.

"I enjoy the product, but not the work." He peered around toward Spot's cage. "And how is the cat this morning? Properly contrite?" He walked over to stand beside Esme.

Esme laughed. "Not contrite at all, I'm afraid. Actually, she seems to be sleeping late this morning. No doubt her exertions of last night tired her." She felt her cheeks redden at the mention of what had gone on the night before. "And how are you?" She dared to look up into his eyes, and had that strange feeling in the pit of her stomach again. It almost took her breath away.

"I didn't sleep very much," Lovatt admitted. "Esme . . .

Miss Darling." He paused, uncharacteristically at a loss for words. "I need to discuss something with you." His words sounded short.

"Shall we sit on the bench over here?" Esme pointed to the bench beside her dahlia patch. She removed her gloves, wishing that she looked better. She wondered if Lovatt were going to offer for her—dirty dress, old bonnet, gardening gloves, and all.

Lovatt stared straight ahead. "First, Miss Darling, I want to apologize for my actions last night. It was unpardonable, I know, but I simply lost my head." He held up his hand as Esme started to say something. "No, let me say this before I muddy the waters any more." He turned to look at her. "Miss Darling, I've been committed to the single life since I was a young boy. As you know, Redferne and I have little in common. To be blunt, he's a roué and a philanderer. I hate to say it, but there it is. He's caused my mother no end of grief, and I've never known what a real family and father were. I decided early on that marriage and family were not options for me." He stopped abruptly.

"And?" Esme said, wondering if he were going to tell her that her dazzling beauty, her wonderful personality, and her warmth had changed his mind.

"And I simply can't get involved with a woman on any basis except a casual one. I wish us to be friends, Miss Darling, much as we have always been. I apologize for my actions last night, and I assure you that I will never mention it." He paused again. "If, however, you feel that the slight done to your reputation requires other amends, I am quite prepared to do whatever you wish."

Esme felt her world crashing around her. Like Aunt Penny, she felt as if everything were falling down around her ears. She fought the urges to cry and to run, and tried to gather her thoughts. "You have no need to worry, Lovatt," she heard herself saying briskly. "I felt that the incident was purely one that happened without either of us thinking. I believe we should put it behind us."

"Thank you." Strangely, there was no relief in his voice. "Are we still friends? I wouldn't want to lose you as a friend, Esme."

She managed a smile, managed to look at his face as well, although she couldn't yet look right into his eyes. "We're still friends, Lovatt. Haven't we been friends for years? I expect things to continue as they have." She turned her head back to look at the dahlias. She didn't want to look at Lovatt—he looked as miserable as *she* felt. "Tell me, do you have any more thoughts on who might be trying to implicate Papa?"

Lovatt shook his head. "Nothing new. Have you discovered anything?"

"No. Everyone here was busy trying to find Spot. Everyone but Vincent, that is," she said ruefully. "As usual, he was busy chasing one of Mimsy's imagined suitors. Bram found him watching Captain Arno last night. Then, of course he and Bram got into a tussle when he mistook Bram for Captain Arno. You should have seen the two of them."

"Why was he watching? What was Arno doing?" There was a spark of interest in Lovatt's voice.

Esme shook her head. "Nothing. Arno did leave his duty post around midnight and start toward town, I believe. Of course, Vincent thought that he was on his way to meet Mimsy. I gave him what for about it."

"Arno left his duty post?" Lovatt's voice was full of disbelief.

"Yes. I'm sure Bram will tell you about it." Esme remembered the reference to Arno's nocturnal activities, and fought down a blush. She certainly didn't wish to discuss that topic with Lovatt. Especially not now.

Lovatt turned his hat in his hands, his long fingers sliding over the brim in much the same way that they had slid over Esme's skin the night before. She stood and looked down at him, hoping she was being cheerful enough, but not too cheerful. "That seems to be all, Lovatt. Do you wish to come inside? I, for one, have some letters to write, and I believe it's going to rain."

He stood and faced her as if wanting to say something but having no words to express what he felt. "No, I think I'll talk to Bram for a moment. Is he here?"

"I believe he's gone." Esme turned away so she wouldn't have to look at him. That was just too dangerous. "You can probably catch him at headquarters. I believe he was going there." She picked up her gloves and hoe. "Are you coming to supper this evening, Lovatt? I believe you and Captain Arno are invited."

"I wouldn't miss it." Lovatt's voice sounded strangled, so Esme turned around. He looked just the same—miserable. "I'll see you this evening then, Esme." He bowed slightly and left.

Esme watched him go back out through the break in the hedge. She walked over to where she could see him walking back across the field, toward Shad Abbas. She had often heard about people suffering from broken hearts and had laughed, asking how a heart could break. Now she knew.

Slowly she went back to the bench and sat down, pulling off her bonnet and letting her hair loose in the humid air. In the sky thunder boomed, and rain began to fall as she started to cry. She sat in the rain for a quarter of an hour, crying until she was drenched.

It didn't help ease the hurt at all.

Ten

Lovatt walked back to Shad Abbas through the rain. The storm mirrored his emotions, as well. Last night he had made up his mind to talk to Esme and stop any idea of an attachment before it began. The trouble was, he had admitted to himself in the cold light of morning, that he had already formed an attachment. He would, he thought to himself, just have to get over it. No entanglements, ever.

He wasn't Redferne—thank God. Lovatt wondered how many times he had had to wish for his father to notice him as a boy. How many times had he seen his mother cry? How many times had Redferne come home reeking of some doxy's perfume? Lovatt couldn't even count them all.

Early in his life Lovatt had decided not to marry, because he didn't want to cause pain, as Redferne had done. Lovatt had had a satisfactory life up to this point. He had traveled; he had advanced in his career; he had a wide circle of friends; he was respected by people he cared about. Now Esme Darling had come back into his life, and she certainly wasn't the little hoyden she had been when he threw her in the millpond. Now he wasn't a schoolboy with a crush on someone; he was a man grown, and had vowed to have no entanglements in his life.

The word *entanglements* distracted him momentarily—he could think of nothing except tangling his fingers in Esme's thick, dark curls, smoothing them down and taming them.

The word *taming* brought on a whole new set of associations. He shook his head. He had to stop thinking about this and focus on the reason he was back at Shad Abbas. He needed to get on with the job of clearing Major Darling's name.

He stalked inside Shad Abbas, dripping water all over the floor, much to the housekeeper's annoyance, changed his clothes by himself, much to his valet's annoyance, and called for his horse to be brought to him, much to the stableman's annoyance. Quickly he scribbled a note, then set off in the rain to meet Bram and see if he could discover the reason Arno was out wandering the countryside at midnight.

Lovatt was facing the window, looking out at the rain and drinking his fourth ale, when Bram finally came into the taproom at the Three Dogs Inn. The day was still gray and cold, and the rain was coming down in buckets, but Lovatt was feeling immeasurably better.

"God, what a terrible day," Bram said, sitting down and shaking water from his hat and cape. "If you hadn't said in your note that you needed to talk to me, I doubt that I'd have stirred out all day." Bram signaled to the barmaid for ale, and the two men sat comfortably drinking and enjoying the heat from the small fire smoldering in the fireplace. The heat was just enough to dispel the cold and gloom.

Bram finished his ale and motioned for another. "I'm glad I came," he said, stretching his feet out in front of him. "This is a good place to spend a day like this." He turned his head, and Lovatt noticed a scratch down his face. Bram saw him looking and grinned ruefully. "No exciting nights with a lightskirt, I'm afraid. This is courtesy of Vincent," he said. "I stumbled on him and he thought I was Arno, come to ravish Mimsy. We had quite a tussle."

"Es . . . Miss Darling told me that Vincent had seen Arno leaving around midnight. That's why I asked you here. I wanted to see if you knew anything about the man or his activities."

"I know what you said about suspecting everyone, but I think you can safely take Arno off your list." Bram shook his head. "He's been father's aide for months. Father says Arno is one of the best aides he's ever had—organized, intelligent, and very much an army man. I know he has a foreign connection and family still abroad somewhere, but I think they're in Spain or Gibraltar. They're not French." He downed another swallow of ale. "I don't think he's a viable suspect."

Lovatt shook his head. "I don't suspect him directly, but as I said, everyone and anyone might be involved. I don't want to eliminate anyone at this point. It could be that Arno has inadvertently done something, or knows something. After all, wandering about at midnight isn't the rule."

Bram grinned. "Probably a doxy, I'd say. I've seen him at the circus several times, so I think he may have a ladybird there." He chuckled. "I let the cat out of the bag when I said as much to Esme. I think Arno has designs on Esme. He's mentioned her to me more than once."

Lovatt fought down a wave of something that flowed through him, and it took him a moment to identify it—it was pure rage. He had the urge to beat Arno to a pulp. Instead he looked at Bram with interest. "You've seen Arno at the circus. Have you actually seen him with a woman there?"

Bram sipped his ale and shook his head. "No, but you know, Lovatt, that no self-respecting man, especially one who wants to get ahead, is going to be seen with a woman from the circus. No, you're just going to visit there, get what you went after, and leave, hoping no one is the wiser." He grinned at Lovatt. "Don't tell me you've never done that."

It was Lovatt's turn to grin ruefully. "We're all in the army," he said without further comment on that topic. "Bram, when did Major Darling first suspect there was a spy in his command?"

"Intelligence from Whitehall confirmed it about, oh, six

or seven months ago. It was just about the time Napoleon rejected the terms at Frankfurt—maybe November of 1813. That would be about right."

"And there have been things to incriminate Major Darling since then?" Lovatt knew there had—he had even seen the information when he went for a briefing at the Horse Guards, but he wanted to hear what Bram had to say.

Bram nodded. "About the time Napoleon tried to poison himself—that was in April, I think—Whitehall intercepted a letter that clearly let them know there was a spy here. Shortly after that, about the time Napoleon went to Elba, the letter actually naming father was sent to London."

"To throw everyone off the scent."

"Exactly." Bram motioned for his third ale. "I'm of the opinion that it will all stop now that Napoleon's at Elba. Still, if someone's disloyal, he needs to be discovered."

"You discount the rumors that Napoleon may return, then?"

Bram nodded. "I don't see how he can get off Elba. Who would follow him?"

Lovatt thought about the Frenchmen he had known during his travels. A very few were against Napoleon, but the majority of the men who had fought for him were still loyal to the man, although they were thoroughly sick of war. "I think he could get an army together," he told Bram, and the talk drifted into military matters.

An hour or so passed companionably as they drank and talked. Bram finished his ale, while Lovatt declined another but contented himself with a good cigar. Lovatt was facing the window and looking out. Not too many people had come by. The rain had now stopped, and it looked as if the sun might peer out before another hour was over.

Suddenly Lovatt saw Arno walking by, going down the street. Quickly, Lovatt got to his feet and peered out the window, just in time to see Arno veer off down an alley between two shops.

Lovatt tossed some money down on the table. "Could you get my shot out of this?" he asked Bram, reaching for his hat and cape. "I just saw someone I need to speak to right away. I'll be back if I don't catch up to him." He didn't wait for Bram to answer, but hurried out the door.

Glancing around outside, he recognized no one on the street. He hurried across and went down the alley between the shops, but saw nothing except a well-worn path. The back doors to both shops were closed, and Lovatt noted that Arno might have gone into either one. One was a draper's shop and the other a chandler's. He made a mental note, then decided to follow the path. To his surprise, it led him to the edge of the circus grounds.

He walked around there for a while and saw nothing, but something—that intuition that had served him so well in the past—told him that Arno was there. He had to find out more about the circus, but how? He looked around and found a break in the fence that led to a well-worn path by the road. He would be seen if he tried to enter now, but he resolved to come back later. He was deep in thought all the way back to the Three Dogs, trying to come up with a reason why Arno would be frequenting the circus. Once back at the Three Dogs, he discovered that Bram had paid the shot for both of them and left.

Perhaps, Lovatt thought as he rode home in the warm sunshine, he would discover more about the very agreeable Captain Arno at supper tonight. First, he had to discover more about the circus, and perhaps more about Arno's fascination with it. He had hit on a way he might do this, but he would have to be careful. He wondered idly as he dismounted in front of Shad Abbas why he wasn't more cheerful.

Samad was in the library, waiting, his white turban bright against the dark wood and heavy green velvet of the drapes. Lovatt smiled at him. He had had misgivings about bringing Samad to England with him, but Samad had begged to come. Lovatt had once saved Samad's life, and they had been together since. Samad, at Lovatt's instigation, had been at the circus, joining one of the Indian families there. He had nothing to report, but Lovatt described Arno carefully and then sent Samad back to watch for him. Lovatt had found in the past that Samad usually saw things others missed. He fervently hoped that was the case here.

Supper at the Darling house that evening was a strange affair. Vincent, surprisingly, spent the entire time being his most charming. Esme was amazed—she had expected him to glare at Captain Arno during the entire meal. Instead, he was witty, entertaining everyone with *on-dits* and anecdotes. Arno matched several of the stories. Lovatt sat quietly through most of Mrs. Hinson's meal, just observing. After supper, they went to the drawing room for cards. Whist was Bram's game so they played that, with Mimsy, Vincent, Bram, Captain Arno making up four. Lovatt, Esme, and Aunt Penny watched.

After cards, Mimsy sang for them. "Would you honor us?" Arno asked Esme.

"I'm afraid singing isn't what I do best," Esme answered.

"Gardening is Esme's passion," Mimsy said. "She even has dahlias from Spain. Perhaps you've seen them."

Arno nodded. "I have, and they are beautiful. When I was in Spain I admired many dahlia gardens. I understand the flowers were imported to Spain from Mexico."

"Oh," Bram said, frowning, "did someone tell me that you know Esme's friend Señora Romero, General Romero's widow? Her gardens are famous throughout Spain. I believe she and Esme have exchanged several flowers."

"Yes, we've met, but only briefly." Arno smiled. "Spain is such a beautiful country."

"You were there with Wellington?" Lovatt asked. His expression was perfectly blank and his tone innocent, but Esme got the impression that he was asking more than this simple question.

"Yes, briefly. I was sent to Brussels shortly after I was posted to Spain. I speak several languages, and I suppose the army felt I would be more useful in Brussels."

"Umm. The crossroads of Europe," Lovatt said. "Tell me, what did you think of Napoleon's performance in Spain?"

"He was a worthy adversary," Arno said easily, "but let us not speak of war tonight. I would love to hear Lady Evers sing again." He smiled at Mimsy, and she obliged him with a song. Vincent remained perfectly calm. Esme wondered what undercurrents she was missing.

Lovatt left shortly afterward, telling them that he had to rise early the next morning and needed to return to Shad Abbas. Aunt Penny made sure he took his hat with him, then invited him back any time. He left, first telling Esme that he would take a turn around the leopard pen to check on Spot. He wanted, he told her as he said his good-bye to her, to check the lock, just for safety's sake. He looked over Esme's head as he spoke, rather than looking at her face or eyes. She thought she acquitted herself quite well, smiling brightly at him. He would never, she had vowed to herself, know how her hopes had come crashing down. She would never allow herself to care for Chalmers Lovatt in anything but a cursory way. Still, as she sat back down beside Arno to listen to Mimsy sing again, she followed him in her mind out to Spot's cage, through the hedge, and back through the field to Shad Abbas.

Captain Arno left shortly after Mimsy finished her song. Vincent excused himself to go up to bed since, as he told Esme with a grin, he had been up late the previous night. Bram, Esme, Mimsy, and Aunt Penny played cards for a while.

Esme was ready to crawl into her bed when she remembered Lovatt's coat. She retrieved it from under the bed and shook it out. It was, she thought ruefully as she held it up for inspection, quite ruined. "Serves him right," she

We'd Like to Invite You to Subscribe to Zebra's Regency Romance Book Club and Give You a Gift of 4 Free Books as Your Introduction! *(Worth $19.96!)*

If you're a Regency lover, imagine the joy of getting 4 FREE Zebra Regency Romances and then the chance to have these lovely stories delivered to your home each month at the lowest prices available! Well, that's our offer to you and here's how you benefit by becoming a Zebra Home Subscription Service subscriber:

- 4 FREE Introductory Regency Romances are delivered to your doorstep
- 4 BRAND NEW Regencies are then delivered each month (usually before they're available in bookstores)
- Subscribers save almost $4.00 every month
- Home delivery is always FREE
- You also receive a FREE monthly newsletter, *Zebra/Pinnacle Romance News* which features author profiles, contests, subscriber benefits, book previews and more
- No risks or obligations...in other words you can cancel whenever you wish with no questions asked

Join the thousands of readers who enjoy the savings and convenience offered to Regency Romance subscribers. After your initial introductory shipment, you receive 4 brand-new Zebra Regency Romances each month to examine for 10 days. Then, if you decide to keep the books, you'll pay the preferred subscriber's price of just $4.00 per title. That's only $16.00 for all 4 books and there's never an extra charge for shipping and handling.

It's a no-lose proposition, so return the FREE BOOK CERTIFICATE today!

Say Yes to 4 Free Books!

COMPLETE AND RETURN THE ORDER CARD TO RECEIVE THIS $19.96 VALUE, ABSOLUTELY FREE!

(If the certificate is missing below, write to:
Zebra Home Subscription Service, Inc.,
120 Brighton Road, P.O. Box 5214, Clifton, New Jersey 07015-5214)

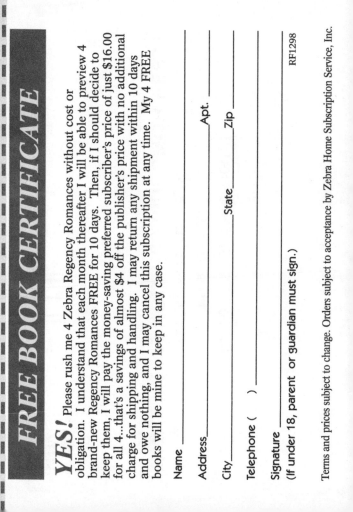

FREE BOOK CERTIFICATE

YES! Please rush me 4 Zebra Regency Romances without cost or obligation. I understand that each month thereafter I will be able to preview 4 brand-new Regency Romances FREE for 10 days. Then, if I should decide to keep them, I will pay the money-saving preferred subscriber's price of just $16.00 for all 4...that's a savings of almost $4 off the publisher's price with no additional charge for shipping and handling. I may return any shipment within 10 days and owe nothing, and I may cancel this subscription at any time. My 4 FREE books will be mine to keep in any case.

Name _____

Address _____ Apt. _____

City _____ State _____ Zip _____

Telephone ( ) _____

Signature _____ RF1298
(If under 18, parent or guardian must sign.)

Terms and prices subject to change. Orders subject to acceptance by Zebra Home Subscription Service, Inc.

muttered as she began to fold the coat. The faintly spicy smell of the soap Lovatt used wafted up from the coat as she handled it. Quite without meaning to, Esme buried her head in the coat and cried bitterly.

When her tears were exhausted, she finished folding the coat and put it at the very bottom of her wardrobe. She would return it as soon as possible. She didn't care for Lovatt, anyway. Her memory of him and her first impression had been right—he was incorrigible and insufferable. She crawled into bed and lay there, determined to put Lovatt out of her mind.

The more she concentrated on dismissing thoughts of Lovatt, the more they filled her head. Finally, she got up and walked to the window, looking out over the landscape. It was moonlit and beautiful. Turning away from the window, she decided to go down to the kitchen and warm some milk to help her sleep.

Quietly, she put on her dressing gown and slipped down the stairs. Mrs. Hinson always left a candle burning in a sconce in the hall as well as one in the entryway, in case anyone had to leave in a hurry. "Army men can get called out any time," she had said. Esme was glad Major Darling had never objected to the expense.

Once in the kitchen Esme had to light another candle, and when she checked the embers in the stove, she saw that she still had enough heat to warm her milk. She was just getting ready to pour the warm milk into a tea dish when she heard a noise at the front of the house. Her first thought was of Lovatt, her second of Spot, so she quickly picked up her milk, blew out the candle, and hurried to the front. To her surprise, she discovered Vincent in the hall, carefully closing the front door behind him.

"Following Captain Arno again?" Esme asked, balancing her cup of milk.

"Yes, but not for the reason you think." Vincent peered into her cup. "Warm milk? Can't you sleep, either?"

"Either?" Esme looked at him and noticed the dark shadows under his eyes. "Are you telling me you followed Captain Arno because you couldn't sleep?"

"Exactly." Vincent sat down on the bottom step and ran his fingers through his hair. "I haven't slept much since Mimsy came here without a word of explanation." He glanced at her milk again. "Does that really work?"

Esme smiled at him. She really liked her brother-in-law in spite of all his foibles, and hoped he and Mimsy would make things up. "Come into the kitchen and I'll warm some for you. You could use a good night's sleep."

"I certainly could." Vincent followed her into the kitchen. Esme stuck the candle's wick into the embers and the candle blazed up, throwing a light around them and making huge shadows on the wall. She put her milk on the table in front of Vincent. "Why don't you drink that, Vincent, and I'll warm more for myself."

Vincent took a sip of the milk and shuddered. "Reminds me of my nursery days," he said, making a face. "I hope it works."

"I think it will." Esme poured herself more milk. "Tell me the truth, Vincent—were you actually following Captain Arno because you couldn't sleep, or because of Mimsy?"

"Because I couldn't sleep," he answered promptly. "I'm finished acting like a lout because I'm jealous of Mimsy. What you said to me last night convinced me that I was being juvenile. I'm still jealous of her, of course, but I intend to try to act like a man about it."

Esme turned and looked at him, astonished. "Vincent, that's wonderful."

"It's not so wonderful, Esme. Mimsy still insists that she's leaving me. But you were right, I don't think it's because of Lovatt or Arno. I do wish you would tell me the reason."

"I can't, Vincent. I promised Mimsy. If she ever releases me from my promise, I'll tell you. For what it's worth, I think you *should* know." Esme sat down at the table and sipped her milk. "Why did you follow Arno if you've stopped showing your jealousy?"

"I couldn't sleep." Vincent sipped his milk and leaned back in his chair. "I thought I'd go out and maybe ride a little through the field, since the moon was so bright." He grinned wryly. "Oh, I know it was a stupid idea, but I'm just not thinking very clearly right now. Anyway, I rode along the field and then went up toward town so I could get on the main road back here. I was worried about footpads and so on, since I hadn't even thought to bring along so much as a whip, so I stopped at that huge tree just outside town and looked down the road. To my surprise, here came Captain Arno, moving along very quietly, almost as though he was afraid he'd wake someone. He passed by me and I decided to follow him. I planned to wait until he got out of earshot of my horse, and then follow him." He grinned at Esme. "You'll never believe what happened next."

"He saw you."

"No, guess again."

"You caught him with a lady friend."

Vincent grinned again and shook his head. "Not so. You'll never guess in a million years, so I'll just break the suspense and tell you. Lovatt came down the road, very quietly as well, quite obviously following Captain Arno." Vincent smirked.

"Lovatt?" Esme couldn't believe her ears. "Are you sure?"

"Positive. I waited until Lovatt was out of earshot and then followed him as he was following Captain Arno." He chuckled. "We made quite a cavalcade."

"Where did they go?"

Vincent frowned. "That's the strange part. Captain Arno went to the circus. Of course it was locked up, but he evidently went inside. I didn't see him, but I did see Lovatt dismount and slide through a section of fencing into the circus grounds. I went up to the fence but nothing happened after that, so I turned around and came back to Rouvray." He looked at Esme and stifled a yawn. "That milk is working, Esme. I'm going up to bed." He walked to the door, turning to look back at her. "I just don't understand who's doing what, Esme. One thing I do know is that there's something odd going on here. Very odd."

Esme finished her milk, wide awake now, her mind reeling with the information that Lovatt was following Captain Arno. Finally she gave up thinking about it and went upstairs to bed. She still couldn't sleep and got up to look out over the field, toward Shad Abbas. "Odd is hardly the word, Lovatt," she said to no one in particular. "You're implicated in this in some way that you're not telling me, and I intend to get to the bottom of it!"

It was almost morning before she finally went to sleep.

Eleven

When Esme woke up, the first thing she thought of was Lovatt, and Vincent's strange story of the night before. Whatever was Lovatt doing? She sat up in bed, the beginnings of a dull ache at the back of her head. Illogically, she blamed Lovatt for her headache as she got up and looked in the mirror. Then she blamed him for the fact that she looked so haggard this morning.

She wasn't feeling much better when she went to breakfast. Over the years, Esme had gone to the breakfast room to eat with her father. Her mother and Mimsy usually ate from trays in their rooms, frequently just having chocolate or tea and toast. Major Darling preferred a hearty breakfast, and Esme had also acquired that habit.

To her surprise, Mimsy was already in the breakfast room, looking sadly at a plateful of food. "It's disgusting, isn't it?" she said sadly, pushing the plate away. "I haven't been able to touch it, although I was starving when I came in here." She looked up at Esme. "You look terrible."

"Thank you." Esme sat down as Mrs. Hinson put a cup of chocolate in front of her. "Nothing like being cheered up this morning."

"I didn't mean that. You look as if you're ill." Mimsy looked at her critically. "Here, have this. I haven't touched a thing, and I hate for it to go to waste."

Esme looked at the food and grimaced. "I couldn't, not

with this headache this morning. Let me take it up to Aunt Penny." She got a tray from the sideboard and put the plate, some silverware, and a cup of tea on it, then took it to Aunt Penny.

Aunt Penny's room looked out across the back. It was, Esme thought, one of the best rooms on the floor. The large tree in the back was close by and shaded the window from the heat, but the tree was still far enough away to allow the room to be flooded with light. Aunt Penny, however, had complained since she first moved in. She preferred, she had said, a nice, dark room for sleeping.

Esme carried the tray into the room. "Oh, thank you, dear," Aunt Penny said, propped up in bed. She adjusted the tray on her lap and looked up at Esme. "You look perfectly wretched, dear. Is anything wrong? No doubt you couldn't sleep. I myself heard things at all hours last night. That's why I'm staying in bed this morning. You know there's not a lazy bone in my body, but I simply couldn't sleep. I could have sworn that someone was scratching at my window. I thought of screaming, but decided I must have been dreaming." Aunt Penny smiled. "I do take my duties seriously, you know. About watching after you children while James and Isabel are away." She nodded and sipped her tea.

Esme took advantage of the lull in her conversation. "Enjoy your breakfast, Aunt Penny," she said hastily, backing out the door. She shut it behind her quickly before Aunt Penny could say anything else.

Back downstairs, she sat and looked across the table at Mimsy. "Aunt Penny thinks someone was scratching at her window during the night." She shook her head. "We're looking after her instead of the other way around."

Mimsy nodded absently. "She told me the same thing yesterday morning. She said that someone had scratched on her window and awakened her. She had the drapes drawn tightly, and was afraid to get up and look." Mimsy looked around at the door as Hinson passed by. "Have you seen Vincent this morning?"

Esme lifted an eyebrow. "Not this morning. Why?"

Mimsy shrugged. "No reason." She pushed her chair back. "I believe I'll go for a walk." She went out the door as Esme stared after her. The only place Mimsy had been known to walk was into and out of shops. Even more amazing, when Esme looked out the window a few minutes later, Mimsy was actually wandering out across the field, toward Shad Abbas.

Esme had just finished helping Ned feed Spot when Captain Arno came by. He looked singularly handsome this morning, his boots polished to a mirror shine, his uniform immaculate. Esme, on the other hand, was dirty from helping Ned, and she was in the process of getting out her gardening tools to work with her dahlias. Not only was her apron dirty, but the hem of her dress was, too. Captain Arno bowed slightly, and smiled at her just as if she were wearing a ball dress.

"Good day, Miss Darling," he said. He started to say something else, but Spot stretched and made a noise. Captain Arno stopped mid-word and glanced at Spot's pen. His expression was not happy.

"Spot won't bother us, I assure you," Esme said, replacing her hoe. She removed her apron and hung it on a nail in the garden shed. "She's just had her breakfast, and will probably nap most of the morning."

"Excellent." Captain Arno turned and smiled at her again. "I . . . I wonder if I might have a few words with you, Miss Darling." He glanced at the house and back. "In private."

Esme motioned him toward the garden bench by her dahlias, and they sat down. Captain Arno appeared uncharacteristically nervous. He fidgeted with his hat, turning it around twice before he put it beside him. Then he patted his cravat and touched the buttons down the front of his uniform. "Is there something you wish to say to me, Captain Arno?" Esme prompted, wishing she had at least had the opportunity to wash her hands. Before she put on her gloves, she had pulled some weeds growing beside her violet dahlia, and her hands were grimy.

"This is very confidential, Miss Darling," Captain Arno began, "and I trust you will divulge my suspicions to no one, not even your brother." He paused, waiting for her answer.

"I would never break a confidence."

Arno turned and smiled at her, his good looks set off to advantage by his uniform. "I knew I could count on you, Miss Darling. I want you to do something for me, and, as it concerns you and your father, as well, I hope you will comply."

"And that is?"

Arno hesitated. "I have reason to believe that your neighbor may be implicated in the plot against your father."

"Neighbor?" Esme couldn't imagine what he was implying.

"Yes, I know it's a delicate matter, and I hesitate to broach it, but . . ." Captain Arno frowned. "Your neighbor at Shad Abbas."

"Lovatt?" Esme was astonished. "What makes you think that?"

Arno put his hand over hers. "I'm not at liberty to tell you that right now, Miss Darling. Just be assured that I would not say such a thing lightly. I do have some evidence, but I need something more concrete. I know the man is over here frequently. I had hoped that you might be able to watch and listen to him, and perhaps tell me if you discover anything."

"You know that I will do whatever I can to help Papa," Esme began, "but what—"

"Thank you, Miss Darling," he said, wrapping his fingers warmly around her hand. 'I knew I could count on you.

As I said, I would never make such an accusation unless I had some proof, but I don't feel I have enough at this point to publicly denounce him." Captain Arno smiled at her again. "Perhaps the two of us can work together, and unmask him for the villain he is."

"Lovatt?" Esme said again, not sure that she and Arno were talking about the same person. "Lovatt truly likes Papa. He told me so."

"Of course he did. What better way to get your confidence?" Arno paused. "You seem hesitant, Miss Darling. Is there . . . is there an attachment there? If so, I'm truly sorry."

Esme waved away his suggestion "Of course there is no attachment. It's just that I've known Lovatt forever. I can't believe he would do something like that to Papa."

"Who better?

Esme sat, stunned at Arno's words. She couldn't think of Lovatt in that way. Was that why he hadn't wished to have their relationship go any further than casual friendship? She turned to Captain Arno to ask for proof of Lovatt's treachery, but stopped as she saw Mimsy coming toward them.

Captain Arno stood. "Lady Evers," he said, bowing. "You look wonderful this morning."

Esme truly looked at Mimsy for the first time in a while. Mimsy did look wonderful. Her hair was tousled and her complexion was glowing. "Thank you, Captain Arno. It's a lovely morning for a walk." She turned to Esme. "You really should take a walk now and then, Esme. It's quite refreshing. Won't you come inside, Captain Arno?"

He picked up his hat and smiled at her. "No, thank you, Lady Evers. I was just passing by and stopped to say good morning to you and Miss Darling. I hope to see you soon."

"Yes, do come dine with us. Perhaps the first of the week?" Mimsy turned to Esme. "You won't believe what a

wonderful idea I had while I was walking. We should have
a party!"

"A party? With Papa in London?" Esme stood to get
Captain Arno on his way, so that she could stop Mimsy.
She walked with him around the side of the house to the
front gate. They stood at the gate for a moment, and then
Captain Arno clasped her hands in his and looked down
at her palms. Esme looked as well—her palms were dirty
and streaked with green from the weeds. "Miss Darling, I
can't tell you how much your friendship means to me,"
he began, then stopped and looked over her shoulder at
something down the road. Esme turned to see Lovatt rid-
ing into view, astride a beautiful gray. He rode up to the
gate and paused, looking down at Captain Arno standing
there, still holding Esme's hands. "Am I interrupting
something?" Lovatt said with a grin that clearly let Esme
know that he didn't care if he were interrupting or not.

"No, not at all." She pulled her hands away and tried
to cover them with the folds of her skirt.

"Good," Lovatt said easily, dismounting. "How are you
this morning, Arno?"

"Quite well." Captain Arno's voice sounded stiff.

"Good." Lovatt smiled breezily at them, tied his horse,
and sauntered through the gate as if he owned Rouvray.
Hinson opened the door for him even before he knocked,
and he disappeared into the house. Esme stared after him.

"He appears to be quite welcome." Captain Arno's voice
was flat and stiff.

"As I said, he's an old acquaintance," Esme said, hedging the truth a little. "He always had the run of the house
when he was a child."

Captain Arno nodded, then smiled at her. "Enough of
Lovatt. Thank you for seeing me out, Miss Darling." He
reached for her hands again and Esme moved, smiling
back at him.

"A pleasure, Captain Arno. I do hope you'll return soon. I hope to have some news of Papa before long."

"As do I." He managed to clasp one of her hands in his and held it. "May I count on you to watch, um, the subject of our conversation? Perhaps between us, we can solve this puzzle." He smiled down at her, and Esme felt strange. She had always thought Arno handsome, but in truth he was decidedly past that. And now there was a strange smile on his lips and an even stranger shift in his attitude toward her. Esme felt thoroughly confused.

"I hope so, Captain Arno," she said sincerely, moving back toward the gate. She smiled at him again as he left.

To her surprise, Lovatt opened the door for her. "Hinson's off doing something for your sister. It's of great importance, I'm sure, so I thought I'd take the door duty." He shut the door behind her after glancing out. "Tell me, what did the dashing Captain Arno have to say?"

"Nothing."

Lovatt looked down at her, started to grin, then frowned and stepped back. "Not so, Miss Darling. I know when you're hedging your bets. What did he have to say?"

Esme looked at him and lifted an eyebrow. Lovatt was the most arrogant, the most supercilious, the most . . . the most of any bad word she could imagine. She decided to take him down a peg. "If it's any of your business, Captain Arno wishes to call on me," she said, glaring at Lovatt with what she hoped was an icy look.

"Good, good." Lovatt nodded his head in approval. "When you're with him, try to find out something." He looked around and drew Esme into the small green parlor to the side of the hall. The curtains were drawn and the room was dark. Lovatt sat down on the sofa and patted the spot beside him. Esme ignored him and sat down in the opposite chair.

"What's on your mind, Lovatt?" she asked bluntly.

"Nothing," he said innocently, but Esme could see his devilish grin in the gloom. "Where's Vincent, by the way?"

"I haven't seen him this morning. I suppose he's tired from all that chasing around you and he did, following Captain Arno."

Lovatt stared at her. "You know about Vincent following me?"

"I know about most of the things that go on around here. But in answer to your question, yes. Vincent told me all about it." She stopped. "How did you know Vincent followed you? He said he stayed behind and you didn't know he was there."

Lovatt laughed. "When it comes to tracking, Vincent has all the finesse of an elephant. I knew he was there from the moment his horse stepped out into the road." He paused. "Actually, I thought he might join me at the circus, but he stayed back. I didn't want him along, so that was the best thing. As it was, I hesitated to do some things, afraid he might decide to barge in."

"What things? What did you do?" Esme hated to ask him, but couldn't stop herself.

"Ah, something you *don't* know."

"Don't be smug, Lovatt. Just tell me." Her voice was tinged with irritation.

"Let me savor the moment a little, Miss Darling." Lovatt stretched out his legs in front of him and leaned back. He sighed deeply in mock contentment.

"Do tell me when you've savored enough, Lovatt," Esme said, standing. "I'll be back to listen to you then."

He stood and caught her arm as she started to leave, then turned her around to face him. That was a mistake. Before Esme knew what was happening, Lovatt's face was close to hers and she was looking into his eyes, eyes that were large and dark in the gloom of the room. He gave her a look she could not identify. "Esme," he whispered, as overcome as she.

Esme licked her lips, feeling the warmth of his chest as she brushed up against him. Her knees felt strangely weak, and she fought against melting into his chest. "Chalmers," she managed to say, barely feeling the sound of his name across her lips.

Lovatt lowered his head slightly, and Esme knew he was going to kiss her. She remembered what he had said about avoiding entanglements, and tried to will herself to pull away and slap him. Instead, she stood there as though mesmerized. Just as his lips were so close to hers that she could feel the gentle touch of his breath on her skin, Lovatt suddenly snapped straight and pushed her into her chair, then fell back onto the sofa.

"What—" Esme began, but Lovatt, glancing quickly at the door, interrupted her. "And I do believe Spot will be just fine, Miss Darling," he said, apropos of nothing, his voice like that of a friendly vicar.

"Oh, there you are, my dear," Aunt Penny said, staggering into the room, her hand to her head., "I seem to have come down with a perfectly dreadful headache. It must have come from my experiences last night." She rubbed her head delicately. "At any rate, I wondered if you could go to the apothecary's and get me some powders." She collapsed on the sofa beside Lovatt. "As I told you, it was that scratching again."

"For the past two nights Aunt Penny has heard something scratching at her window," Esme explained to Lovatt.

He raised an eyebrow. "Someone trying to get inside?"

"Oooh! Listen to that, Esme. Someone trying to get inside." Aunt Penny moaned and turned to look at Lovatt. "Do you think so, too? It's too terrible to contemplate." She began to wring her hands. "Whatever shall we do, Esme? I refuse to spend another moment in that room."

"The room is fine, Aunt Penny." Esme glared at Lovatt and he grinned at her. The thought occurred to her that he knew full well what he was doing—he was encouraging

Aunt Penny in her ridiculous notion just as a distraction. "It must be a limb from the big tree scratching the window-pane," Esme said firmly, trying to look at Aunt Penny with sympathy. She did look wretched. "I'll have Hinson see to it."

"A limb?" Aunt Penny's voice was weak.

"A limb." Esme patted her hand. "Don't you worry about a thing, Aunt Penny. No one has ever tried to break into Rouvray, and I'm sure no one ever will."

"Are you sure?"

Esme nodded. "I'm sure. Why don't you let me go get you some more breakfast? Were you able to eat what I brought up to you?"

"Part of it, dear, although I do believe breakfast while I was so agitated may have brought on this headache." Aunt Penny looked around, relieved. "However, I do believe I might feel better with some more sausage, and perhaps a muffin. And a bowl of strawberries. And I think some eggs." She nodded. "Eggs are always good when one is ailing."

"And I'll be glad to go get your powders," Lovatt said gallantly, standing. "Why don't you rest until I return? I'll be back in a very few minutes." He nodded briefly at Esme, picked up his hat, and left.

Aunt Penny looked gratefully at the door Lovatt had exited. "What a wonderful young man," she said. "Don't you agree, Esme, dear?"

"Just wonderful, Aunt Penny." Esme almost choked on the words. She too, was looking at the door Lovatt had exited, but her thoughts were certainly not the same as Aunt Penny's. Worse, Lovatt had told her that he knew something about the situation at the circus that she didn't, but he had left before he told her what it was. Now she was going to have to get the information out of him.

And she would do it, she resolved. One way or the other.

Twelve

Lovatt must be hiding something, Esme thought when he didn't return from town with Aunt Penny's powders. He sent Samad with them. Esme tried to quiz Samad about what was going on at the circus, but he pretended not to understand her. He merely handed her the powders and bowed, backing out the door.

Esme fumed most of the day about Lovatt's tantalizing lack of information about his nocturnal shadowing of Arno. Just what was Lovatt doing? Why was Lovatt following Arno? What were the things Lovatt said he hesitated to do? Esme worked in her dahlia patch with a vengeance, weeding and grooming the ground, all the while pondering. Finally, there was nothing more she could do to the garden, so she took Spot for a walk. Spot was sluggish, almost as if she were tired. Esme led her to the back field, toward Shad Abbas, and they stayed there for a while, Esme sitting while Spot dozed in the shade of a tree. Hard as she tried to deny it to herself, Esme was hoping Lovatt would come by.

After almost an hour, Esme was getting hot and was beginning to perspire. She thought for a moment, then gathered up Spot's leash. "Come on, Spot," she said, pulling on the leash, "we're going to Shad Abbas."

To Esme's surprise, Spot got up and loped along the path that led to Lovatt's house. The closer to the house the leopard got, the faster she went. Esme was having a difficult time controlling her.

As they neared Shad Abbas, Spot decided to cut off the path and go along a wooded ridge toward the back. Esme tried to hold her back, but Spot was not to be deterred. She charged forward, heedless of Esme running into brambles and trees. Esme's bonnet caught on a limb, and she barely had time to untie the ribbons as Spot bolted ahead. Briars and brambles pulled at her clothes, but Spot hurried on. Esme didn't have time to yell at Spot—she was too busy dodging obstacles.

Finally, they came to a low-lying limb and Spot jumped up on it as though accustomed to using it. Esme walked up to the limb, and looked down over Shad Abbas. They were directly above the stables, looking right down into the paddock. "Lovatt must have been right," she muttered to Spot. "No doubt you were terrifying his horses every time the wind blew across you toward the stables."

Spot stretched along the limb. Esme tried for a moment to persuade her to hop down, but Spot was not to be moved. Esme gave up and leaned against the limb until such time as Spot felt ready to get down. Esme smoothed her clothes, removed a few brambles and leaves, then felt her hair and pulled some twigs from it. From the feel of it, she knew that her hair was in terrible disarray, standing out around her head. There was nothing to be done for it. "Come on, Spot," she said, trying again, tugging at the leash. She stopped and dropped the leash as she saw a flash of white in the woods behind the stables, not far below them. In a moment, Lovatt appeared from the stables and strode off into the woods below her. From the other side, her right, Esme saw two men in white turbans walking up to meet him. She recognized Samad, but she did not know the other man. The stranger looked much like Samad, and was also dressed in Indian clothing.

The three men went out of her line of sight, so Esme

scrambled up onto the limb beside Spot and looked down. The limb was slick from use. "Spot," she muttered, "is this where you've been hiding when I've missed you?"

Spot merely stretched and closed her eyes. Esme could see the three men from overhead, but she was unable to see their faces clearly. She leaned over and tried to listen to what they were saying, but they were too far away for her to hear. She did see Lovatt pull a pouch from his pocket and give it to the stranger. Then Samad and the other turbaned man left at a lope, headed deeper into the woods. They seemed to be going toward Rouvray. Lovatt sat down on a rock and took a small notebook from his pocket, wrote something in it, and then left, heading back toward Shad Abbas.

"Very peculiar, Spot," Esme muttered. "Do you think Arno could be on to something? Could Samad and the other man be spying? Why else would Lovatt be paying them? Neither Samad or the other man is English, that's for sure." She sat on the limb and thought.. If either of the turbaned men were the spy, or both, then Lovatt was, as Captain Arno had said, definitely implicated.

The thought brought no joy, and she kept rejecting it. Still, the idea Arno had planted kept nagging at her.

"Come on, Spot," she said finally, pulling on the leash. "Let's go home."

Spot was ready. She jumped down and began running through the woods, Esme in tow. Esme did manage to slow her down long enough to disentangle her bonnet from the limb. Then they hurried on home, Spot leading Esme and her bonnet across the field.

Esme put Spot in her pen and collapsed on the garden bench to catch her breath. "You do look frazzled," Mimsy called out. She was sitting at the small table in the garden, reading a book. "What have you been doing?"

"Walking Spot." Esme gasped, then went to sit down at the table. To her surprise, Vincent came out of the house carrying a glass of lemonade and placed it in front of Mimsy. "We were just talking," he said, sitting down carefully across from Mimsy. "Lovely weather, isn't it?"

"Lovely." Esme paused, trying to think of a way to ask Vincent about details of the previous night. She had to find out what Lovatt was doing. It was imperative now. She had to know.

"Vincent and I were just talking about Papa," Mimsy said. "We got a letter from him, and he said nothing has been done so far. Evidently he and Mama are just sitting in London waiting to be questioned."

Vincent frowned. "I have some influence in London. I think I may go to town for a week or so and see if I can talk to some people."

"Let's wait a bit," Esme said slowly. "Papa seemed to think that he would be exonerated. No point in bringing any pressure to bear if there's no reason."

"What we need to do is find the spy," Mimsy said, nibbling on cake and sipping lemonade. "By the way, Vincent had a most interesting experience last evening. He should tell you about it."

"I mentioned it to Esme," Vincent said hastily, not saying that the mention had been made in the dead of night.

"You mentioned it, but didn't give me any details." Esme smiled at him. "Do tell me everything."

Vincent looked decidedly uncomfortable. "Oh, as I told you, I was merely outside and saw Lovatt breaking into the circus through a hole in the fence. That's all."

"All!" Mimsy put down her cake. "Vincent, you said the man looked around guiltily before he went inside. I can't believe it of Chalmers Lovatt! I've known him since we were children, and I know he'd never do anything the slightest bit wrong."

"I didn't say he did anything wrong." Vincent's tone was defensive.

"Why don't we watch and see what he does?" Esme said.

"We could go tonight to the village and hide, then watch for him. If he comes to the circus again, we can follow him. If he doesn't, perhaps we can do some investigating on our own."

Mimsy turned to her and grinned. "What a wonderful idea, Esme! We'll go tonight. I'll wear my new dark blue cape, and no one will see me at all. I'd better bind up my hair as well, don't you think?" She turned to Vincent. "Isn't that a wonderful idea, Vincent? We could have such an adventure!" She stood up and stretched. "I'm truly sleepy, and if we're to stay up tonight, I should get some sleep. I'll see you at supper and then we'll decide when we should leave." To everyone's surprise, she patted Vincent on the head as she passed by him.

"I take it things are improving," Esme said dryly, watching Mimsy go inside.

"Yes, but I've been watching every word I say. It's been quite a strain, to say the least."

"Then how did you let slip the story about Arno and Lovatt?"

Vincent grimaced. "I didn't mention Arno, and by all that's holy, I can't figure out how Mimsy got the story about Lovatt out of me. We were talking about her childhood, and she mentioned Lovatt. Then I said something about him, and before I knew what I was doing I was blabbing about seeing him skulking around the circus fence." He looked sheepish. "Mimsy has a habit of doing that to me."

Esme laughed at him. "Mimsy always gets exactly what she wants. You should know that by now."

"I do. I'm usually the one providing exactly what she wants, no matter what it is." He frowned. "Do you think we should try to talk her out of this silly notion of trying to follow Lovatt?" He paused and reddened. "Oh, I'm sorry. It was your suggestion, wasn't it?"

"Yes, but on reflection, it is a silly notion." Esme grimaced.

"True. He may not even be out and about tonight."

"Silly or not, though, Vincent, it's the only plan we have. Can you suggest something better?"

"Just to wait." He grinned ruefully. "That's not a very good plan, is it? It doesn't matter, I suppose. Mimsy will want to go pretend she's a Bow Street Runner, so we might as well give in gracefully."

Esme stood up. "Vincent, silly or not, I wouldn't miss this for the world. If Lovatt isn't out and about tonight, then I intend to watch every night until he is. I'm going to discover just what he's up to." She couldn't resist—she patted Vincent on the shoulder as she went inside, chuckling to herself. Lovatt should know better than to try to hide anything in a small town.

That night, the three of them slipped out of Rouvray and went across the field that joined Shad Abbas. Then they turned left and took the little path that led to the village. Once there, they settled behind some bushes near the circus fence, right where they could see the break in the fence where Vincent said he had seen Lovatt enter.

"I'm damp," Mimsy muttered. "My hair will fall down."

"Of course it will," Esme whispered back. "Be quiet."

They sat in silence for all of three minutes. "My legs are cramping," Mimsy said. "I'm going to have to stand up. Besides, I'm getting my new cloak all dirty."

"Stay down," Esme hissed. "Someone's coming." She grabbed Mimsy's arm and pulled her to the ground. "Ooofff," Mimsy said, plopping right into Vincent's lap. Esme held her breath, afraid the person had heard them. Esme peered around the leaves of the bush. "It's Captain Arno," she whispered, watching his shadowy figure as he looked around furtively, then entered the break in the fence. "What do you suppose he's doing?"

She got no answer and, as soon as Arno had disappeared behind the fence, asked her question again. "Whatever could he be doing?" she whispered, turning to Mimsy and

Vincent. Mimsy was still draped over Vincent, but Vincent seemed to have taken things well into hand. He was holding Mimsy firmly and kissing her as if this was the first time they had ever kissed. Esme shook his shoulder. "This is hardly the time, you two. Come with me and follow Captain Arno. He's gone behind the fence."

Vincent waved her away as he kept on kissing Mimsy, but Esme persisted, shaking Vincent's shoulder. "Stop that and come on. We're going to lose Captain Arno if we don't hurry."

Vincent stopped kissing Mimsy long enough to glance up at Esme. "I'm busy. Besides, I'll wager that Arno is probably going in to see some lightskirt. Enough of them are with the circus to keep the entire garrison entertained." With that, he began kissing Mimsy again, and the two of them fell back on the grass.

"Disgusting," Esme muttered. "You two are simply disgusting. I'm off to follow Arno myself." She turned back toward the circus and just caught a glimpse of someone else going inside through the break in the fence. She hadn't seen enough to be able to identify the person, so she waited a moment, then crept toward the opening.

The fence was broken, and its wooden edges were rough and jagged. She had to pick up her skirts almost to her knees and step high to get through. At that, she snagged her stockings and had to pause before she could go on. Inside, everything was very dark and quiet. Off to one side she could hear snuffles and scrabblings. Her heart stopped for a moment until she identified those as the sounds of the animals in their cages. Evidently some of them were nocturnal, and were pacing and scratching on their cage walls.

She glanced left and right to get her bearings, and saw absolutely no one. Carefully she headed for the row of hastily thrown together shanties and huts that housed the circus folk. Her heart was pounding in her chest so hard that she thought it could be heard outside her body. There was no sign of Arno or of the other person she had glimpsed entering the fence. For a moment, she considered going back. If anyone caught her here alone, her reputation would be in shreds. "Think of Papa," Esme muttered to herself. "He wouldn't be craven. He would do his duty." Besides, she decided, she had a choice. If necessary, she could run back to Vincent and Mimsy or she could scream. Vincent and Mimsy were probably too involved to hear her if she screamed, but surely someone would. Resolutely, she walked on.

Lights were burning in only two of the shanties. One was on the far end, and as Esme drew closer she noted that the window covering was pulled back. She would be able to see inside. Carefully she skittered sideways, skirting the neighboring shanty, and came up from the dark side next to the fence. She tiptoed around to the side of the shanty so she could peer inside without being seen. She shuddered when she saw two very coarse men playing cards. That in itself wasn't bad, but the men were accompanied by two women in various stages of undress, and they were all drinking from two bottles that stood on the table. Blue ruin, if Esme was any judge. Arno certainly wasn't in this group. Silently, Esme drew back into the shadows and walked back up beside the fence to the other shanty where she had seen lights.

She was preoccupied, hugging the fence on her right side and watching carefully on her left to make sure there was no one there. As she got to the corner of the shanty, she ran into something that was only about knee high and she fell forward, right over whatever was there.

Before she could scream, someone clamped a hand over her mouth. She had clattered into the side of the shanty as she fell, and the noise sounded deafening in the quiet. The man who held Esme kept one hand over her mouth, then quickly wound his other hand around her waist and grabbed her up unceremoniously. He clutched her to his body, then ran. Esme couldn't make a sound, and she couldn't move out of the man's grip. He was terribly strong. He reached the animal cages and paused. She could hear him breathing hard from the exertion of running with her clutched in front of him. He started to put her down, but the animals began howling and making all sorts of noises in the quiet night air, and Esme found herself dragged again.

This time she realized that the two of them were at the fence, near the place where the break was located. She could hear noise behind them, the sounds of the animals mixed with the voices of men. If only she could scream, she would be safe, but the man still had his hand over her mouth. They reached the broken spot in the fence and Esme thought he was going to shove her through the hole, but he instead heaved her over his head and tossed her over the top of the fence as if she were a sack of flour. She felt herself flying through the air, and landed on the ground on the other side with a thud so hard that it knocked the wind out of her. She tried to scream for Vincent and Mimsy, but had no breath.

The man leaped through the fence and scooped her up. He jerked her around, and was as surprised as she was. "Lovatt!" She gasped. "What?" See didn't have time to finish her sentence, as Lovatt clamped his hand over her mouth again.

"Come on," he whispered hoarsely as he glanced behind them. The voices of the men inside were closer. "We have to get out of here."

"Ummm!" Esme muttered underneath his hand. In desperation, she pointed to the bush where Vincent and Mimsy were. Lovatt looked at her blankly, and she pointed again, jabbing her fingers into the air. Finally he moved his hand. "Vincent and Mimsy," she whispered. "There!" She ran over to the bush, Lovatt right behind her.

She was about to get Vincent and Mimsy when Lovatt threw himself onto her from behind and she landed right on top of Vincent, who was on top of Mimsy. "Everyone be still," Lovatt muttered. "They're looking outside the fence. Don't move."

"But wha—" Esme almost choked as Lovatt clamped his hand over her mouth again.

"Be still," he hissed, pressing down hard on her.

Esme tried to sort out the sensations she was feeling, but she could feel nothing except the length of Lovatt's body against her back. They fit together like pieces of a puzzle. As she was thinking of this, strange things were happening to her body.

Lovatt released her and moved slightly. "Don't move," he whispered. "I think they've gone, but I want to check. They may be just inside the fence, and we don't want to give ourselves away."

He moved away from Esme and she felt the cool night air against her instead. It was only then that she realized that her cloak and gown were bunched up around her thighs. She scooted back a little to move her clothes and glanced up at Lovatt. He was peering out around the edge of the bush, looking intently, not moving.

Mimsy made a strange sound and Esme looked back down at them, suddenly realizing that she was on top of Vincent. She rolled off to one side.

"What?" Esme started to ask, but Vincent interrupted her. "Move away," he muttered, his voice sounding strange.

"Why?" Esme asked. Lovatt looked back at them and then came over to her. "Come with me a minute, Esme," he said, his voice holding a hint of laughter. He was grinning as he pulled her to her feet and led her away.

"What do you find so funny?" Esme demanded, straightening her clothing as he dragged her out of the way. He stopped when they got to a large tree, and he pulled her behind it so they couldn't see the bush, the fence, or Vincent and Mimsy. "What's wrong with you, Lovatt?"

"I believe your sister and her husband needed a moment of privacy," he said, still chuckling. "Their clothing was, shall we say, disarranged?"

"Privacy! Are you out of your mind? Why would they need privacy? After all . . ." Lovatt's meaning hit her, and she felt herself blush. "Oh," she said.

"Indeed." Lovatt's shoulders were shaking with laughter. "Why don't we walk on ahead a bit, Miss Darling? We'll give them time to, ah, rearrange and catch up with us." He glanced back at the fence. "Then I'll see you home. While we're waiting for Mimsy and Evers, perhaps you can tell me what you were doing out at this time of night, wandering around such an unsavory place as the circus." He looked down at her, grinning, his teeth very white in the faint moonlight. He was dressed all in black, his hair was rumpled, and there was a smudge of dirt on his cheek. From their tussle, Esme knew that he also had a faint stubble of beard, and she had caught that whiff of scent that was always Lovatt—citrus and soap.

She felt that strange feeling in the pit of her stomach and had to look away. She had the strangest thought—she could imagine herself and Lovatt doing the same thing that Mimsy and Vincent had been doing. She had to catch her breath.

She turned away from him, trying to escape, but he put his hand on her shoulder and turned her around to face him. "Don't run away from me, Miss Darling. I want to know why you were here." He smiled at her again and his hand slid down her arm to cup her elbow. Esme felt her knees go weak.

"If I know you," Lovatt said, "it should be quite a story."

Thirteen

Esme glanced over Lovatt's shoulder and, to her intense relief, saw Vincent and Mimsy walking toward them, holding hands. "I believe we can go home now," Esme said stiffly, not looking at Lovatt. She knew if she looked at him, she was lost. "Vincent and Mimsy are ready now."

Lovatt turned around and let go of Esme's elbow. He nodded at Vincent and Mimsy. "Good to see you," Vincent said formally, as though they were meeting in the Holland House drawing room.

"Yes," Lovatt answered, standing ramrod straight. "Delighted to see you, as well." He bowed slightly toward Mimsy. "Lady Evers."

"Lovatt." Mimsy inclined her head.

"I can't believe this," Esme said, looking from one to the other. "I've just discovered Lovatt skulking around a shanty at the circus, crawling around on his hands and knees. I've been tossed over the fence like a sack of flour, and we've been hunted by circus people. Now we're pretending that we just met after midnight here under a tree in town."

"Oh, well," Vincent said. "It really doesn't matter. Are you going our way, Lovatt?"

"I wouldn't miss it," Lovatt said with his maddening grin. He offered his arm to Esme, and the four of them set out across town toward the path that led to Rouvray.

All the way home Esme kept waiting for Lovatt to say why he was at the circus, but instead he and Vincent exchanged small talk about mutual acquaintances, the dirt in London, the Prince Regent's doings, and hunting. Esme was ready to shriek when they got to Rouvray.

"Thank you for walking with us, Chalmers," Mimsy said, elegantly sweeping into the front hall. Hinson had left the usual candle burning in the sconce, and Esme could see that Mimsy had dirt, bits of grass, and leaves clinging to the back of her cloak and her hair.

"Quite welcome, Lady Evers." Lovatt grinned devilishly again. "Any time." He turned to Vincent. "I'll see you tomorrow." With that, he turned and took a step toward Shad Abbas.

Esme grabbed his arm. "No, you don't, Lovatt. You come inside right this minute and explain yourself. Exactly what were you doing at the circus, and more importantly, whatever were you doing skulking around on your hands and knees behind that shanty? I insist you tell us, and do it right now."

Mimsy ran her fingers up Vincent's arm and looked at him from under heavy-lidded eyes. "Now, Esme, if Chalmers is tired, let him go on home. There will be plenty of time to talk another day." She batted her eyes at Vincent, and he looked back at her adoringly.

"Will you two stop that!" Esme said crossly. "Lovatt, I insist. Come in here right this minute and explain yourself."

He grinned at her, but she refused to be taken in by his charm. "If you insist, I suppose I must," he said. "Only I think turnabout is fair play—you're going to have to explain to me why you were wandering around alone there, and tripped over me."

"There's a perfectly good explanation for that," Esme said.

"I'm sure there is, and I can't wait to hear it." Lovatt

stepped into the hall and took Esme's hand. "The drawing room? The parlor?" He looked at Mimsy and Vincent, who were still gazing at each other. "You two are joining us, aren't you? I don't believe it would be quite the thing for me to be meeting at this time of night with Miss Darling without a chaperone."

"What?" Mimsy said, looking at Lovatt with unfocused eyes. "Of course. Whatever you say, Chalmers. Do have a nice walk home."

Esme gave her a disgusted look. "Mimsy, don't be such a featherwit. You know that—"

She was interrupted by a bloodcurdling scream from upstairs. Lovatt immediately shoved her into the small parlor. "Wait here and don't move," he said firmly. Then he bounded up the stairs, going out of sight as another scream echoed through the halls.

Mimsy clung to Vincent and they hurried into the parlor with Esme. "You two can stay here if you want, but I'm going upstairs. That was Aunt Penny." Esme grabbed her skirts and dashed up the stairs, almost colliding with Bram, who was rushing down the hall dressed in his nightshirt, carrying his sword. He pushed past her and ran into Aunt Penny's room. "Stop, there, you!" Esme heard him yell as he ran into the room.

There was a terrible crash, then Bram and another man wrestled on the floor. All the while, Aunt Penny kept screaming.

"Stop it, Bram!" Esme yelled, reaching out to grab him. "That's no burglar! You're wrestling with Lovatt!"

Bram jerked back suddenly and crashed into Esme. She went sideways into Aunt Penny's washstand, and the pitcher of water and bowl on it went sliding off the end. Lovatt had started to get up, and the pitcher of water hit him right on the head with a terrible *thunk*. He fell to the floor without a sound, and didn't move. Aunt Penny was still screaming.

"Oh, good Lord," Esme gasped, horrified She scrambled to her feet and ran to kneel at Lovatt's head. "Is he dead?" She reached down to smooth his hair from his head and discovered that his head was bloody. "Bram, have we killed him?" She turned toward the bed. "Aunt Penny, do stop. You're fine." She put her arms under Lovatt's head and cradled it in her lap. "Lovatt. Chalmers, speak to me. Please." She moved as her lap felt wet, and was horrified to see blood all over her skirt. "Bram, he's going to bleed to death if we don't do something."

Bram knelt by Lovatt's side. "Head wounds always bleed like the devil. They usually look worse than they are." He felt along Lovatt's head with his fingertips, then leaned down and listened to Lovatt's breathing and his heart. "His heart's steady," he said, sitting back up. "He's going to have Old Nick's own headache tomorrow, though."

"If he doesn't bleed to death first. Go get some water and some bandages."

Bram stood. "I'm no good at finding that sort of thing. I'll get Mimsy."

"Do you know what you're saying?" Esme fixed him with a glare. "As if Mimsy could ever do anything in a crisis. Besides, she and Vincent are probably . . . are . . ." She stopped suddenly, remembering the scene behind the bush. "Never mind about Vincent and Mimsy. Just go get some bandages. And do it now!"

Aunt Penny crawled out of bed and came over to sit beside Esme. "I feel so terrible. This is all my fault." She began to cry. "I promised James and Isabel that I'd take care of you, and now look what I've done. And all because of the burglar."

"Burglar?" Esme stared at her. "There was a burglar in here? Are you sure?"

"Yes, it was terrible. I left my window open to catch the night breeze. I thought it might be efficacious for my headache, you know, and evidently the burglar came in that way. I heard a noise—you know that I've had trouble sleeping—and sat up in bed. I saw the black shadow crawling across the floor, and I screamed."

"Then what?" Esme shifted as Lovatt moaned. "Where *is* Bram?" she asked anxiously, looking at the door. "He's had time to find some bandages and get back here." She looked at Lovatt, deathly pale in the candlelight, his blood a dark stain down the side of his face and in her lap. "Go help Bram, will you, Aunt Penny? I'm afraid Lovatt is losing too much blood."

Aunt Penny peered across Esme's arms. "Dear me," she gasped, rocking back on her heels. "I fear I'm going to faint."

"Don't faint until you help Bram get some bandages," Esme said. "After you do that, you may go over to your bed and faint." She pinned Aunt Penny with a look. "Now go. Please."

Aunt Penny stood and tottered out into the hall. Evidently she met Bram outside the door, as he came right in, Aunt Penny following him. "You certainly took your time," Esme said.

"I had to get some water, and I didn't want it to be icy cold. And these bandages were hard to make. I think I've torn up a tablecloth."

"No matter." Esme moved and put Lovatt gently down on the floor, then wet a strip of cloth in the water and began sponging his head lightly. Even with her light touch, he groaned and tried to move his head. "I'll have to hold him," Bram said, moving to the other side.

"I believe I'll just go lie on the bed," Aunt Penny said faintly. "I'm not well at all."

"The very thing for you to do, Aunt Penny," Esme said absently. "Bram, did you bring bascilicum powder and some scissors?"

"No, but I do know where those things are. As soon as you've sponged the blood, we'll put a pad on the wound, and I'll go get the powder." He grasped Lovatt's head in his hands and held firmly as Esme sponged. She tried to be gentle, but Lovatt kept moaning softly. He did not open his eyes. As much as it hurt her, Esme was almost glad to hear his moans. At least he was alive.

The water in the bowl was dark red by the time she finished sponging his head. The cut was jagged where the pitcher broke against his head, and Esme wondered if they should send for a doctor. "It wouldn't hurt," Bram said, frowning, as he returned with the bascilium and scissors. "Although how we're going to explain this to the doctor is another story."

"I'll think of something. Can you go for the doctor?"

Bram bit his lower lip and looked again at the wound. "It really isn't a very long gash, and as I said, head wounds bleed terribly. Why don't we get him into bed and bandage this carefully? We can take another look at it when it gets light, and if we think he needs a doctor, I'll go get one then." He handed her the bascilicum powder and cut the rest of the tablecloth into strips for her. Esme cut Lovatt's hair around the wound as best she could, sprinkled bascilicum powder liberally on the cut, then wound a bandage around his head.

Bram grinned. "The man looks as if he's come out the worse in a duel. Where did you ever learn to apply a bandage?"

"You know good and well that I'm no nurse." She tied off the end of the bandage. "I just wanted to use enough strips to stop the bleeding."

"That should do it," Bram said, still grinning. "I can't decide if he resembles a snowball or a mummy."

"I fail to see your humor." Esme looked at him anxiously. "Where can we put him? All the bedrooms are full."

"I have an idea. Wait a minute." Bram ran out of the room and was back in just a moment. "Vincent's room is empty," he said with a smirk. "We'll put Lovatt in there."

Esme left Bram with Lovatt while she went to supervise the changing of the sheets on the bed. Then she had Hinson and Bram put Lovatt into bed. When they had him undressed and under the covers, she went into the room.

"You can go to bed, Esme," Bram said. "I'm sure he'll be all right."

Esme put extra candles on the table, pulled up a chair next to the bed, sat down in it, and covered herself with a quilt she had brought. "I'm going to stay here, Bram. He may be hurt worse than we think. One of us should stay with him."

"Lord, Esme, think about your reputation!" Bram stared at her. "You can't stay here with a man all night."

"I hardly think Lovatt is in any shape to harm my reputation," she said dryly. "If it will make you feel better, you can sit in the other chair."

Bram looked at her, then at Lovatt, and sighed. "All right. Aunt Penny would have an attack if you stayed here alone. I'll be right back."

Esme was smoothing Lovatt's covers and trying to give him a few drops of water when Bram came back. He had brought his coverlet with him. "By the way," he said as he sat down, "I don't suppose you'd want to tell me why you're up and dressed, and what Lovatt's doing here at this time of the night, would you? You might also explain what happened to Vincent and Mimsy. I suppose the divorce is off?"

"Yes, I do believe the divorce is off, and, no, I do not wish to explain tonight. I'll tell you everything in the morning." She leaned over and blew out all but one candle. "Goodnight, Bram."

The only reply she got was a muffled grunt as Bram snuggled farther down in his coverlet. Soon he was snoring gently. Esme couldn't sleep. She left Lovatt once to go check on Aunt Penny, who had taken some laudanum and gone back to sleep. Esme quietly closed Aunt Penny's window and the curtains, then went back to Lovatt. She felt his forehead gently, and he moved slightly under her touch, putting his hand up to hers. He grasped her fingers and she pulled her chair closer to the bed with her other hand, then sat close beside him, holding his hand. Sometime toward morning, she fell asleep.

A touch on her head woke her. The sun was shining in the window, and it took her a moment to realize what had happened and where she was. She had fallen over onto Lovatt's chest, and she could hear his heart beating steadily. Then she again felt the touch that had awakened her. It was Lovatt, gently stroking her hair. With a start, she turned her head and looked right into his eyes. "Good morning," he said, giving her a wobbly smile. His hand was still on her head, smoothing her hair.

She sat up and felt his face and forehead. "Are you all right?"

"I feel as if someone hit me with a cannon. What happened?"

"Aunt Penny's bowl and pitcher fell off the washstand and hit you. You have a terrible cut on your head." She leaned over and peered at the bandage. There was a little blood on it, but not as much as she had expected. "Do you think you need a doctor?"

"What I need is a new head." Lovatt tried to rise, but had to stop and hold his head. He looked down at his body, naked under the covers. "You didn't—?"

"No, Hinson and Bram did that." She looked over at Bram, who was still sleeping peacefully. "Bram, wake up!" Esme walked around the bed and shook Bram. He leaped to his feet and knocked her backward across Lovatt. *"En garde!"* he yelled, drawing back his arm. Then he stopped and blinked.

"The first rule of being a soldier," Lovatt said with a weak smile. "Never wake up a man when he's dreaming about fighting someone." He peered down at Esme. "Are you all right?"

Esme got up stiffly. "Perfectly fine." She looked at Bram. "I want to take off the bandage now that Lovatt is awake. You can help me."

"Um, much as I thank you for your efforts, Miss Darling, I would appreciate if it you would allow me a few moments of private time before you begin. Bram, could I rely on your assistance?"

"Let me help you. What do you want to—" Esme began, then realized what he wished. "Oh," she said, backing toward the door. "Oh. I'll see to some breakfast." She hurried out the door and closed it behind her. As she passed by Mimsy's bedroom door, she heard Vincent giggling.

Esme waited a good half an hour before she went upstairs with a breakfast tray for Lovatt. She knocked at the door and Bram opened it. Lovatt was sitting in the chair, wearing his breeches and one of Bram's shirts and looking the worse for the wear. Hinson had just finished shaving him.

"I told them I would just go home, where my man could attend me," Lovatt said with a weak grin, "but both of them insisted that I'd do no such thing."

"You're as pale as your bandage," Esme said, putting his tray down on the table. "Do you want me to send to Shad Abbas for someone to come get you?"

"I think I can walk there after I eat something."

Bram lifted a sausage from the tray and popped it into his mouth. "Excellent," he said, savoring it. "Mrs. Hinson is a wizard with sausage." He looked back at Lovatt. "Don't be an ass, Lovatt. You're not going to get about for a day or so, and you know it. Right now, I'll wager you have a headache."

Lovatt touched his bandage and smiled his thanks at Hinson. "A headache hardly describes it. That pitcher must have been made of iron."

"Just pottery," Esme said, smacking Bram's fingers away

from the sausage left on the tray. "Eat your breakfast, and I'll send someone to Shad Abbas to tell them you're coming home when you feel better. You can go then, in our carriage."

Ned was just coming in to feed Spot when Esme went back downstairs. She helped him feed the leopard and then dispatched him to Shad Abbas with a message about Lovatt.

Esme and Bram thought Lovatt should stay another night at Rouvray just to make sure that he was fine, but he was anxious to get home. Shortly before noon Lovatt insisted he was ready. Esme wanted to ask him why he had been at the circus, but felt she really couldn't impose on him while his head hurt so. Still, she couldn't resist when he was waiting with her in the drawing room for the carriage to be brought around.

The second that Bram left the drawing room to go check on the carriage, Esme turned to Lovatt, who was sitting on the striped sofa. "So, why were you at the circus last night, Lovatt? You promised to tell me."

"I don't recall any such promise." He held his head and moaned.

Esme walked over to him and moved his fingers. "I think you're doing it up a little brown, Lovatt. I heard you telling Bram that you were much better, and thought you'd be recovered completely by tomorrow morning at the latest."

Lovatt moved his hands and grinned wickedly at her. True, it was only a shadow of his usual grin, but it had his touch of the very devil in it. "I can't fool you at all, can I?" he asked sadly. "I don't recall a promise, but I will tell you, since you asked." He paused, listening.

"That's just the carriage. Now tell me." She bent down toward him and he reached up and touched her hair. "It was very nice waking up to find you atop me, Miss Darling." The wicked grin flashed, and Esme felt herself blush.

"Lovatt," she said, standing up in front of him, "I do believe you're cured."

He stood up facing her. "Let's see about that."

Before Esme knew what he was doing, he had swept her into his arms and was kissing her. In spite of herself, she put her arms around his neck and began kissing him back. One part of her mind told her that she shouldn't be doing this, but the other part of her mind and all the rest of her body urged her to get more involved. She heard a sound of contentment, and realized that it was coming from her throat. She leaned farther into Lovatt's body as he tightened his arms around her. Vaguely, she heard another sound in the background, and realized that it was the sound of the front door opening. She quickly stepped back, putting a safe distance between them.

"Esme," Lovatt said thickly, reaching out and clasping her hand.

"Good heavens, Chalmers! I thought to find you at death's door."

Lovatt released Esme's hand and looked over her shoulder, toward the door. His face went carefully blank. "Good day, Mother. What brings you here?" he said calmly.

Fourteen

Esme whirled around, her face flaming. "Lady Redferne," she stammered. "I was just, we were just—"

Bram, Mimsy, and Vincent came into the room just then. "Lady Redferne," Bram said, bowing. Mimsy and Vincent welcomed her as well, while Esme closed her eyes and thanked the stars and the druids and the heavens and everything else she could think of for rescue. After a few minutes of idle chatter, Lady Redferne looked at Lovatt. He had seated himself opposite his mother, and Esme noticed that a touch of blood was showing through his bandage.

"Much as I hate to cut my visit short," Lady Redferne said, standing, "I do believe we should return to Shad Abbas now." She leaned forward, touched Lovatt's knee, and smiled at him. "It isn't good to tire oneself out after an injury."

Everyone agreed, and Bram saw Lovatt and Lady Redferne to their carriage. Esme wondered just what Lady Redferne must think of her, standing that close to Lovatt, unchaperoned, in the room with the door closed. Worse, she wondered just what might have happened had Lady Redferne not interrupted them. Her lips tingled at the thought.

"And why are you sitting here smiling so?" Mimsy asked, coming into the room. She sat down in the chair Lovatt had used and leaned back. "That's the first time I've seen Lady Redferne in ages. She never gets out in society anymore, you know. I suppose she's afraid she might run into Redferne and one of his paramours. He flaunts them all over London."

"Really? I had never heard that, but of course I never go into society, either. Lovatt remarked once that Redferne had humiliated her."

Mimsy nodded. "I think she's come to terms with it, though. Lovatt is very protective of her. That's a good thing because I understand that the other son—the heir—is just like Redferne. Most think he won't last until he's forty, and Lovatt will inherit."

"I don't know that Lovatt would want to inherit," Esme said.

"Oh, you're probably right." Mimsy leaned sideways and peered around Esme until she could see out the window. "I do believe that your pet is wandering the yard again."

Esme turned quickly, just in time to see Spot slither into the patch of foxgloves that was just about halfway grown. She jumped up and ran out the door, yelling at Spot. The leopard turned around in the crushed foxgloves and, happy to see her owner, rolled over on her back, then got up and trotted over to Esme.

"And how did you get out of your pen?" Esme asked as Spot flopped alongside the garden bench. "Did someone leave the latch off again?" She went to inspect the pen. It was locked, just as she had left it when she and Ned had fed the leopard. Puzzled, Esme walked around the pen, but saw nothing. "Surely," she said to Spot, slipping a leash on her and tying her to a tree, "you haven't acquired the fine art of unlatching and relatching your gate." Spot merely looked at her, round-eyed, then closed her eyes and stretched out in the shade. Esme inspected the ruins of the foxglove patch and did what she could to straighten them up. Most of them would recover, she decided.

Vincent and Mimsy were already eating by the time Esme got back indoors. Actually, Vincent seemed to be spearing tiny bites and feeding them to Mimsy, while she batted her eyes at him and giggled. Esme did not wish to interrupt them, so she went in search of Aunt Penny. "Would you like to eat outdoors with me on the garden table?" Esme asked.

Aunt Penny put her hand over her heart. "I don't believe I can eat anything, dear. I'm still in a state of shock from last night. There's no way I can sleep in that room another second, so I plan to sit up all night in the parlor." She brandished the heavy poker from the kitchen. "I'll arm myself with this."

Esme took the poker from her. "Aunt Penny, you don't need to worry about this. What you need is some nourishment," she said firmly. "Come with me and eat lunch. Then we'll change rooms if you wish. You can have my room for a few nights, and I'll sleep in yours. I don't believe the burglar will return, but I'll keep watch."

"Would you do that, dear?" Aunt Penny asked, her voice grateful. "I don't want to put you out at all, but—"

"You're not putting me out, Aunt Penny. I would much prefer to know that you're safe in my room. I assure you that I won't have a moment's trouble sleeping." She took Aunt Penny's hand and started down the stairs beside her. "Now, let's go have something to eat. I'm sure Mrs. Hinson has all your favorites ready. And," she said, glancing down at the poker in her hand, "I'm also sure she'd want this back."

"You're just too good to me." Aunt Penny sighed. "I can't wait to tell James and Isabel just what a pattern card you are. Such perfect manners and sense of propriety! I must admit, child, that I was worried when James first asked me to stay here because I thought you might be the independent sort, but I'm happy to say that notion was wrong."

"Thank you," Esme said demurely, not daring to look Aunt Penny in the eye.

The afternoon was spent switching Aunt Penny into Esme's room. When Esme got herself settled in Aunt Penny's room, she looked out the window and wondered why she hadn't taken this room years ago. From the window she could look right down into Spot's pen, and right across the field to Shad Abbas. A glance to the left, and she could see the edge of the road to town; a glance to the right, and she could admire her dahlias. It was quite a nice room.

The evening was quiet. Vincent and Mimsy went upstairs to talk, while Aunt Penny and Esme stayed in the parlor. Aunt Penny worked on her embroidery while Esme wrote a letter to her parents telling them that all was quiet and orderly at Rouvray. She didn't mention Lovatt.

It was so quiet that she was startled when Hinson announced that Captain Arno had stopped by. When Hinson ushered him into the room, Esme was struck again by the fine figure he presented in his uniform. Arno was born to be a soldier, and she couldn't imagine him dressed any other way.

"I realize it's rather late, and I hope I'm not intruding," he said with a smile, handing Hinson his hat. "I believe we concurred it would be allowed for me to stop by." He glanced at the mantel clock. "I was in the neighborhood and saw the lights."

"Of course. We're delighted." Esme smiled at him, wondering just how she could turn the conversation around to the circus and perhaps discover why he had been there at such an ungodly hour the night before. If Vincent was correct and Arno *was* visiting a lightskirt, he certainly wasn't going to admit it, and Esme couldn't ask. It was a puzzle.

The puzzle wasn't solved by the time Arno left. To Esme's disappointment, he and Aunt Penny exchanged pleasantries the entire time he stayed. Aunt Penny did mention his family, and Esme noted that Captain Arno evaded the question and began talking about other things. He didn't stay long, and when he made his excuses Esme walked with him to the door, in hopes of slipping a question into the conversation. It seemed Arno had his own question to ask.

"Did you discover anything about Lovatt?" he whispered hoarsely, looking around to see if they were observed.

Esme started to say something when Arno nudged her arm. "Thank you," he said in his normal voice, smiling at her. "I hope to return soon." He glanced toward the bottom of the stairs. Esme followed his glance and saw Hinson standing there. "Good," she said, annoyed that she hadn't been able to discover a single thing about him or Lovatt. "Do come again."

As soon as Arno had gone, Esme went back into the parlor and looked out the window, hoping to see which direction he took. "He is a fine young man, isn't he?" Aunt Penny asked.

"What? Oh, certainly. Very fine." As Esme peered out the window, it seemed that Arno was heading toward town. She wondered if he were going again to the circus, and briefly flirted with the idea of following him.

"He would make James a fine son-in-law," Aunt Penny said coyly. "And it's that time for you, dear."

Esme turned and stared at her. "I don't know that I'll ever marry, Aunt Penny. Entanglements merely complicate one's life." To her horror, she realized that she was sounding exactly like Lovatt.

"Perhaps," Aunt Penny said, standing up and folding up her embroidery. "But then, dear, it is so nice to have another person in one's life, isn't it? Think of James and Isabel. They're such a happy couple." Left unsaid and hanging in the air was Aunt Penny's comment on her own life.

Esme gave her a hug and walked up the stairs with her. "And then there are those like you, Aunt Penny, who are wanted by everyone. I'm really glad you came to stay with us."

Aunt Penny smiled at her, a sweet smile that made Esme glad she had said something. "Thank you, my dear. I do my best." She turned to go sleep in Esme's room. "If you're bothered tonight by the burglar, just call out and I'll be there in just a moment." She paused and turned to Esme. "I have not one, but two pokers at the ready." Esme stifled a smile. "Thank you, Aunt Penny."

Esme awoke the next morning to discover that she had slept soundly and nothing at all had happened during the night. She was somewhat disappointed.

The day was as uneventful as her night had been. The weather was terrible—cold and foggy all day—so that Esme did little except go out and feed Spot. Inside, she picked up things and put them down again, then tried to read but lost her place, then tried mending but kept pricking her fingers.

"You're going to pace a hole in the carpet," Mimsy told her. Mimsy was cuddled against Vincent on the sofa in front of the fireplace in the drawing room. They had directed Hinson to build a small fire to keep away the damp, and now they were holding hands and giggling at each other. Esme had planned to stay as far away from them as possible, but the fire was too inviting and the other rooms were too cold.

"I seem to have an abundance of energy today," Esme admitted, sitting down. In just a moment she was up poking at the fire, then rearranging some dahlias in a bowl. "I don't know what's wrong with me."

Mimsy and Vincent looked at each other and broke into foolish grins. "I'll make the supreme sacrifice and go outside for you," Vincent said. "Would you like me to go get him?"

"Him?"

Mimsy and Vincent looked at each other and giggled. "Lovatt, of course," Mimsy said. "Isn't that the reason you're wandering around like your penned leopard?"

"Don't be silly." Esme was affronted. "The only time I've thought about Lovatt today was to wonder how he's getting along. That blow to his head might have been more serious than we thought."

"Oh, that," Vincent said. "He's fine. I saw him in town early last evening, and we shared an ale or two at the tap-room. He was pale and said his head still ached a little, but he was out and about and fine."

"Well, you could have told someone!" Esme snapped, jabbing at the fire with the poker. "I'm sure Aunt Penny would have liked to hear that. After all, it was her pitcher that did the damage." She put the poker down and marched toward the door. "I'm going upstairs to read, and don't want to be disturbed." As she closed the door, she could hear Vincent and Mimsy giggling again.

The nerve of the man! she thought as she went up the stairs. Here he had gotten out and evidently wandered all over while she and Aunt Penny languished at Rouvray and wondered if he were going to survive or not. He wasn't worth wasting a thought on. Not one thought. She slammed the bedroom door behind her and sat down to read. After an hour or so her feet were freezing, but she refused to go back downstairs until it was suppertime.

They kept country hours at Rouvray, so supper was out of the way early. They all went to the drawing room to sit after supper. Hinson had built up the fire a little, and the temperature was just right. The four of them spent an hour or so there. Mimsy and Vincent played cards, Aunt Penny embroidered, and Esme read aloud to her. Mimsy and Vincent were the first to go up to bed. Aunt Penny stayed up until ten, then yawned and went upstairs to sleep.

The fire was almost out, but there were still enough

smoldering embers to keep the room warm. Esme got another book, one she had been reading off and on for several days, slipped off her shoes, and propped her feet on the fender in front of the fire to warm them. She started to read, then decided the book wasn't that interesting. Instead, she blew out all the candles except one and then curled up in Papa's big wing chair, watching the red-gold patterns the embers made. She was comfortable, the room was warm, and she soon dozed off.

Something woke Esme. The fire was still warm, but was almost out. Even the embers were almost gone. There was only a hint of a red glow here and there. Her candle had gone out at some time during her nap. A faint breeze from the open drawing room window nuzzled Esme's curls, and she absently pushed her hair from her face. *A breeze?* she thought, and then she stiffened—the French doors hadn't been open when she dozed off. She stayed quiet for a moment until she was fully awake. There was a noise in the room—a noise that wasn't supposed to be there. Could it be Aunt Penny's burglar? She peered around the edge of the wing chair and saw a dark shadow quietly and carefully going through her father's desk drawers. The papers made a soft rustle as the intruder riffled through them. The room was dark and there was no moon, no light at all in the room, so Esme couldn't see who was there. She moved slowly, very slowly, and put her feet down on the floor, one at a time. Than she slid slowly off the chair and down onto the floor, taking care not to touch any of the furniture or knock against anything. Carefully, she reached for the poker an inch at a time, worried that it would clang against the fireplace or the fender. She held her breath when her fingers finally touched it and slowly, ever so slowly, she slipped her hand around it. Finally she had it in her grasp, and she very carefully lifted it over by her side. All the while, the intruder kept going through her father's desk drawers, tossing papers into a pile, as though he knew exactly what he was searching for.

Esme wondered how to stop him. Should she try to crawl across the floor and risk being seen? It was almost certain that he would see her. Or should she simply leap to her feet and run across the floor, screaming? That might disconcert him long enough for her to land a hit with the poker. She opted for that stratagem. With a screech loud enough to wake the dead, she leaped to her feet and brandished the poker. She leaped toward the desk, the poker over her head, then brought it down hard, trying to hit the burglar. Instead, the poker hit the desk hard, and Esme couldn't stop. She ran right into the desk, fell across the top, and tumbled right onto the burglar. They rolled and wrestled on the floor for a moment until the burglar managed to roll on top of her and hold her facedown on the floor. He ran his fingers down her side, feeling her breast, as he cursed under his breath. Esme kept on screaming.

Quickly the burglar got to his feet, dragging her along. He ran to the window and grabbed the drape there, jerking it from the rod across the top. He wound it around Esme and stuffed the corner in her mouth, all the while standing behind her so she couldn't see him. Then he tossed her down on the floor and stepped out the French door. She could hear Spot rumbling in her cage, and the sound of a horse galloping down the road. Then the inside door was thrown open. Vincent and Mimsy came in, holding candles.

"Oh, good God, Papa's desk!" Mimsy said in alarm. "Just look, Vincent."

"Whatever is going on?" Aunt Penny cried from the door. She held her hand over her heart. "Oh, the shock! My vinaigrette! Quickly!" Vincent caught her just as she crumpled delicately against the doorframe. He scooped her up and disappeared, calling behind him. "Find her vinaigrette, Mimsy, and bring it up."

"Oh, no, you don't, Vincent. I'm not staying a moment in this room by myself," she cried, running out the door behind him. The room was pitch dark again.

Esme was still on the floor, wrapped like a mummy, with the corner of the drapery stuffed in her mouth. She made some inarticulate noises, but no one was there. In desperation, she rolled around on the floor, but that was difficult. If she could only loosen one hand, she thought, she would be able to free herself. She rolled into a chair and hit her head. "Ooooff," she mumbled, tears coming to her eyes.

She bent her knees and tried to stand. It was difficult, but she managed to scoot against the wall and then slide upward. Once upright, she tried to move across the floor, hopping along, hoping to make it to the closed door. She hopped once, then wobbled, weaving from side to side. She was losing her balance, and was in danger of falling into the fireplace. She tried to swing the other way, but wound up falling right, toward the sharp edge of the mantel. There was no way to stop herself. Her head hit the mantel's corner and she felt a terrible pain that jolted from one side of her head to the other. Something warm and wet covered the side of her face, and she slipped to the floor, unconscious.

Esme tried to open her eyes, but they didn't want to open. In the distance, she could hear people talking. "And to think she was there all the time and we didn't know it until Vincent and Hinson went back downstairs to make sure the French door was closed," Mimsy was saying.

Strong fingers smoothed her hair away from her forehead. She wondered for a moment if they were her father's, then remembered that he was in London. It had to be someone who worried about her—the touch was too gentle, too concerned, to be a stranger's. She tried again to open her eyes. This time they opened, but she couldn't see anything except fuzzy images. She blinked, trying to

fix the image so she could see who it was. Slowly, the edges
of the image sharpened. It was Lovatt.

He smiled at her. "So you're back with us," he said, the
frown lines between his eyebrows vanishing. "Tell me, are
broken heads going to be contagious around here?" He
grinned as he touched the bandage around her head.
Esme reached up to feel the bandage, as well, and their
fingers touched.

Mimsy peered over Lovatt's shoulder. "Are you all
right?"

Vincent peered over Mimsy's shoulder, and Bram walked
over to stand on the other side of Lovatt. "You still look
like death," Bram said, frowning.

"Bram, hush!" Mimsy glared at him. "You look just wonderful, Esme. Believe me."

"She knows she can't look wonderful." Bram scowled
at Mimsy. "After all, she's taken a devil of a lick to the
head." He looked back at Esme. "What did he hit you
with? The poker? We found it stuck in the desk."

Esme tried to shake her head, but a pain so sharp that
it hurt her teeth overwhelmed her, and she felt tears fill
her eyes. Lovatt put his hand on her head again. "Don't
move. It hurts too much. I know." He grinned at her again,
and Esme realized that he no longer wore the bandage
that had been around his head.

"Are you better?" she whispered.

"I'm fine," he said, leaning down toward her. "Can you
talk enough to tell us what happened? Did you surprise
someone in the library?"

"Yes." Words were more of an effort than she had realized they could be. "Tried to hit him with the poker . . .
he ran away. Fell against the mantel."

Lovatt ran a finger along her bandage. "You got a nasty
lick there. You were lucky it wasn't lower on your temple,
or you might have been . . ." He stopped and shook his
head.

"What are you doing here?" Esme whispered, putting her hand up to her head.

Lovatt took her fingers in his. "I was with Bram when Vincent came to get him. Vincent was going for the doctor and stopped to tell Bram that you'd been hurt."

"So it wasn't you?"

His eyes grew wide. "Good Lord, no! If I wanted something from your father's desk I'd either ask you for it or write him and get permission." He looked hurt. "I may do many things, but burglary isn't in my repertoire."

"Then who?" Her voice was a whisper.

Bram made a face. "We were hoping you could tell us. Did you see anything that might identity him? I'm assuming our burglar was male."

Esme tried to nod her head again, but stopped. "Yes," she whispered, "but I didn't see who it was. I didn't see much of anything. He was searching Papa's desk for something."

Lovatt and Bram looked at each other. "Do you think he found what he came for?" Lovatt asked Esme.

"No. I think I surprised him. Then when I screamed, he left. There was a horse . . ." She winced as she moved her head.

Lovatt put his hands on both sides of her face. "Don't. Don't try to move or talk. Bram and I will go to the drawing room and see what we can find. Mrs. Pennywhistle will sit here with you. I want you to go to sleep. Tomorrow we'll talk." He looked at her anxiously. "Promise."

"Promise," she mumbled, glad to close her eyes. In just a moment she felt herself drifting to sleep, Lovatt's hands still on her face.

In spite of the pain, she felt strangely comforted.

Fifteen

When Esme woke up, it was the middle of the afternoon, and it took her a moment to remember where she was and why she was there. She was in the room she was using now—Aunt Penny's room—and the sunlight was streaming in through the open windows. The faint scent of flowers from the garden blew in on a soft breeze that billowed the lacy curtains. The drapes had been pulled back and tied, as had the lace undercurtains.

Quickly Esme closed her eyes again. The sunlight was too much against her eyes. The smell and the soft touch of the breeze against her skin felt good, but a thousand hammers were beating inside her skull and behind her eyes. She moaned softly and put her fingers to her head, wishing she had the soft touch of Lovatt's fingers against her skin, touching her the way he had before. She ran her fingers along the side of her head to feel the bandage, stiff and unfamiliar. She wondered how she looked, and if the cut would leave a scar. Would Lovatt care? She opened her eyes again, prepared for the sunshine, and looked to her right, hoping to see Lovatt. No one was there except Aunt Penny, who was dozing in the chair, her embroidery about to fall off her lap.

Esme pushed herself up to her elbows, gauging the level of pain in her head. She stayed quiet for a moment as the pain peaked and ebbed, then peaked and ebbed again.

She felt the need to get up—to attend to the necessities and to try to get her feet back under her and find out what was going on. And Spot—dear heavens, Esme could almost wager that no one except Ned had looked after Spot. The poor thing must be frantic to get out of her pen and go for a walk.

Taking it in slow stages, Esme moved to the side of the bed, away from Aunt Penny. Esme didn't want to wake her. Carefully, Esme slid off the edge of the bed and stood for a full five minutes, waiting to see if she would be dizzy or if something terrible would happen. Finally, satisfied that her head really wasn't going to fall off, she tiptoed out of the room and down the hall to her usual room to get some clothes.

Dressing took longer than she thought it would, but by the time she had washed her face and changed from the skin out, she felt better. Finally, she worked up enough nerve to look into her mirror, and was horrified. The bandage was wrapped around her head, and her dark hair contrasted with it. Her hair stood up on top of her head, sticking out of the bandage like a carelessly tied shock of wheat. The skin on the side of her face was bruised and purple all around her cheekbone and eye. She looked terrible, and realized that she couldn't go out and about looking this way. The pain in her head was lessening, and she was beginning to feel more herself, but she would frighten children, not to mention her family, if they saw her like this. She picked up the comb and tried to tame her hair, but it was no use. The more she combed, the more her hair stood on end, sprouting up from the bandage. In desperation, she got her scissors and snipped the bandage loose. It stuck a little to the cut on her head, and she had to pull carefully. That made tears come to her eyes, but she got it off. Then she got her mirror and went to the window to take a good look.

Her face looked worse than the cut did. Evidently, as

Bram had told her, head wounds bled profusely, even small cuts. The wound on her head wasn't large, but the swelling and bruising were extensive. Esme put the mirror down and reached for powder and paint. Perhaps she could repair some of the damage, inexpert as she was.

After a half an hour, she was on the verge of giving up when Mimsy walked in. "Whatever are you doing?" Mimsy asked. "Are you putting something on your face?" She walked in and glanced critically at Esme. "I thought it was worse," she said matter-of-factly. "Give the paint and powder to me and let me see what I can do." Esme, recognizing an expert, handed everything over silently.

A few minutes later, Mimsy stood back to admire her work. "There, much better. By the way, I came up to see how you were getting along. Lovatt is downstairs waiting to find out."

Esme jumped to her feet, then put her hand to her head, suddenly dizzy. She sat down again. "Why didn't you tell me? I want to talk to him. He promised to tell me why he was at the circus the other night. There's something havey-cavey going on with that man, Mimsy." She tried to stand up again.

"Ummm," Mimsy said, giving her a thoughtful look. "So true. We have a half hour or so—I think Lovatt is going out to check on that horrid animal you keep around. Do sit still and let me do something with your hair. It looks rather like fireworks exploding from a canister."

"I resent that," Esme muttered, but she sat down in the chair all the same and stayed still while Mimsy worked on her hair, pulling it gently this way and that.

"There," Mimsy finally said, "that looks a little better. At least you won't frighten Lovatt into running back to Shad Abbas." She put down the brush and stretched, looking out the window. "Lovatt should be back inside by now, so let's go down and get some food. I told Mrs. Hinson to fix something substantial for us to eat with tea. I'm starving." She leaned forward and peered out the window. "I do believe that may be Captain Arno making his way along the road. Perhaps he's planning to stop here."

Esme sighed. "Probably not. Let's go have some tea."

Lovatt was out, Hinson informed them, but would return shortly. "He's still checking on that atrocious animal," Mimsy said with a nod. "Hinson, will you bring in tea?"

Esme and Mimsy sat in the drawing room to await Lovatt's return. Mimsy had already begun on a plate of small biscuits, some cold ham, two pieces of fruitcake, and some peaches when Hinson appeared at the door. "Captain Arno is here," he announced solemnly.

Esme put down her tea dish. "Show him in here, Hinson," she said, "and have Mrs. Hinson bring another cup so we can give Captain Arno some tea."

Captain Arno came in, bowing to the two of them. "My apologies, but I was just passing by, and—" He stopped and looked at Esme, his expression horrified. "My dear Miss Darling! Did you fall?"

"We had an intruder last night," Mimsy said as Hinson brought in another cup.

"And he did that to you?" Captain Arno came over and sat down beside Esme, taking the cup of tea she poured and handed to him. He glanced at it absently, then put it down without touching it.

"No," Esme explained, "The intruder didn't do this. I fell against the mantel."

Captain Arno looked at her with concern. "I would hate to think that anyone would want to harm you, Miss Darling." He paused. "Are you sure it was an intruder?"

"Oh, yes." Esme nodded. "Someone was in the drawing room going through Papa's desk."

Captain Arno's eyes widened. "What did he take? I know your father had some valuable papers there. He had even asked me to file or copy some of them." He paused. "Perhaps you might like me to take a look. I know most of what he had here."

Esme almost said yes, but then held back. For a reason she really couldn't identify, she wanted to look through the desk first. Perhaps the intruder wasn't after anything of Papa's in the desk. Perhaps there had been another motive for the attempted burglary. "Thank you, Captain Arno," she said with a smile, "but I don't think anything was taken. I interrupted the burglar, so I don't think he was able to get whatever it was that he came after."

Arno frowned. "Perhaps, but do you think there might be another attempt? I would hate to think that the intruder might consider coming back for whatever he didn't find the first time. I'll be glad to go through the desk and remove anything that might be sensitive. Your father kept many papers here that dealt with army matters."

"It might be an excellent idea, Esme," Mimsy said, turning at a sound from the garden.

"Yes, I think that I—" Arno stopped and looked out the door toward the garden. Lovatt was walking toward the house. His coat sleeve was half torn off, and his cravat was dangling down the front of his body. He seemed to have lost his hat, as well.

He came inside, banging the door behind him, stopping only long enough to pull the bell rope. "Bring another cup if you don't mind, Hinson," he requested with a smile, sitting down in the chair next to Mimsy and stretching out his legs. He hefted the teapot. "And a fresh pot of hot water." He ran his fingers through his hair to smooth it, but that only tousled it more. "Esme, that damned cat of yours has about finished me. I thought I'd take it on a turn around the yard, but it ran through the hedge and into the field. It was over every rock and up every tree it could find. I even splashed through the stream trying to restrain the thing." He paused as Hinson brought his cup and Esme poured him some tea. "You might as well face it—Spot is getting entirely too large to keep here. You're going to have to find a home for her somewhere. A zoo, perhaps, or a large enclosure where she can run and play."

"I know." Esme sighed. "I can barely hold her when we go out for walks."

"Another of your misguided rescues," Mimsy said, peeling her peach. "Just like the litter of puppies you saved when you were ten. Or how about the horse you rescued from the glue factory and then didn't know what to do with? Or then there was the parrot you saved from that inn on the Bath road. What was its name—Figi? The parrot that spoke only profanities."

"And wouldn't learn anything else. I almost fainted when the minister came and Figi wouldn't hush. That was when Papa said I had to get it out of the house. I was certainly glad when Captain Bowe offered to take it with him on his next voyage." Esme tried to stifle a giggle as she remembered.

Lovatt reached for more tea, then stopped and looked at his hand and sleeve in horror. The entire side of his sleeve was caked with mud, and he had gotten mud on the furniture. "Why didn't you tell me I looked as if I'd been on the battlefield?" he asked, standing. "Do you think Mrs. Hinson would allow me access to the kitchen so I could clean up?"

Vincent stood in the door and greeted them, his eyes widening when he saw Lovatt. "Good afternoon," he said, smiling. "I'm sorry to interrupt, but I'd like to have a word with my wife." He grinned as he looked from Lovatt's boots to his hair. "And I'd like a word with you as well, Lovatt, if you can spare the time."

"But of course, Vincent." Mimsy practically purred. "I'm sure both of us can spare a moment. I'm sure Esme won't mind entertaining Captain Arno until we return. We weren't discussing anything important, at any rate. Merely commenting on Esme's leopard." Mimsy shuddered visibly as she walked toward the door. "Perhaps, Vincent, you can come up with a way to dispose of the animal. You know I don't like it, and it doesn't like me." Mimsy paused at the door and smiled. "Do come back soon, Captain Arno." With that, she disappeared around the corner of the door. In just a moment, Esme saw Mimsy and Vincent outside the window, strolling along arm in arm. She smiled, thinking that she had known all along that they would patch things up. As she and Captain Arno watched, Lovatt came up to them, and they moved out of sight, laughing.

"How did you happen to acquire your leopard?" Captain Arno asked, bringing her back to the conversation. "I seem to recall your father mentioning it some time back, but I don't remember the details."

"I went to the circus and saw the poor thing. The owners had almost killed it. It was malnourished and sick, and they had beaten it almost to death. The poor little thing was just a cub, and they were ready to kill it. I rescued it from the rubbish heap and brought it home. I thought it was going to die."

"The circus?" Captain Arno sipped his tea and grimaced slightly. Esme assumed that his tea was lukewarm by now. "Did you know the leopard's owners?"

"Two men named Sikes and Bradshaw. Thoroughly disreputable characters. They're still there, although I wrote several letters to the authorities about them." She paused. "Perhaps I should send my complaints again. I have copies of my letters in Papa's desk."

Captain Arno looked excited. "That must be it, Miss Darling! Those two men must have been the ones who broke into the desk. They were probably looking for the information you had against them."

Esme looked doubtful. "I don't know. The only time I confronted one of them he told me that I could, as he so elegantly put it, 'law and be cursed.' I think he would have used a stronger word if he hadn't been afraid of Papa."

"Your father *can* be formidable." Captain Arno smiled. "Did you sue them?"

Esme shook her head. "No, and I haven't heard from either of them since." She frowned. "But they didn't break into the house. There was just one man, and I got the impression that he knew what he was looking for, and where it was in Papa's desk. I can't imagine who would know that."

"I'm sure in his position in the army, your father has communicated with all sorts of people. I fear your intruder could be any one of hundreds."

"You're probably right." Esme sighed. "At least, I don't think the man will return any time soon." She put her hand to her head and touched it. It was beginning to throb again.

Captain Arno looked at her sympathetically. "I've tired you, Miss Darling. I do apologize." He leaned over and took her hands in his. Esme glanced down, surprised at how brown his hands were. Her own hands looked small and very white in his fingers. "It's just that I've been very worried about you."

Esme looked at him. He was looking at her with an expression of care, his dark brown eyes warm. "Thank you, Captain Arno. I appreciate your concern."

"And, I hope, my warnings." There was a very slight pause while he increased the pressure of his fingers on her hand. "Have you noticed anything unusual about our suspect?"

It took Esme a moment. "Do you mean Lovatt?"

"Of course." He looked at her with a worried frown. "Has the blow on your head bothered you, Miss Darling? We discussed Lovatt's possible involvement yesterday afternoon. I warned you to be on the watch for him." He lowered his voice. "Do you think he might have been the intruder? I understand he came here last night after you had been wounded. It's certainly odd that he would have been so close by, or would have been up and awake at that hour."

Esme stopped in mid-thought, speechless. It was true—

and yes, it was odd. She hadn't considered that before. Lovatt said he had been with Bram, but for how long? Immediately she dismissed the thought. Lovatt would never do anything like that. As he had said, if he wanted something, he was the type to just ask for it, or walk right in and tell everyone that he was planning to go through the desk and look for something specific.

Before she could reply, Captain Arno squeezed her fingers lightly. "I've distressed you, Miss Darling. I would never do that intentionally. I apologize. My only concern and care is for you." He paused. "Since I've been posted here with your father, you've become very special to me." He turned Esme's hand over, palm upwards, and, to Esme's surprise, brought her hand to his lips and kissed it gently.

"I don't want to talk about my feelings at a time like this, Miss Darling. Perhaps when all this is over . . ." He left the sentence dangling.

"Perhaps," Esme answered weakly. She really didn't know what else to say.

Captain Arno stood and smiled down at her. "That tells me that my attentions may stand a chance." He picked up his hat. "I'll return tomorrow, if that's all right with you, Miss Darling. I am concerned. And I want to assure you that I'll do everything I can to capture the person who terrified and injured you."

"Thank you," Esme began, but Captain Arno had taken her hand again, bowed low, and kissed her palm. Esme looked over his shoulder and past him to the door, where Lovatt was standing. Lovatt turned on his heel and went back outside without a word. Captain Arno didn't even know he was there.

Hinson showed the captain out, and Esme pondered for a moment. Then she finished her tea and stood, testing her head and her legs. Her head had stopped throbbing, and she was feeling much better. She went to the French door and went outside, wondering if Lovatt had stalked off to Shad Abbas.

He hadn't. He had started that way, and had gotten as far as the break in the hedge that opened onto the path into the field. Vincent and Mimsy had detained him there, and were talking to him. He glanced up at Esme as she approached.

"I see you've recovered," he said coolly. Then he turned back to Vincent, as if Esme weren't there. "Bram and I will meet you then," he said. Vincent nodded, and Lovatt turned to leave.

"Wait!" Esme said, reaching out for his sleeve. She didn't touch him, but everyone turned toward her. Esme looked around helplessly. "I wanted to talk to Lovatt about Spot," she said lamely. It was the best she could do on the spur of the moment.

"Spot is fine. Better than I am, after our walk." He glanced down at his coat and tucked in the dangling ends of his cravat. "As you can see, she exercised herself thoroughly."

"You shouldn't be out, Esme," Mimsy said with a frown. "Should she, Vincent?"

Vincent gazed at Mimsy. "Whatever you say, dear."

"Bother," Esme said, waving their objections away. "Lovatt, would you come look at Spot for me?"

"I just left her. She was fine." He made a half turn, but this time Esme caught his sleeve.

"She may appear that way, but I think there may be a problem. I thought you might give me your advice."

They all looked at her for a long moment. Finally Lovatt stepped back inside the yard. "If you're asking my advice, Miss Darling, then I suppose it's such a remarkable occurrence that I should help you. Do you need my assistance in walking?" He offered his arm.

Esme slipped her arm through his and they walked slowly toward Spot's pen, leaving Vincent and Mimsy staring after them. As soon as they were out of earshot, Esme whispered to Lovatt. "I didn't really need to talk to you about Spot."

"I gathered as much." His voice was still very formal. "Just what is it that you want, Miss Darling?"

Esme looked behind them to see that Vincent and Mimsy were going into the house. She let go of Lovatt's arm and turned to face him. "Last night you promised to tell me everything. I'm holding you to your promise."

He stared at her with cold eyes. "So you might share that with Captain Arno?"

Esme felt herself blush. "He just stopped by. I certainly didn't know he was coming."

"And no doubt the Captain had just stopped by to inquire most solicitously after your health. Is kissing your palm a new form of treatment?" Lovatt moved back a step and glared at her.

Esme felt anger flare through her. "Enough, Lovatt," she snapped. "Either you trust me, or you don't. I would think we have enough of a friendship to know and trust each other."

"And do you?" His tone had a strange, questioning note.

"Do I what?"

"Do you trust me?" His eyes met hers and held her gaze.

Esme paused a fraction of a second while she considered what he was asking. "Yes, Lovatt, I trust you implicitly. I believe I could trust you with my life, and you wouldn't harm me in any way." She realized that what she said was completely true. In spite of Arno's insinuations, she knew Lovatt would never lie to her, or try in any way to hurt her.

He let his breath out in a long exhale and smiled at her. "That's good to know. And quite true." He reached over and took her arm and linked it through his. "Shall we sit on the garden bench, and I'll tell you everything you ask of me?"

They sat down in front of the dahlias, and Esme picked up a few violet petals that had fallen and let them drift through her fingers. "Why did you ask if I trusted you, Lovatt? I would think that is one of the things you can take for granted."

"In my line of work, Miss Darling, I've discovered that nothing can be taken for granted, no matter how much one may wish it to be so. As for why I asked—I was at the door long enough to overhear Captain Arno's intimations that I might be implicated in some way in this unpleasantness."

"You're not." It wasn't a question. Somewhat to Esme's surprise, it was a flat statement.

"No, I'm not at all, but I *was* sent here to try to clear your father. And now it seems I'm also going to have to try to find out who was breaking into Rouvray. I think the same person in responsible for both acts."

"Perhaps, but—" Esme stopped as Lovatt's words sank in. "You were *sent* here to help Papa? What do you mean, Lovatt?"

He turned so that he was looking right at her. "White-hall thinks your father is being blamed to divert attention from the real spy. They've sent me here to find out. I'm not here on a holiday, Esme. I'm not here to see to the last renovations for Shad Abbas. I'm not here to visit my family. I'm working."

"Working?" She was confused and frowned, trying to understand exactly what he was saying.

"Yes, working. I've been sent here to uncover a spy."

Sixteen

Esme echoed his words. "You're working to catch a spy?" She was having difficulty with this. Lovatt was many things, but she had never considered him a spy catcher, not even when he had offered to help.

He nodded. "Yes. Trust goes both ways, you know." He paused. "I helped solve a thorny problem in India at the beginning of my career, so was recommended to the Home Office as someone suited to intelligence. I've done that type of work since, and, at the risk of sounding immodest, I'm fairly good at it. Officially, I suppose you could say that I'm . . . I'm . . ." He stopped abruptly.

Esme looked at him, her eyes wide. "You're a spy, Lovatt?"

"Not exactly." He looked uncomfortable. "I merely . . . discover things."

"And they sent you here to find out about Papa?"

He took her hand in his and his fingers wrapped around hers, strong and firm and warm. "Not to find out *about* him. As I told you once before, when I found out that he had been accused, I volunteered to come here. The Major Darling *I* know would never do such a thing. My official assignment, though, isn't to clear your father—I need to uncover the spy."

Esme felt a stab of fear run through her. Above all things she didn't want Bram or her father to have to fight Napoleon, a man who had no compunction about destroying those who opposed him. She didn't want Lovatt to have to fight and risk his life. "It's something to do with Napoleon again, isn't it?"

Lovatt nodded. "We think he plans to come out of exile and try to raise an army. Most people think he's done for, but I have my doubts. However, the last thing we need is for him to know about our troop strength and our plans."

Esme looked at him solemnly. "You promised to tell me what you were doing, Lovatt. Now I promise not to divulge a word of what you tell me, not even to my father."

"All right, although you do understand that I can't tell you everything." At her nod, he went on. "I think Arno is involved in this," he said bluntly. "And it isn't just because I don't like the man. I don't. But I haven't let that cloud my judgment. I think the circus is operating as a center for spies."

"An excellent hiding place," Esme said. "I recall that once you or Bram pointed out that the circus would be ideal because people are always coming and going. There would be no way to trace someone who came in and disappeared. No one really notices oddities there, because there are so many."

"Exactly." Lovatt looked at her with approval.

Esme blushed slightly. "But how do you think Captain Arno is involved?"

"I'm not sure, but all my instincts tell me he is. I'm going to London tomorrow to try to find out more. While I'm gone, I want you to stay here at Rouvray. Promise me you won't be out alone with Captain Arno, and you won't go to the circus. I've even made arrangements for Ned to walk Spot every day until I get back."

"And how long will that be?" The thought of Lovatt being away was devastating.

"Not long—only a few days, if I can manage it. I need

to get back, in case something happens. If anything does, Samad is at the circus and he's to get in touch with Bram immediately."

"Samad? The man in the turban? There are several of those at the circus. I remember seeing them."

"True. One of them works with the animals and is completely honest, Samad says, but he told Samad that strange things go on there at night. He's taken Samad in with him on the pretext that Samad is some kind of relative from India."

"That sounds reasonable."

Lovatt grinned. "Actually, if they were in India they'd be bitter enemies because of where they live, but here, since they're countrymen, they're friends. I don't think anyone will know that they're from rival factions."

Esme looked down at the bench between them. Lovatt's fingers were still twined with hers, and she resisted the urge to squeeze his hand. She was aware of him all over, just as she had been before. She could almost feel the length of him along her body, the wool of his coat barely scratching the tender skin at her throat. She felt herself growing warm all over and quickly looked up, staring fixedly at the panes of the bedroom window where she slept now. "What do you want me to do, Lovatt?"

"I want you to stay right here and not go out. Promise me that you will."

Esme sighed. "I promise. But only for a week or so."

He grinned. "Good. I hope to be back in five or six days. If you need anything, Bram knows where I'll be, or Mother is still at Shad Abbas." He picked her hand up and turned it over, his expression suddenly serious. "Bram plans to stay here at Rouvray in case anyone else tries to break in, and Vincent will be here, as well."

"I can't imagine who the intruder might be, Lovatt." She frowned. "Those different nights in Aunt Penny's room, and then at Papa's desk. It has to be someone who knows the house well."

Lovatt chuckled. "I agree with you about the intruder, but I don't think that a person tried to break into Aunt Penny's room. The desk, yes, but not her room."

"Then who did?"

"Not who. What." Lovatt gestured toward Spot's pen.

"Ridiculous." Esme shook her head. "Spot has no way to get up there. She certainly can't scale the side of the house. No, Lovatt, I think you're wrong on that head." Her voice was decisive. "I can stay up and watch. I promise to waken Bram if I see anything."

"We can leave it at that, then." He ran his thumb across her palm and Esme shuddered slightly. "I'm not good with talk in the way Captain Arno is, but—" He stopped.

"But?" Esme prompted.

"Nothing." Lovatt released her hand and scooted an inch or so over toward the end of the bench. "Tell me, Miss Darling, what is in your father's desk that is of such interest to a burglar? Do you have any idea?"

"No." Esme bit back her disappointment. She had been so sure he was going to say something important, so sure that he was going to kiss her hand or her lips, so sure that he was finally going to realize that there was more between them than mere friendship. "Nothing." She kept her voice flat.

"Do you recall what was in there?"

"Just my father's letters. He keeps all his correspondence in there, as well as copies that he has me make of important things. There are copies of the letters implicating him in the spying for Napoleon."

Lovatt grimaced. "That doesn't sound promising. Is there anything else?"

"A little household money. And a few papers of mine."

"Such as?" He looked at her frown. "Bear with me, Miss

Darling. Often something that seems trivial will prove to be important."

"Nothing in there would be important. I keep letters I get, primarily about dahlias. People write me from other countries." She tried a weak smile. "We dahlia fanciers are a rabid lot, you know. We're always after a tuber of a new color or variety. Señora Romero and I have been writing regularly about her coming visit. She's going to bring me a new tuber—a brilliant red, she says." She thought a moment more. "There were two or three letters from Señor Morillo in Mexico and, of course, my correspondence about those two ruffians at the circus who mistreated Spot. Sikes and Bradshaw."

Lovatt became very still. "And what was that about?" he asked carefully.

Esme shrugged. "Nothing, really. As you know, I found Spot there, and she was in terrible shape. I thought those two men should pay for doing that to an animal, so I wrote letters to everyone I could think of, complaining about them and asking for an investigation into the circus."

"Did anything come of it?" Lovatt frowned and bit his lower lip as he thought.

"No, nothing was ever done. I still think they should be punished. I wrote another letter a fortnight or so ago, but again, I've heard nothing."

Lovatt smiled at her again. "I doubt anyone would be looking for a letter of that sort, then. I would not like to be on the receiving end of your wrath, Miss Darling. I pity Bradshaw and Sikes."

"Oh, I intend to see that they have a comeuppance someday. No one should be allowed to treat an animal the way they treated Spot. I'm surprised she didn't die."

"She's certainly healthy now, and we'll figure out something to do with her to ensure she lives to a ripe old age." Lovatt stood up and offered his hand to help Esme. "I must be going."

Esme reached up and touched his hand, and it seemed that a current ran between them. She looked into his eyes, and their gazes locked. For an instant the world spun about her, and she felt transported, strange. It took her breath away. She stood and looked at Lovatt, the instant broken. He turned and looked across the yard, and Esme wondered if he had felt the same short burst of intense feeling. He showed no sign of it. Instead, he offered her his arm, and they walked across the yard to the French doors.

"I hold you to your promise, Miss Darling. I'll be back as soon as possible, and bring you news of your father. In the meantime, I want you to recover." He touched her head lightly, a feathery touch that she barely felt.

"Take care, Lovatt." It wasn't what she wanted to say, but it was all that seemed fitting in the situation. She wanted to touch him and kiss him good-bye, but he wanted no entanglements.

She turned and went inside quickly. If she didn't, she knew she would throw herself onto him, and that would be embarrassing beyond measure. She didn't even allow herself the pleasure of turning around and watching his broad back as he went through the break in the hedge, walking toward Shad Abbas.

Mimsy was in the small parlor, doing some embroidery. "Has Lovatt gone?" she asked, glancing up at Esme.

"Yes." It was more a sigh than a statement. "Where's Vincent?"

Mimsy stabbed her needle through a flower, making a center. "He's gone to see Bram. They're doing something for Lovatt, I think. Or perhaps with Lovatt." She frowned. "I'm hazy on the details." She bit her lip. "Lovatt has asked that Vincent stay here, but he wants to return to Eversleigh House for a few days to attend to some business."

"Heavens, it seems that everyone is going somewhere. When are you going?"

"I'm not going." Mimsy bent over her work and attacked it with a vengeance. "I just can't go back there and endure his mother again."

Esme looked at her slowly. "Have you told him this, Mimsy?"

She shook her head. "How can I ask him to choose between me and his mother? Besides, she's right—I shouldn't keep Vincent from fathering an heir."

Esme walked over and sat down beside Mimsy, then took the embroidery and mangled threads away from her and sat them on top of a small table. "Mimsy, look at me." She waited a moment until Mimsy looked into her eyes. "Don't you think you should be honest with Vincent and let him make up his own mind? After all, he's a man grown, and he should know what's best for him. If he chooses his mother's path, then you can get on with your life. If he wants you, then you know he's decided for himself and he can live with the consequences."

"I don't know." Mimsy looked down and twisted the rings on her fingers. "Vincent has always cared very much for his mother."

"And for you." Esme put her arm around Mimsy's shoulders. "You've got to do something about this, Mimsy. I've seen how happy you are with Vincent. You can't let yourself be in this situation. Talk to him."

Mimsy took a deep breath. "All right, I will. I promise. I'll talk to him this very evening." She turned and looked at Esme. "What did Lovatt want? Has he offered for you? I know all the signs, and I thought that might be what he was doing. That's why I hurried Vincent inside."

Esme shook her head and moved her arm from Mimsy's shoulders. "No, he hasn't offered for me, and he won't. He's spent his whole life seeing what Redferne did to his mother and vowing that he would never be in a situation like that. 'No entanglements,' he always says, and he's said he'll never marry."

Mimsy patted the back of Esme's hand. "Poor Esme.

We're a pair, aren't we?" She smiled weakly at Esme. "Why don't we go into town and get some new ribbons? I want to refurbish my blue straw hat, and it will do both of us good to get out." She paused and glanced at Esme's head. "On second thought, perhaps we should just have some lemonade out near the dahlias and let me read to you." She paused. "Oh, by the way, you got a letter from Señora Romero. It's on the little table in the hall."

By the time Vincent returned, Esme had read her letter aloud to Mimsy. Señora Romero was coming to London and to Rouvray, and would be here in a week, bringing the red dahlia and possibly a yellow. Esme was ecstatic. In turn, Mimsy had read aloud two chapters from Mrs. Radcliffe's newest, and they had drunk an entire pitcher of lemonade.

Esme gave Mimsy a nudge as Vincent sat down with them at the table they had Hinson move near the dahlias. Esme got up, vowing that she was aching all over and needed to go to bed. As she went into the house, she looked back to see a determined look on Mimsy's face. "I do hope they settle this," she murmured as she went inside.

"You do hope what, dear?" It was Aunt Penny, sitting on the sofa, her fingers to her head. "I apologize for not joining the two of you, but I do have such a dreadful headache. It must be from not getting the proper sleep for the last few nights."

"Why don't you go upstairs and take a nap, Aunt Penny?"

Aunt Penny smiled wanly. "Thank you, dear. I believe I shall." She tottered off up the stairs. Esme went up behind her, and went to the room Aunt Penny had occupied. She looked out the window toward Shad Abbas, and thought of the predicament she was in. She traced some letters on the glass with her fingertip, then looked down, and realized that she had written Lovatt's name.

She turned away from the window, angry with herself.

Why Lovatt? she asked herself. Stopping to assess her feelings, she felt the truth wash over her.

She was in love with Chalmers Lovatt. And he wasn't in love with her. He had vowed never to marry, never to have entanglements.

Here she was, she thought bitterly, giving advice to everyone in the household while she was in need of advice herself. She closed her eyes and, in her mind, saw Lovatt walking across the field. She could see every detail—his long stride, his slightly long hair glinting in the sun, his confident demeanor. Esme shook her head and opened her eyes. Lovatt wanted to be a friend only. How many times had he made that perfectly clear? She could hardly count them all.

She went back to the window and looked at the top of Shad Abbas again, then put her forehead against the open window, feeling the breeze touching her face. The afternoon perfume of the flowers scented the breeze. *A perfect afternoon for lovers,* she thought. She turned away from the window, brushing at her eyes with the back of her hand. She would not allow herself to make a complete fool of herself over the man. She wouldn't.

On that note, she threw herself across the bed and tried to keep from crying.

Lovatt had been gone for four days and everything had been quiet. Too quiet, Bram had said. The only thing of note that had happened was that Vincent had left Rouvray immediately after he and Mimsy talked.

Esme heard him order his horse brought around and she feared the worst. As soon as she heard him leave, she went to find Mimsy and comfort her. She discovered Mimsy by the door, looking out the window, watching Vincent ride away toward Eversleigh.

"I'm sorry, Mimsy. I truly am."

"Sorry?" Mimsy's shoulders shook with sobs.

"Yes, I shouldn't have made you talk with him. What did he say?"

"He said he loved me, Esme." Mimsy turned from the window, her smile radiant. "He said he loved me." Mimsy's eyes were red-rimmed and her skin was blotchy from crying, but her expression was beautiful. "He's going to tell his mother to leave Eversleigh and move to their house in Kent." Mimsy smiled through her tears and hugged Esme. "And to think, Vincent and I would never have sorted this out if you hadn't made me talk to him. How can I ever thank you, Esme?"

"Just be happy, Mimsy," Esme said, returning her hug.

"If you only knew how very happy I am," Mimsy said, turning to run up the stairs. "If you only knew."

Esme watched Mimsy turn the corner and then sat down slowly on the bottom step. *And I will never know,* she thought sadly.

The afternoon of the third day of Lovatt's absence, Ned returned early from taking Spot out on her walk. Mimsy and Esme were sitting outside in the shade of a tree, enjoying the soft summer air and the flowers. Esme, feeling quite recovered, had considered taking the leopard for her walk, but Mimsy had forbidden it. "I promised Lovatt I would make sure you were quiet until he returned," she divulged guiltily, looking around to make sure Ned had penned Spot up securely. Mimsy had never become comfortable with the leopard. More accurately, she was terrified of Spot.

Esme had started to reply when Vincent came into the yard, followed by Captain Arno. "I discovered Arno on the doorstep and brought him back with me," he explained, sitting down beside Mimsy and looking at her fondly. He nodded at Mimsy, letting her know that all had been accomplished at Eversleigh, then turned and smiled at Esme. "I saw Mrs. Hinson and I've already sent for lemonade and some of her wonderful macaroons."

Captain Arno sat down beside Esme and smiled approvingly as he looked at her wound. "I see you're healing nicely, Miss Darling."

She nodded and laughed. "I'm perfectly well, thank you, although the family is trying to turn me into a chronic invalid."

"Fiddlesticks!" Mimsy said. "We're merely trying to keep you from dashing across the fields at a dead run or spending the day in the hot sun digging in your dahlias."

Captain Arno looked at the riot of color behind Esme. "You have some beautiful specimens."

"And I'm about to get another, perhaps two," Esme told him, turning to follow his gaze. "Señora Romero is bringing me one or two plants in a few days."

"Oh?" Captain Arno lifted an eyebrow. "She's bringing them? From Spain?"

"Oh, she isn't making the trip just to bring flowers. She's going to visit, too, although I own that her visit *is* a surprise. She had written that she would be coming to London sometime, and I had planned to meet her there and get the dahlias. However, now she's written that she's coming here and bringing me a red, and possibly a yellow, dahlia. I'm truly excited."

"Spoken like a true gardener," Vincent said, helping himself to two macaroons from the plate Mrs. Hinson placed in front of them. "Tell me, Arno, is everything rubbing along well at the post while Major Darling is in London?"

"Perfectly." Captain Arno glanced at him, then back at Esme. "And when will you be getting your plants, Miss Darling? I'd love to see them. I'm something of a flower fancier myself."

Esme frowned slightly. "In her letter she said she would be here within a week. That was three days ago, so I expect her almost any time." She looked at Mimsy in surprise. "Heavens, we need to get a room ready for her."

Mimsy gestured toward the room Esme had been using, the one vacated by Aunt Penny. "Why not that one? Aunt Penny certainly isn't going to stay in there again."

They all looked up at the window, so they didn't see Spot coming around the edge of the dahlias. She came up to the table and put her front paws on it, trying to sniff the macaroons. Mimsy looked at her in horror, leaped to her feet, screamed once, and fainted dead away.

Vincent leaned over the table in a vain attempt to grab her, but he missed and Mimsy crumpled to the grass. Vincent didn't wait to go around the table, but crawled right over the top, knocking macaroons and lemonade everywhere. Spot, confused by all the noise, tried to slide under Esme's chair.

Mimsy moaned as Vincent picked her up and bellowed for someone to fetch a doctor. Then Vincent turned to Esme, his expression furious. "You knew she was terrified of that creature and yet you kept it around. If one hair of her head has been harmed, I intend to shoot the thing before nightfall!" With that, he stalked into the house, carrying Mimsy in his arms.

"I think," Captain Arno said delicately, "that perhaps I should go for the doctor." He looked nervously down at Spot as he backed toward the edge of the yard. At the corner of the house, he turned and gave Esme a cursory good-bye. Then he almost ran toward the road.

Esme was left sitting at the table, lemonade and macaroons on her lap and Spot under her chair. She closed her eyes and took a deep breath. After a while, she reached down and scratched Spot on the head. The leopard crawled from under the chair and put her head on Esme's knee.

"My poor, misunderstood Spot. What a fiasco," she said, as Spot stared up at her contentedly. "What else could possibly happen to us?"

Hinson appeared at the door. He didn't care for Spot and wasn't about to come out into the yard, so he simply called out his message. "Señora Romero is here. What shall I do with her?"

Seventeen

Esme looked from Hinson to Spot and back. "I'll be right there, Hinson," she called out. "In the meantime, have Mrs. Hinson give the Señora the room that Lord Evers occupied." Hinson nodded and backed farther into the house, obviously relieved that he didn't have to go out on the lawn.

Spot put her paws on Esme's knees and then around Esme's neck. She nuzzled Esme's neck and tried to lick her face. Esme hugged her and stood up so she could walk Spot back to her pen. "Just how did you get out of there?" Esme asked, examining the lock on the pen. The door was shut and locked firmly. Esme unlocked it and shooed Spot inside, then waited a moment to see if Spot could leap over the top. Instead Spot ambled over to her favorite tree and stretched out in the shade.

Mrs. Hinson, with her usual efficiency, had already placed the Señora in a chamber. "There's only one maid, so she can use the little room beside that one," Mrs. Hinson said, nodding.

"As usual, you have everything well in hand, Mrs. Hinson," Esme said, as they walked up to the bedroom to see if Señora Romero needed anything else. Mrs. Hinson rapped on the Señora's door and took a fresh pitcher of water inside. Esme followed her.

There were two women in the room—the Señora, who

had aged years since Esme had seen her, and another woman who was unpacking. Esme paused, surprised at the Señora's appearance. Her hair was almost gray, and there were lines of care and worry across her face. Still, when the Señora looked up and saw her, a smile brightened her expression. "My dear child!" the Señora exclaimed, hugging her. "How good to see you again." She stood back. "And you've changed so. You've turned into a beautiful young woman."

Esme started to answer her, but her eyes were caught by two pots containing lush plants. There were no blooms on the plants, but they were covered with buds. "The dahlias! And aren't they beautiful!" She touched a bud and could see the soft red just beginning to show around its tips. "How on earth did you get them here in such lovely condition? I expected tubers, or at most a tiny plant."

The Señora chuckled. "You have no idea how difficult this has been. I believe it would have been easier to travel with children." She yawned before she could stop herself.

"Thank you, and thank you," Esme said, moving to the door. "I know you need to get unpacked and rest. We keep country hours here, so supper will be early. I'll send Mrs. Hinson up to wake you."

"You are too good to me. Do send your man up to get the dahlias. He brought them up before I knew it. I had intended to have them placed directly where you planned to plant them."

Esme left the Señora and went down the hall to Mimsy's room. She was in bed, and Vincent was holding her hand and fretting over her. Mimsy looked perfectly fine to Esme, but Vincent seemed to think she was suffering from a dire condition brought on by shock. He was promising to take her to Italy for the sunshine. Esme started to reassure him, but was interrupted by Mrs. Hinson.

"That captain is downstairs. He's fetched Dr. Beeson."

Esme dashed down to send Dr. Beeson right up. "Probably a case of the vapors," he grunted, "and a complete waste of my time. A little hartshorn and vinegar should do the trick." He stomped up the stairs, Esme right behind him. She turned to see Captain Arno still standing in the entry.

"Do wait a moment, Captain Arno. I'll be right down," she called back over her shoulder. "Mrs. Hinson will bring you some tea if you wish."

Captain Arno glanced from Mrs. Hinson to Esme and smiled. "I'll just be on my way. Don't bother to see me out at a time like this. I'll return at a better time." He opened the door and gave her a last smile. "I hope Lady Evers recovers soon."

"I'm sure she will. Thank you for your help." This last was called over the stair railing as Dr. Beeson began opening various doors looking for his patient. Esme heard Mrs. Hinson close the door behind Captain Arno, and hurried to show Dr. Beeson Mimsy's room. Dr. Beeson took one look around, frowned at Vincent, and promptly sent him and Esme out of the room. They didn't speak until they were downstairs in the parlor.

"You're going to have to do something about that leopard. It needs to be shot." Vincent's voice was flat.

Esme rounded on him. "You touch one hair on Spot, Vincent, and I promise that you'll regret it! That leopard has had enough trouble in her short life, and I intend that she lives in comfort and peace while she's here."

"Even if she terrorizes people? You saw what she did to Mimsy."

"She did nothing to Mimsy. You know yourself that Mimsy faints at the drop of a kerchief. She always has."

Vincent collapsed into a chair. "I know, but I still worry every time she does it." He looked around. "I apologize to you, Esme. And to your animal, as well." He rubbed the side of his face, as though to wipe away the worry.

"Where did Captain Arno go? I thought he returned with the doctor."

"He did, but he excused himself and said he'd come back another time. I didn't even have time to tell him Señora Romero is here. Of course, she's resting, so there wouldn't have been a chance for them to talk. He told me that he had met her in Spain."

Vincent didn't answer. Instead, he went to the door and looked around. "I thought I heard someone," he said, coming back into the room. "Did you hear a door close?"

"It was probably Hinson or Aunt Penny. Poor Aunt Penny has taken to her bed again. I'm afraid life at Rouvray is proving too much for her." She turned as they heard the doctor coming down the stairs. Vincent dashed out to the hall to talk to him while Esme went to the drawing room to finish straightening her father's desk. She had worked on it the day before, and almost had things put back in order.

To her surprise, her neat stacks of papers had been moved and shuffled. The stack of all her correspondence was missing. She put her hands on her hips and scowled. Mrs. Hinson was always complaining about papers around the house, but this time she had gone too far. Esme went to find her, but stopped when she saw Vincent sitting on the bottom step. The doctor had gone, and Vincent was just sitting there, looking at the door.

"What is it, Vincent?" Esme asked in alarm. "Is it Mimsy? Is something wrong?"

He looked up at her, a dazed expression on his face.

Esme sat down on the step beside him. "What is it? Tell me, Vincent. Is it serious?"

He nodded as Esme grabbed his arm and shook him. "A baby," he croaked. "Mimsy is going to have a baby."

Esme felt her jaw drop, and she stared at Vincent with an expression that was as shocked as his. "A baby? Mimsy? Are you sure?"

Vincent nodded again and stood unsteadily. "Yes, the doctor said he was sure. I'd better go up. She might try to get out of bed." He dashed up the stairs, taking them two at a time.

Esme was still staring at the door when Bram and Lovatt walked in. Lovatt looked at her and grinned. "Don't tell me that there's been another catastrophe."

"Many," she said, grinning back at him. It was so good to see him again. "But this news is a trifle different." She told them about Mimsy. Lovatt got a strange, faraway look on his face. "A family," he said. "How wonderful."

"At least it will give Mimsy something else to think about," Bram said. "Is there anything to eat in this house? I'm starving."

"You have to wait. Señora Romero came today, bringing my dahlias—two of them, nice, bushy plants in pots. You should see them. Beautiful plants, and they're going to bloom this year."

"Good, but I'm still starving." He looked toward the kitchen. "She'll probably want to eat late, so perhaps I should—"

"Don't even think of it," Esme said. "I told her we would eat early, so supper will be at the usual time."

"Good, I can't wait much longer." He turned to Lovatt. "Would you care to join us?"

"No, I'd best be getting on to Shad Abbas. You forget that I haven't been home yet."

Esme walked over and stood in front of the door. "And you're not going until you tell me what you discovered. Why did you go to London? It took me a full day to realize that you hadn't told me a single thing about your reason for going. What do you know?"

Lovatt chuckled and looked around. The only open door led into the front parlor. Esme took his arm and Bram's and herded them into the room. "Now, tell me everything."

Lovatt selected the chair that was the least uncomfortable and sat down. "I can't." He looked at her. "I do believe you've recovered."

"Oh, Esme was better the next day," Bram said. "She was even wanting to go walking with that leopard. I understand she was even entertaining Captain Arno this afternoon."

"Who told you that?" Esme's tone was peevish.

"Arno." Bram's voice was full of satisfaction. "He saw me this morning and asked if I minded if he visited you often. It seems he's attracted."

"Bram!" Esme felt her face flame, and she risked a glance at Lovatt. He didn't appear nearly as entertained by the idea as Bram was. In fact, he was glowering.

"You can do as you wish, Miss Darling," he said formally, "but I don't believe I'd be alone with the Captain if I were you."

"Lord no, Esme. If only half of what Lov—" Bram stopped himself quickly and looked over at Lovatt, aware that he was about to tell tales out of school.

"What?" Esme said. "What are you saying?"

Aunt Penny wafted into the room. "Good afternoon, gentlemen. Esme, my dear, it's still an hour until supper. Do you think it would be amiss if we had a cup of tea? I'm peckish today." She sat down in the chair next to Lovatt. "You've been to London, I understand. Do tell us all the *on-dits* from town. I do hope you're planning to stay and dine with us."

Lovatt hesitated a moment. "I'd be delighted," he said with his most courtly smile. "Just let me send word to Shad Abbas."

Aunt Penny smiled and rang for Hinson. Esme gritted her teeth and sat there, waiting for an opportunity to quiz Lovatt, and wondering why he had changed his mind.

They had almost finished eating. Most of supper had been spent in congratulations to Mimsy. Then the Señora told about the horrors of her trip from Spain to London. After that, Mimsy and Aunt Penny pressed Lovatt to recount the gossip current in the *ton*. Dessert had just been served when a messenger came from Shad Abbas. Hinson came in and murmured something to Lovatt, and he immediately got up to talk to the messenger. In just a moment he was back, his face pale and his mouth taut. "There's been an accident," he said shortly. "My man, Samad, has been injured. So if you'll excuse me . . ." He bowed and left the room.

Esme could stand it no longer. She jumped up and ran after him, catching him beside the front door. "Was he hurt badly?" she asked.

"I don't know." Lovatt's expression was grim. "I fear the worst."

"Was Samad hurt at the circus?" At Lovatt's nod, she went on. "If this has anything to do with Papa's case, come back and tell me what happened. Do you promise?"

"I will. It may be late." He looked at her for a moment, his eyes a deep color that was almost black in the candlelight. "I may not be able to come back if he's . . . if it's serious."

"I understand." Esme watched him hurry out the door. He mounted his horse and set off at a gallop toward town and the circus.

At one o'clock in the morning, Esme finally gave up waiting and went upstairs to go to bed. She had put on her nightdress and dressing gown, and was busy brushing her hair when she heard a rattle at the window. *The burglar!* she thought. She tossed the brush aside and grabbed the poker, stationing herself at one side of the window.

The window rattled again and opened a fraction. "Miss Darling! Esme!" It was a hoarse whisper. "Are you in here?"

Esme almost dropped the poker. "Lovatt? What are you doing coming in the window at this time of night?"

He pushed the window further open and swung his legs inside. "You said for me to stop by, and there were no lights downstairs. However, there were lights here and I saw someone through the curtains, so I assumed you were here." He stepped into the room and brushed off his coat with his hands.

"How did you get up here?" Esme peered out the window and down into the darkness.

Lovatt grinned. "The same way Spot keeps coming in here. I climbed the tree outside the window. I noticed the other day how very convenient those limbs are, and how easy it would be to get to this window. I think Spot was Mrs. Pennywhistle's burglar."

"And mine too, I suppose?"

"No, yours was real, unfortunately." Lovatt sat down in the chair where Esme had been brushing her hair. "You need to close the draperies, but leave the window open. If I have to leave in a hurry, I don't want to hurtle through glass," he said with a grin. "Is the door locked?"

"No. But how could Spot climb up here?" Esme peered down into the darkness once again, then pulled the heavy draperies closed. Lovatt locked the door and then sat down again. "The limbs of the tree are low enough for her to leap up on them, and it's easy for her from there. In India I've seen leopards go straight up a fifty-foot tree trunk. Leopards are the most agile animals I've ever seen."

"I've never seen Spot do anything like that." Esme shook her head.

"All the same, she does. When I took her for a walk the other day, she was sunning herself on top of the little house in her pen. From there, it's just a short hop to the tree. I think she gets back inside by jumping on the garden bench and then leaping over the fence. Leopards are able to leap long distances."

"And you really think she can jump into the pen? It must be six feet high."

"Exactly six feet. I found some fur stuck on the top, so I know she's jumping inside, just in time to get fed." He looked at Esme and ran his fingers through his hair. "But enough of that. You wanted me to come tell you about Samad. He will be fine, I think, although it might have been much worse."

Esme sat across from him and pulled a little table up so she could set the candle down. Lovatt looked unbelievably handsome in the candlelight. The shadows caught the planes of his face, and there was a lock of his hair hanging over his forehead. Esme laced her fingers together to try to keep from touching it and smoothing it back. "What happened?"

"He was pushed from behind, and fell under a rolling wagon. He could have been killed, but he's very quick. He managed to roll under the middle of the wagon. The wagon went over his leg and broke it. I had Dr. Beeson set it for him. He'll be all right in a few weeks, I'm told."

"Pushed? Is he sure? Couldn't he have just fallen?"

Lovatt shook his head. "Not Samad. His agility is on a par with Spot's. I've seen him climb unbelievably tall trees and cliffs that had no visible handholds for yards. He can leap from limb to limb just like Spot. No, he wouldn't have fallen."

"Then who pushed him?"

"That's the question I'd like an answer to." Lovatt raised an eyebrow and shook his head. "No one saw, and no one knows. Samad has no idea. He heard a sound behind him and started to turn. He was pushed before he could see his assailant." Lovatt paused for a moment. "He thinks it might have been Arno."

"Captain Arno! How ridiculous! Lovatt, I assure you that he wouldn't do such a thing. I've known him for a while, and he's always been a perfect gentleman."

Lovatt looked at her slowly. "Do you care about him?"

It took Esme a moment to realize what he was asking. "Care about him? Why do you ask?"

"Because what I tell you will depend on your answer. I prefer that you be honest."

A touch of anger lit her voice. "All right, Lovatt, I'll be perfectly honest. I like the man very much, but no, I don't have any feelings for him. None whatsoever."

Lovatt released his breath in a long sigh and eased further back into the chair. "Good, because I think Arno isn't really what he seems. I'm still asking questions, so please don't ask me to explain, but I will tell you as soon as I'm sure."

Esme shook her head. "I know you suspect him, but I can't imagine him doing anything to hurt Papa. What would be the point?"

"He said he knew Señora Romero. You know he's not from England."

"Good heavens, Lovatt, how could those two small things add up to anything? Most of the world is from somewhere besides England, and the Señora must know hundreds of people, me included."

Lovatt stretched his legs in front of him and looked at the tops of his boots in the candlelight. "You know the Spanish rules of propriety would question the Señora's coming all the way to England with only a maid and a groom in attendance. Have you wondered why she's done that? I think there must be something very urgent for her to come here with such a small escort."

Esme frowned, thinking of what her father had told her about Spanish customs. "Perhaps Rodrigo brought her. He prefers to stay in London when he visits this country."

"No, I checked. She came alone. Just the Señora, her maid, a groom, two trunks, and two plants."

"Perhaps she's just getting away from tradition. I'm sure that many of the old customs have changed because of the war in the Peninsula." She shrugged. "After all, these are modern times."

"One thing hasn't changed in Spain. Napoleon still has an active faction there. His army was there so long that there was a great deal of intermingling. Napoleon will get help from Spain when he returns."

"When?" Esme seized on the word. "Don't you mean *if?"*

"When." Lovatt's tone was flat. "I've gotten the information from reliable sources. I also have a feeling that the Señora is somehow involved, although I don't know how. He ran his fingers through his hair again and stood. "I have to leave. The questions about the Señora's reputation will be nothing compared to what might happen to yours if I'm caught in here." He grinned. "I'd feel honor bound to offer for you, and you know how I feel about that."

"I know. You've told me—no entanglements." Esme carefully kept her expression blank. She stood, reached out, and touched his arm. "Lovatt, when will you know something else to tell me? I want to know what you discover about the Señora and Captain Arno."

"I should know by tomorrow night. Day after tomorrow at the latest." He looked at her in the candlelight and caught his breath. There was a connection between them, something that didn't want to be denied. "Esme . . ." he said, slowly.

She took a step toward him. "Chalmers," she whispered in reply, her hand still on his arm. Her fingers slid up to his upper arm and across to his chest. "Chalmers," she said again.

Before he could think or stop himself, he pulled her close to him and lowered his head to hers. Her soft cheek rubbed against his, feeling like silk touching his skin. He wanted to say her name, but the only sound to come from his throat was a moan. He buried his face in her hair, feeling the curls crush against his cheeks and lips. He brought his hands to her head, lacing his fingers through her hair, holding her face to his. The candlelight made shadows on her face, highlighting her lips that were waiting for him, and creating shadows in the hollow of her throat. He tried to stop himself, but he kissed the base of her throat, feeling rather than hearing the moan in her throat.

He moved to her lips, feeling along the way how her jawbone moved against the faint stubble of his beard. He tried to take her lips softly, but couldn't restrain himself. He crushed her to him, trying to hold back, but unable to deny the emotion she always aroused in him. He thought his emotions had reached a peak, but when Esme put her arms around his neck and answered his kiss with one of her own, parting her lips to receive him, he lost all reason. He moved his hands, fumbling a moment with the ties on her dressing gown until he opened it. Slowly, softly he ran his fingers up her sides, feeling the warmth of her underneath the thin cotton.

"Chalmers," she whispered again, clinging to him, her mouth open against his.

Beyond reason, he turned her and pushed her back against the bed. She fell back, pulling him with her, moaning his name. Her knees opened and he leaned into her, pressing his body to hers.

There was a noise behind him, but he ignored it. In a moment, Spot leaped up on the bed, swatting playfully at Esme's hair. Lovatt stood, his arousal painfully evident. He turned and grabbed the back of the chair for support, breathing heavily. "Spot seems to have come at an opportune time, Miss Darling," he said, his voice shaky as he gripped the chair. "I want to apologize."

Esme crawled up on the bed and huddled there, trembling with emotion. She said nothing.

Lovatt turned and looked at her, his breathing slowing.

"Are you all right?" He stepped back a step further and put the chair between them.

"Fine," Esme managed, although she didn't feel fine. She wanted Lovatt, more than she had ever dreamed. He didn't want her, but she wanted him. It was humiliating.

"I'd better leave." His voice sounded almost normal. "Do you want me to take Spot with me?"

Esme glanced over at Spot who was sprawled on the bed on her back, all four paws in the air, her white belly fur lustrous in the dark. "No, just leave her. She'll go back down when she's ready."

There was an awkward silence. "Good night, Miss Darling. I'll keep you informed." With that, he went to the window and let himself out.

Esme waited for a moment, but heard nothing else. She touched herself down her side, on her breasts, and on her lips. She wanted Lovatt. But, she reminded himself, he didn't want her. He wanted no entanglements.

She put her head down on Spot's soft, white belly and sobbed.

Eighteen

When Esme woke the next morning, she and Spot were still curled up on top of the bed. Esme waited a moment as she heard the clock chime in the hall. It seemed very bright outside, and she waited and counted. "Good heavens, Spot, it's half past ten! I never sleep this late."

Spot stretched and yawned, waving all four paws in the air. She swatted affectionately at Esme and then licked her up the side of the arm. "It does appear, Spot," Esme said, rubbing her swollen eyes, "that you're destined to be my only companion, especially here in my bedroom."

She got up and slid off the bed just as Abby, the maid, came into the room. Abby was followed by Aunt Penny. "Esme dear, are you sick? It's past the usual time that you . . ." Aunt Penny took one look at the bed and shrieked. In less than a minute, Bram and Vincent were at the doorway with drawn pistols in their hands.

Esme jumped up and stood between the bed and the door. "Put those things away." Esme tried to keep calm, but it was a strange feeling to be staring at the front end of a pistol, and she could hear her voice quiver.

Bram strolled into the room and looked at Spot. The leopard gave him a superior look, jumped over to the open window, and disappeared from view.

"Oh, my heavens," Aunt Penny cried. "That animal has gone to slaughter something! Or someone!"

"Don't be ridiculous, Aunt Penny," Esme said, peering out of the window. Spot had gone down the tree and jumped into her pen. She was calmly washing her paws, waiting for Ned to come with her breakfast.

Esme turned around. "Now, if you will please leave. I'm hardly dressed for company."

"But fetching, anyway," Bram said with a mock leer as he went out the door. Esme wished she had something close by to throw at him. He deserved it.

When she dressed and went downstairs, she decided to wait and eat with the others at their midday meal. In the meantime, she contented herself with a cup of tea.

After tea, she went upstairs looking for the Señora, intending to apologize for being such a terrible hostess and to ask what the Señora would like to do during the day. To Esme's surprise, Señora Romero wasn't there. Spanish ladies never went anywhere alone, so Esme was afraid that something was drastically wrong, and tried to question the Señora's maid. The maid was obviously terrified at being in a strange land, and her English was execrable. Esme finally got a word in and asked the girl to speak in Spanish. The maid seemed surprised that Esme was fluent, but was overjoyed that someone else could speak familiar words.

The maid, Juanita, told Esme that the Señora was acting very strangely, and had gone out about an hour ago without saying where. Esme was puzzled. Spanish ladies simply did not go out and about without an escort. Surely the maid had been wrong, and Señora Romero was somewhere on the grounds.

Esme found Señora Romero in the small parlor, peering out the window as though searching for something. Esme walked up and smiled at her. "My dahlias are over there." She gestured to the left. "I know they can't compare to any of yours, but you're welcome to take whatever you wish."

"Gràcias." Señora Romero nodded, the picture of carefully cultivated Spanish manners. She seemed strained and tense, and barely noticed the dahlias. Esme was more and more convinced that Lovatt was right—something had to have forced the Señora to come to Rouvray, accompanied only by her maid and groom. Esme determined to discover what was happening. Before she could say anything, Mimsy came bouncing into the room, glowing with health. "There you are, Esme, and you, too, Señora! I have the most wonderful day planned for us! We're going into town to shop for ribbons and cloth. Esme, you must help me with my layette, and I know the Señora will enjoy the outing."

"I do not know. I am truly fatigued from the journey." Señora Romero's voice seemed stilted to Esme, but Mimsy didn't notice that, or the Señora's hesitation. She chattered on, informing them that they would leave right after they had eaten luncheon. Then they would shop and then meet Vincent, Bram, and possibly Captain Arno for tea at the inn.

"Yes," Señora Romero said, her voice stronger and more animated now, "I would very much enjoy seeing the shops in town. English goods are so much different than ours." She hurried out of the room, leaving Mimsy still chattering about the baby. Mimsy didn't notice she was gone.

The shopping trip was not a success for Esme or Señora Romero. Mimsy enjoyed it tremendously, chattering about everything she saw. Señora Romero answered perfunctorily. She seemed distracted, and looked from left to right in every place they stopped. Esme once asked her if she felt well, and she smiled brightly, saying that she had never felt better.

At the inn, Vincent, Bram, and Captain Arno were waiting for them. "You are, I believe, acquainted with Señora Romero," Bram said to Captain Arno as the ladies were seated in the small private parlor.

Captain Arno bowed slightly. "We have met, but I'm afraid I cannot say that we're closely acquainted." He smiled at her. "Perhaps after this visit Señora Romero and I will be able to really call ourselves acquaintances." The Señora nodded regally in Captain Arno's direction. "Perhaps so," she said, not smiling.

"Good day. What a pleasant surprise to see all of you out." Lovatt stepped into the parlor. He stopped and looked around at them, smiling pleasantly. "I do hope I'm not intruding, but I came in and the innkeeper directed me in here. He's seen us together, and must have thought I was to join you."

"Do sit and join us," Bram said promptly. "Our ladies have just arrived, and I've ordered tea for everyone."

Lovatt got a chair from the side of the room and sat down between Captain Arno and Señora Romero. "Thank you for asking me." He turned to the Señora. "At supper last evening, I meant to ask you about your dahlias. Tell me, do you have any of the tubers from Mexico, or have all yours been grown in Spain?"

The Señora looked at him, startled, then visibly relaxed, and the conversation fell into generalities. They spent the better part of an hour just talking about travel, flowers, and differences in weather. Lovatt seemed to do most of the talking, recounting several of his adventures in India and telling them about the weather and strange customs there.

Vincent finally drew out his watch, flipped the lid to check the time, then looked sternly at Mimsy. "It is," he informed her, "time for you to go back to Rouvray and go to bed."

Esme had thought that Mimsy would protest, but instead she looked at Vincent, smiled, and agreed. Señora Romero put her hand to her head. "Yes, and much as I hate to leave such pleasant company, I do fear I'm getting something of a headache. It will be good as well for me to return with you to your house and rest before supper."

Everyone stood and drifted toward the door. Captain

Arno slipped up to walk beside Esme. "Have you noted anything suspicious about your neighbor yet?" he whispered, leaning slightly toward her. "I thought you might have been watching."

"Do you mean Lovatt?" Esme whispered back, trying not to look directly at Lovatt. "As you know, he's been gone, so I haven't had a chance to watch him." This was true as far as it went.

"Do keep your eyes open, and let me know what he's doing," Arno whispered as they reached the door. He touched Esme's arm and gave it a familiar squeeze. Shocked, she looked up into his eyes. He was looking down at her, a faint smile at the corners of his mouth. "Until later, Miss Darling," he said, giving her a slight bow. Then they were all out the door, Lovatt headed up one street, Captain Arno went in another direction, and Esme, Señora Romero, Mimsy, and Bram started back to Rouvray.

"Do you know the Captain?" Señora Romero murmured.

Esme nodded. "Quite well. He's often been at Rouvray, both in his official capacity with my father and as a visitor."

"So you are close." The Señora's voice was flat.

"I wouldn't exactly use that term, but I am well acquainted with him."

"Are you and the Señora discussing Captain Arno, Esme?" Mimsy asked. "If that's so, then you must tell the Señora the truth." She laughed and looked at Señora Romero. "Captain Arno has asked if he may call on Esme," she said with a smug smile. "I think it would be safe to say that they are very close acquaintances, indeed." She laughed and patted Esme's hand. Esme said nothing.

"I see." Señora Romero gave an odd inflection to the words.

Supper was an ordinary affair with just Esme, Vincent, Mimsy, and Señora Romero. Bram left right before supper, telling them that he was going to Shad Abbas to dine with

Lovatt. Esme wondered what the two of them were discussing. Perhaps Lovatt had received confirmation of his suspicions. Hadn't he said that he would know for sure by tonight? Perhaps he would be back to tell her.

After supper, Esme went out to check on Spot and found her stretched out on a tree limb, quietly washing her paws. She looked down at Esme and swatted at her playfully. Esme picked up a stick and waved it in front of Spot, while Spot tried to catch it. After a few minutes, Esme decided to leave Spot alone and go inside. She left her window open for Spot, in case the leopard wished to make another visit to her room—at least, she *told* herself the open window was for Spot.

Esme was ready to climb into her bed when there was a faint knock at her bedroom door. She thought it was Bram or Mimsy, and just called out for the visitor to come inside. She threw back the bedcovers, then turned, expecting to see one of them. Instead, Señora Romero stood there, her face as pale as the white of her dressing gown, her expression no longer the carefully polite mask Esme had seen since the Señora had arrived. Now she looked positively haggard. Señora Romero closed the door behind her. "You know the captain well," she stated flatly.

Surprised, Esme looked at her. "Captain Arno? Yes, but . . ."

Señora Romero let out a long sigh of relief. "Then you must be the one who should pass this on to him." She pulled a letter from her dressing gown. "They told me that it must get to Captain Arno, and no one must know. I thought today that I would be able to give it to him, but he was very careful. I know nothing about how to do this. Then, when I saw you talking privately to him I knew that there must be more between the two of you than mere friendship. That was why they sent me to your house."

"Señora Romero, you mistake me—" Esme began, but she stopped, as the Señora seemed on the verge of tears.

"If not you, then who? I must get this to him. I *must*. Please tell me that you are the one who can deliver this. If Captain Arno does not get this, they will kill my son."

"Kill your son?" Esme was trying hard to figure out what the Señora meant.

She nodded. "They have him now. They said they will kill Rodrigo if Captain Arno does not get this letter. They said if I tell anyone that they will kill Rodrigo." She fell to her knees in front of Esme. "I beg you. I beg you as a mother. You know that my husband is dead. My brothers are dead. Rodrigo is all I have left." She reached out and clutched Esme's knees. "I will do anything you ask. Just please see that Captain Arno gets this letter. You are—how do you English say it?—lovers with the captain, I could tell. Give this to him and tell him that I have spoken of it to no one." She held out the letter to Esme.

Esme took the letter. "I will see that the letter is delivered," she said, bending down and putting her arms around Señora Romero. "I will see to it tonight, so you may rest easily." She pulled the Señora to her feet. "You said *they* had Rodrigo. Who are these people?"

"You do not know?" The Señora looked at her sharply and gestured slightly, as though to retrieve the letter.

"Oh, of course." Esme paused and then hazarded a guess. "I hesitate to mention it because I don't know how much you know. It has to do with Napoleon."

Señora Romero nodded and looked sadly at Esme. "Yes, those are the ones. I wondered today when I saw you with Captain Arno how you could follow such a man. I did not believe that either you or your father would ever help Napoleon. But then, I do know that love makes people do strange things."

"I assure you . . ." Esme stopped. She had been ready to denounce Napoleon, Arno, and spies in general, but that wouldn't do at all. The Señora was frantic enough already. "I assure you that Rodrigo will be safe. You can tell the people who hold him that the letter was delivered to the proper person."

Señora Romero kissed her hand. "You have helped me more than you know, Miss Darling. As a mother I thank you. Rodrigo thanks you."

"It's all right, Señora." Esme helped her to her feet. "I will see that the letter is delivered tonight. All will be well." She put her arm around Señora Romero. "Let me help you to your room."

Señora Romero shook her head. "No, I go myself. If anyone sees, then I can simply say that I could not sleep." She paused at the door and turned. "Thank you again, Miss Darling." She slipped out the door and closed it behind her. Esme looked at the door in astonishment. The whole episode seemed unreal, like something out of one of Mrs. Radcliffe's novels. Still, the proof was right in her fingers—a heavy square of cream-colored paper that bore a seal of blue wax. The imprint was an eagle. Quickly she went to her candle and looked at it.

There was no address, nothing on the face of the letter. The eagle seal seemed to be the only identifying mark. She remembered that her father and Bram were always talking about Napoleon's eagles. Esme hesitated only a moment. She had been taught never to open others' mail, but this was not addressed to anyone. She broke the seal and opened the letter. It was written in French. As she read it, she caught her breath. Napoleon was going to leave Elba and form an army. Whoever had sent the letter—and he identified himself only as The Eagle—wanted Arno to send him an estimate of the current troop strength along the coast, as well as the state of morale. Esme sat down heavily in her chair, the letter still in her fingers.

"Arno," she muttered to herself. "Arno has done all this." Fury rose in her at the thought that Captain Arno had been at Rouvray, had been befriended by her father, had eaten at his table, and had betrayed him. She forced herself to stop and think logically. Lovatt needed this letter, and there was only one way to get it to him.

After she dressed in her dark dress and a cloak, she peered out the window. Spot and Lovatt might be able to go down the tree, but she wasn't going to chance it in a dress. She slipped the letter into the front of her bodice and blew out her candle, then slowly edged out the door and went into the hall. Quietly she went out the French door in the back and across the yard. Spot saw her from the tree limb and jumped down to join her. Together they went across the field, toward the lights of Shad Abbas.

At Shad Abbas, Esme knocked on the door. The butler answered and informed Esme that Lovatt was not at home. Bram wasn't there, either, although both gentlemen had been there earlier. The butler looked down his nose at her, letting her know quite clearly just what he thought of unescorted females who knocked on doors at midnight. He shut the door just as soon as he finished what he had to say.

Esme stood in front of the door, wondering just what to do. She looked around for Spot and saw the flash of the white on Spot's ears. Spot was going back toward Rouvray. Esme paused. She certainly couldn't wait for Lovatt here on his doorstep, and she certainly couldn't go searching for him. He could be anywhere. She touched her bodice, feeling the letter safe there, and began trudging back toward Rouvray, keeping a watchful eye on Spot, who was loping along in front.

At the field Spot veered off toward the stream, and Esme walked on. As she neared the edge of the woods, she heard a sound and stopped, her heart in her throat. The sound came again, and Esme, who had never been afraid of the dark, sensed something dangerous. She unfastened her cloak and held it closer to her, then left the path and began skirting close to the woods. She fervently wished that Spot were with her. Whatever was there would never bother her as long as the big cat was near her.

Suddenly someone grabbed her from behind, clamping one arm around her shoulders and trying to put a hand over her mouth. He covered her eyes, instead. Esme screamed as loud as she could, and the man cursed fluently behind her. "Shut her up," someone else growled, running up to her.

Esme twisted out of her cloak and tried to run, but the second man jumped right on her and brought her down. The two of them rolled in the grass, and she tried to jump up and run away, but he clutched her ankle and she fell again, hitting the ground so hard that the breath was knocked out of her.

This time both men seized her and jerked her to her feet. She tried to move her hands so she could push her hair from her face and eyes, but they held her fast. One of them grabbed her hair and jerked her head backward. Tears sprang to her eyes as he pulled hard on her hair.

"Come on," he said to the second man. "He's waiting for us."

Esme blinked her tears away as the second man came into her view. She caught her breath as she recognized Bradshaw, one of the men from the circus who had mistreated Spot. The other one, she thought instantly, must be Sikes. She had no time to wonder why they had done this, or where they were taking her. They dragged her along the path toward Rouvray. There, in the woods behind the house, someone else was waiting. As they got closer, she saw the moonlight glint off the buttons on his uniform.

"I see you found her." Captain Arno smiled at her and took out his handkerchief. He gagged her securely and smiled. "I trust that's not too uncomfortable, Miss Darling." He looked at Bradshaw and Sikes. "We're going to have to take her somewhere until we find what she's done with the letter. Señora Romero swore that she gave it to her." He put a finger under Esme's chin and lifted her head so that she was looking into his eyes. "Is that true, Miss Darling? Did Señora Romero give my letter to you? It will not go well with either the Señora or her son if you lie."

Esme nodded her head to signify yes, and Arno grimaced. "The old Spanish fool! Never send a woman on an errand." He glanced back at the house. "I told the Señora that I would murder the entire household if she so much as made one sound or told anyone a single word. I think she'll do as she should. I'll take care of her tomorrow." He turned back and smiled at Esme. "But for now, Miss Darling, I think you're our first order of business. Much as I hate to do this, it's necessary. Good night, Miss Darling." With that, he smiled again and hit Esme sharply on the jaw. She felt a moment of intense pain. Then the world went dark.

Nineteen

When Esme awoke she was lying on a rough plank floor, and the smells were strange. She seemed to be piled on a pallet of rags. She slowly opened her eyes, turned over stiffly, and looked up. There was a high window open above her, and she could see the stars. *Not too much time must have elapsed, then,* she thought. She ran her tongue across her lips, and realized that the gag in her mouth was gone. That was a relief. She had not known that something so simple as a gag would be so painful.

She heard voices behind her, and rolled over the other way so she could see. There was a small, rickety table in the middle of the room, and three men were there. Bradshaw and Sikes she could see. The other had his back to her, but she knew that uniform. It was Arno. He was, she knew, waiting until she woke up so he could quiz her about the letter.

They had untied her hands. Slowly, she touched her bodice to make sure the letter was safe. She caught her breath as her fingers found nothing there except her skin and underclothes. What had happened to the letter? Had they already searched her and found it? She felt sick and violated.

Carefully she moved her head so that she could see around the room. The door didn't appear to be bolted, but it was across the room and there was no way to get to it. The window was too high for her to get out. She might as well face Arno now, she decided. She sat up, testing every move to see if her body was still working as it should.

"I see the bird is up," Bradshaw said, nodding in her direction.

Arno turned around. "Ah, good morning, Miss Darling." He glanced out the window. "Or at least it will be in an hour or two. I trust you had a pleasant nap."

Esme tried to stand, wavered, then forced herself to get to her feet. "I demand that you release me, Captain Arno. Others know of your treachery. You won't get out of this coil."

"Oh, but I plan to do just that, Miss Darling." His voice was soft and low. He got up and came to stand in front of her. "Now about that letter, Miss Darling."

"I don't have it. I assumed that you did."

He slapped her across the face. "Don't play games with me, Miss Darling. I don't have the time. Today promises to be a busy day. Now give me the letter."

Esme bit her lip to keep from crying. "I don't have it."

Arno slapped her again on the other cheek, then grabbed her shoulders. "You'll tell me, and you'll tell me now." He shook her until her she thought her teeth would rattle.

She gasped. "I don't have it."

"Do you take me for a fool?" Arno hissed. His fingers dug into her shoulder and he flung her away, knocking her against the wall. "It would serve no purpose for me to kill you," Arno said, his voice vehement. "But I will do it, Miss Darling. Don't think yourself necessary to my efforts. You're expendable."

Esme made herself stand up against the wall. "I don't have the letter, Captain Arno. If I did, I wouldn't give it to you. How could you betray your country? How could you betray Papa?"

"My country? I would never betray my country, Miss Darling. As for your father—how could I betray him? Quite easily, I assure you." He advanced on her. "Now, if you don't have the letter, who does? I want that letter, and I want it now." He stood close to her, grinned at her, then slapped her again. Esme's head hit hard against the wall.

At that moment the door crashed open, and Lovatt appeared in the doorway, a pistol in his hand. "It's over, Arno. Leave her alone and come out."

Arno whirled and pulled Esme in front of him. "Shoot if you wish, Lovatt, but I don't think you will. Come inside and put the pistol on the table." He pulled his own pistol and held it to Esme's head. "If you try to shoot, I believe I can get off a shot of my own."

Lovatt wavered, then stepped inside and placed his pistol on the table. "Is anyone with you?" Arno asked.

"You'll have to look for yourself," Lovatt said levelly, never taking his eyes from Arno.

Esme heard a click as Arno pulled back on his pistol. "I asked you a question, Lovatt. Is there anyone else?"

Bram walked into the room and placed his pistol on the table beside Lovatt's. "There's no one else," he said quietly. "Leave her alone."

Arno nodded to Bradshaw, who shut the door and bolted it. "And now we have three," Arno said, moving his pistol but holding onto Esme. "What brought you here, Lovatt? How did you know?"

"I checked. Your family is French, Arno. Your brother and sister are still in France, working actively for Napoleon. That much was easy to discover. What I don't understand is how you got this far in the army without anyone discovering about you."

"I'm quite an actor," Arno said with a smile that was half grimace. "I was almost discovered by Whitehall at one time."

"And that was why you implicated our father," Bram said. "To draw any suspicion away from you."

Arno glanced outside. "It will be daylight in an hour or

so, and I need to be on the move. Gentlemen, I had hoped I would never have to resort to murder, but I believe my options have ended." He leveled his pistol at Lovatt.

"Don't!" Esme cried. "Don't! I'll tell you where the letter is. Don't hurt them!"

Arno released her and stepped back, his pistol still covering Lovatt and Bram. Bradshaw pulled out a pistol and held it on them as well. As soon as Arno saw that Lovatt and Bram were well covered, he turned back to Esme. "Well, now we come to it. I thought lying was above you, Miss Darling, but I misjudged you, it seems. Where is my letter?"

"It's . . . it's . . ." She looked around helplessly. "It's hidden in Spot's pen."

"You didn't have time," Arno said flatly. "Señora Romero said she gave you the letter, and then just a short while later, we found you in the field. You took it to him, didn't you?" He nodded to Lovatt. "You have it, don't you?"

"I do." Lovatt's voice was calm.

Arno put the pistol against Esme's head again. "Now, Lovatt, you know that—" He was cut short by a streak of gold and black fur hurtling through the open window. Spot landed on the table, her hind legs bunched under her, and looked at Sikes and Bradshaw. She recognized them as her tormentors, and in an instant, with a roar, was on Sikes, mauling him. Lovatt leaped across them and knocked Arno to the floor, while Bram tackled Bradshaw. Esme was knocked into the wall and from somewhere she heard the deafening crack of a pistol fired at close range.

She scrambled to her feet and saw Lovatt slumped against the table, blood staining his coat. Sikes suddenly stopped screaming, and Spot moved away a moment, looking at him. The man was inert on the floor, in a puddle of blood. Spot swatted at him a time or two, but he didn't respond, so Spot looked around, still enraged. She saw

Bradshaw at the door, frantically trying to unbolt it so he could run. He got the bolt open and knocked the door wide open, but then Spot tackled him from behind, and the two of them rolled out the door. Arno scrambled to his feet, his smoking pistol still in his hand, and grabbed for Esme. She dodged him as Bradshaw and Spot came rolling back into the room. Bradshaw was bleeding heavily from his head, and was screaming.

Lovatt staggered to his feet, his arm bleeding. He threw himself between Esme and Arno, knocking her backward against the wall. Arno snarled at Lovatt and hit at him with the pistol. Lovatt dodged the attack and lunged for Arno. The two of them fell across Bradshaw and Spot. With a roar, Spot twisted and slashed out with her paw at Arno. He screamed as she raked him across the face. He staggered to his feet, wiping blood from his eyes with his sleeve, and ran for the door. Lovatt tried to get to his feet, but Bradshaw clung to him, pulling him back down. "Save me!" he screamed. "That thing's trying to kill me!" Spot looked at him through slitted eyes and bared her teeth. There was blood all over her long canines, and blood stained the fur around her mouth. Spot growled and gathered herself to lunge at Bradshaw again, but the man cowered and frantically crawled underneath Lovatt.

"The cat, Esme," Lovatt gasped. "Try to calm the cat."

Esme put her hand on Spot's back. Spot spun around, and for a moment Esme thought the leopard was going to attack her. Spot looked at her, paused, and then hopped up on the table and stretched out, her eyes going from Sikes to Bradshaw.

"Can you get her out of here?" Lovatt murmured, trying to keep his voice low and calm. "She'll kill both these two if she can get to them." He looked at Bram and spoke in the same controlled tone. "See if you can get Sikes out of here, then Esme can get Spot out. We've got to get out and find Arno."

Bram dragged Sikes outside and then came back to get Bradshaw. Lovatt stayed between Spot and Bradshaw until they were out the door, then he ran to try to find Arno. Esme stayed inside, soothing Spot for a few minutes until the leopard was calm and nuzzled her affectionately along the side of her face. Only then did Esme allow herself to walk quietly to the door and go outside, her hand still on Spot's head.

Outside, day was breaking. Bram had things well in hand. He had men holding Sikes and Bradshaw, and had sent to the post for help. "Get Spot home," he said to Esme. "There's nothing you can do here, and I'm afraid that cat will kill someone if she gets angry again. Even if she doesn't, she'll terrorize half the men in town." He paused. "Can you go by yourself? I wouldn't ask, but you're the only one who can handle Spot, and I'm needed here. I will send Private Buckness with you." He nodded toward a young soldier who was looking at Spot, obviously intimidated by the leopard.

Esme nodded. "We'll be fine." She looked around. "What about Lovatt? Where is he?"

"Gone chasing after Arno. I've sent all the men I can spare after him. I've also sent word to post the road from here to London, just in case Lovatt doesn't catch him."

"He was wounded. I saw the blood." Esme shuddered.

"Arno?" Bram made a face. "That should slow him down so we can catch him."

"I didn't mean Arno, Bram. I was talking about Lovatt. There was blood all over his arm. Arno *was* scratched badly, though. Spot raked him across the face."

"Good, that should make him easier to recognize. He won't be able to hide scratches on his face. But are you sure Lovatt was wounded?" Bram frowned. "I don't remember seeing that, although I *was* keeping an eye on Sikes and Bradshaw. They were bloody enough. Could the blood you saw have been from either of them?"

Esme shook her head. "No, I think Captain Arno shot Lovatt in the arm. I just don't know how bad it is."

Bram reached out and touched her shoulder. "Go home, Esme. You've had a terrible night. Buckness will help you. Try to keep Spot inside if you can." He smiled briefly. "I'll be home with news as soon as I can."

The first half hour after Esme got home was spent in telling what had happened. The next fifteen minutes were spent in reviving Aunt Penny. After that, Esme went to her room and had water for a bath sent up. While she was bathing, Spot jumped in the window and stretched out on the bed. She looked at Esme and began licking her paws. "I suppose I should thank you," Esme said to her, standing up as she toweled dry. "I saved you once from Bradshaw and Sikes, and now you've returned the favor." Spot looked at her and blinked.

Esme put on fresh clothes, brushed her hair back, and waited. She needed to sleep, but she was too edgy to rest. She rushed to the window at every sound from outside. Finally, she saw Bram coming in. She ran downstairs and met him at the door.

"Bradshaw and Sikes are both mauled badly, but the doctor says they'll recover in time to stand trial and hang. Arno escaped," he said wearily, tossing his hat aside and sitting down on the stairs. Esme sat beside him.

"And Lovatt?" She hardly dared to ask.

"He's fine. You were right, though—he was grazed on the arm. I made him stop and have it dressed before he went back to Shad Abbas." He hit his fist against his knee in frustration. "Arno must have gone to ground somewhere. Lovatt and I just worry that he has a contact somewhere in the neighborhood. Someone who would hide him. There are all kinds of gypsies among the circus people."

"The letter! Bram, he was asking me about the letter. I don't know what happened to it, but I did read it."

"Oh, Lovatt and I found the letter. It was in the grass near your cloak. That was how we knew you'd been kidnapped. Lovatt didn't even have to think. He put the letter in his pocket and we headed straight for the circus. I don't know how he knew Arno would take you there, but he did." Bram chuckled. "You should have seen him when the butler at Shad Abbas told him that you'd been there. He was a man possessed. I think he would have horsewhipped the man if Lady Redferne hadn't intervened. Lovatt was so agitated that he dashed right past his mother and went out the door, searching for you. When we found your cloak . . . well, suffice it to say that he was then more than agitated."

Esme didn't know how to respond, so she said nothing.

Bram stood. "I'm going back to the post to file a report. I just wanted to come by and give you the news, and station two soldiers here. They'll be on guard for a while."

"Why? Lovatt has the letter, and there should be no other worry."

Bram raised an eyebrow as he retrieved his hat. "May I remind you that Arno is still at large? He may try to come here and do harm. He may think that you still have the letter somewhere around here. He may just try to come here and murder all of us in revenge. Who knows?"

Esme shuddered as he went out the door. She could see one of the soldiers standing at the entrance gate to the house, watching up and down the road.

There had been no word from Lovatt. Esme thought briefly about going to Shad Abbas, but that just wouldn't do. Instead, she went for a walk with Spot in the afternoon, hoping to see him. One of the soldiers went with her, keeping a safe distance from Spot. They saw no one.

Bram returned at nightfall, but had nothing to report. They had found one soldier who had seen Arno and recognized him from his badly scratched face. The soldier reported that Arno was on the run. The man knew that

Arno had relatives abroad, and Arno had once told him that if he ever needed to, he would go to them. Word had gone out to all the ports to be watching for him, but Bram wasn't hopeful. "Do you know how many people manage to get on board ships?" he complained. "Do you know how many ships leave England on any given day?" He grimaced.

"Perhaps he won't leave the country," Esme suggested.

"Oh, he will. What's here for him now? I think he'll head straight for France and join Napoleon, if he can. Of course, we've sent word, as well, that there's a plan in the works to reinstate Napoleon, but that's something that's been bandied about since the little Corsican was put on Elba." He shook his head and then grinned at Mimsy as she came into the room. "I even sent a letter to Papa telling him about the events here." He looked at Esme's horrified expression and laughed. "About most of the events, at any rate. You may rest easily—I was very selective, dear sister."

Mimsy looked at her and shook her head. "I can't believe that you, Esme, have turned into such a madcap." She grinned. "And I've turned into such a settled, old matron."

Esme looked at her and made an ungracious sound.

That night Esme went to bed early, leaving her window open. *For Spot,* she thought, but deep inside she knew that she hoped someone else would pay her a visit. She stayed awake for a long time, but nothing happened. Exhausted, she finally dropped off to sleep.

Someone was speaking gently to her in her dreams. She recognized the voice as Lovatt's, and mumbled in return. "Esme, Esme," the voice called.

"Coming, I'm coming," she murmured back, turning to get more comfortable in her soft bed.

Someone shook her shoulder. "Esme, wake up," he whispered.

Her eyes flew open and she sat bolt upright, crashing right into his head. It made a terrible noise, and Lovatt pulled back. Esme heard him sit down in her chair. She fumbled with the flints she kept on the little table beside her bed. It seemed to take her minutes upon minutes to get the candle lit.

Lovatt was sitting in her chair. There was a bandage on his arm, and Esme saw a touch of red on the bandage. "Oh, I've hurt your wound," she said, scrambling out of bed to be near him.

"The arm is nothing. Right now, I'm afraid you've cracked my head again. I may never recover."

"But your arm is bleeding."

Lovatt glanced down at his arm and shrugged. "A result of trying to climb a tree at my age, I suppose. I'm going to have to take lessons from Spot if this keeps up."

"Why are you here, Lovatt? Do you have any news?"

He shook his head. "No 'How are you?', no 'I've been worried about you', no 'My concern knows no bounds?' Just 'Do you have news?' I'm hurt deeply, Miss Darling."

"Fudge. Do you? Have news, that is." Esme leaned against the bed.

"Arno has escaped, and we think he's headed for France. I've sent the letter and my report to Whitehall, so your father should be home in a day or two, completely cleared. Bradshaw and Sikes will probably be hanged or transported for treason, if that's any comfort. Everything seems to have finished up nicely."

"And you? What about you, Lovatt?" She hardly dared to ask.

He shrugged. "I'm probably going to London to work for a while. If another battle comes up with Napoleon, I'll be there. That's all."

Unsaid things hung in the air between them. Finally Lovatt broke the silence. "I want to talk to you about something."

"Yes?" Esme held her breath.

"Well, we've discussed this before, but you know that you're going to have to make some arrangements about Spot."

Esme tried not to let her disappointment show. "I know. I thought she was going to strike at me. She was that angry." She paused. "I see now that she could be dangerous at any time."

"Samad is going back to India next month, and has agreed to take Spot with him. I have a friend who has a huge plantation there. There's plenty of jungle with leopards in it. Spot could have the run of the plantation and, if she chooses, go into the jungle."

"Do you think she could live on her own?" Esme drifted across to the window and looked down. Spot was nowhere to be seen.

"She's in the tree, if you're looking. In answer to your question, yes, she could survive."

Esme paused. "Then I agree. It's the best thing for her. I told her today that I once saved her life, and now she probably saved ours. She's repaid the favor."

"I think it's the best thing." Lovatt stood and came over to stand beside her. "Now, there is one more matter."

"The llama?"

"What?" He looked down at her, puzzled.

"The llama at the circus. Don't you remember? We talked about it."

"Oh, Lord." He grimaced. "All right, Miss Darling. I'll go see if we can do something about the llama. I don't know just what, but I'll think of something."

She smiled at him. "Thank you, Lovatt." She looked into his eyes for a moment, then couldn't bear to think of never having him. She turned around so she didn't have to look at him.

Lovatt put his hands on her shoulders, turning her back around to face him. "I've been thinking."

"Yes?" Esme steeled herself to look at him. She didn't dare let her emotions show in her eyes.

"I've always . . . you know that my life has been planned and ordered. . . ." He ran his fingers through his hair, and winced as he raised his arm. He flexed his arm at the elbow. 'I wanted to . . ." He grimaced. "Oh, hell, why can't I do this?" He looked at her for a moment and then pulled her into his arms and crushed her to him, covering her mouth with his. A flood of emotion raced through her body, and before she could stop herself she clung to him and returned his kiss. His tongue touched hers, and she was exquisitely aware of him all over, from the way his hair felt as she ran her fingers through it, to the feel of his tongue and lips, to the warm hardness of his body pressed against hers.

With a rough sound, he broke the kiss and turned his head to rub against her cheek. "I love you, Esme," he murmured against the softness of her cheek. "Oh, God, how much I love you."

Esme was so shocked she couldn't answer him. She stood there, clinging to him and trying to sort out her thoughts. He pulled away slightly, then she looked at him, unable to speak, her whole body a jumble of emotions.

He brushed her hair back softly with his fingertips, then let his fingers slide down the side of her face and neck. 'I know I've been an idiot," he said, holding her shoulders. "I know I was afraid to let myself fall in love, afraid I'd turn out like Redferne. I promise, Esme, if you marry me that I'll never do that. I'll be a good husband and father, I swear it." He put his fingers under her jaw. "Please forgive me and tell me that you'll marry me. When I saw you there in that shanty at the circus, I knew that nothing would ever be as precious to me as you are. I want to spend my whole life letting you know that." He looked at her again, pleading. "What do I need to do to make you believe me?"

Esme finally found her voice. "You could kiss me again."

He promptly did so, thoroughly and with great enjoyment. Esme hadn't thought that anything could be better than the kiss before this one, but they just kept getting better and better. She held on to him and pressed herself close to him, greedy for sensation. Lovatt finally broke the kiss and moved back a step, still holding her. "Does this mean that you accept me? You'll be my wife?" he asked, a dazed expression on his face.

She nodded, feeling as dazed as he looked. "Yes," she said, catching her breath. "Yes, yes. Forever yes."

He smiled, and she saw love and joy in his.eyes. "As soon as possible? I don't want to wait a minute longer than we have to."

"As soon as possible." She stayed back from him, but reached out to touch him with her fingers, as if she were afraid he would disappear. "I want you, Chalmers," she whispered. "You don't know how much." He started to move toward her, but she took a step away from him, then stopped when her back touched the bed. She looked around, grinned, and turned back to face him. "There's just one more thing you need to do for me."

"Anything," he said fervently. "Just name it."

She smiled wickedly at him, sat on the edge of the bed, and smoothed the covers next to her with her hand. "I believe, Chalmers Lovatt, that it's time to lock the door."

Thanks so much for reading *A Touch of Magic*. Regencies and readers of Regencies are special people. I've noticed throughout the years that readers of Regencies are quite discriminating and have very definite likes and dislikes. I hope this book will be one of those you like and that it will keep a place on your shelf. If you did enjoy it, be sure to watch for my next book, *The Fifth Proposal*, which will be out from Zebra next year. It is scheduled to be on the shelves at your favorite bookstore in November of 1999. *The Fifth Proposal* involves Shelby Falcon, a heroine who is coping with her very eccentric family. There are also four cousins chasing an inheritance, a mysterious stranger, an old mansion, and a cache of jewels from India—the fabulous Jewels of Ali. I think *The Fifth Proposal* will be an entertaining romp, and I hope you will be sure to watch for it.

If you would like to write me with a comment about *A Touch of Magic,* or if you have a question about any of my other books, just write me at the following address:

Juliette Leigh
Box 295
Pineola, NC 28662

A stamped, self-addressed envelope would be appreciated.

If you prefer to e-mail, my address is:
romance@sff.net

My web page has information about all my books, a pub-

lication list, and some frequently asked questions and answers which might be of interest. It is located at:
http://www.sff.net/people/romance

Again, thanks for reading *A Touch of Magic*, and I look forward to hearing from you.

Best,

Juliette Leigh